The Aldoran Saga

The Prophecy

Dedication

I've been on a long journey of my own and
this story is indeed the magical version of it
and people have even departed this land
along the way with new people coming along
to help the process so it is to all of them
that this dedication goes.

Book Two
The Prophecy

Contents

Introduction

Thirty years on, and an ever-growing presence of a dark foreboding burdened the land. But it seemed that it was nothing more than a fear, a rumour, the makings of mythology – until the threat became real, opening the door to fulfilment of the Wyrd Sisters' Prophecy concerning the newly orphaned child, Tama, descended from the Great Queen Aleeah.

The Dragons had all but disappeared from the realm at the passing of the Crown to Aleeah and Alden, but they were getting older and too wearied for active service against any foreboding. The dark force that Aleeah had released in her search for the dragon artefact – had destroyed the mage guild and entombed Cullen, the guild master, in the wreckage.

The mages to whom Aleeah's decedents must turn for help in their new quest, were scattered throughout the kingdoms of Caragh and so Aleeah's grandchild, Tama, takes the reins from her to fulfil the Prophecy: Come the Pretender.

CHAPTER ONE:
The New Era

A great crackle of thunder exploded above the city; the startled young princess sat bolt upright. The tail end of summer was upon them, and this raging storm marked the passing of mid-summer's eve.

"Where's mother?" asked the child, slightly panicked by the noise. Her pulse had quickened. Tama was making only a half-hearted attempt to sleep; it wasn't that late, nor was she tired, and now the storm had begun there was even less chance she would sleep.

"Shush, close your eyes and roll over. They've just popped out to see your uncle." Ada quickly realised this information was not going to help the child sleep.

"What? Uncle Tris is here? I have to go and see him." The excitement of her uncle's visit lifted her already high young voice to a squeal.

"I don't think so," Ada sharply replied. "You'll remain right here. It's an urgent call from outside the city's walls and he is just passing through with some grown-up news." How annoying her old nurse could be, thought Tama, when she shut her out with talk of "grown-up" things.

"But, I want to see him," Tama demanded, and thumped her fists against the bed.

"No! Your father said you shouldn't leave the city," replied Ada commandingly.

"It's not fair! I never get to see him." Tama thought to herself that Ada had far too much control over her life. She wished she was an adult, so she did not have to take orders from them.

Reluctantly rolling over, she looked out at the flickering storm as another burst of lightning charged the air. The rain was beginning to lash through the open doors, so Ada closed them. Tama thought to feign sleep and started to breathe slowly and rhythmically. This was usually all she had to do to trick the old woman into leaving her in peace after dark. As soon as the door-handle turned, Tama's eyes sprang open. She drew the belt around her soft creamy robe, slipped on her shoes, and opened the balcony doors so she could climb over to the next balcony and into the room behind hers, where the lights were dimmed. It was her parents' room, and she knew it would be easy to slip out of their private entrance unseen.

In the quiet of the large bedchamber her heart pounded at the sounds of multiple voices in the hallway. Though the door was closed, she quaked as the voices drew nearer, and slipped behind a dressing screen to wait for them to disappear. They finally became distant, so she tiptoed out into the private hallway and down to the ground floor, hiding like a thief in the night before racing for freedom down the wet and empty avenue. By now the rain had come on much heavier, and Tama realised she was greatly under-dressed; but the prospect of spending a few moments with her uncle was too good to miss.

She ran as fast as her ten-year-old legs would carry her through winding streets with cobbled pathways and flickering candles behind crystal windows. At the battlement's east gate, she hid behind the right side of the gatehouse and waited for the sentry to reach the far left of the gate, then she ran on, hoping not to be seen. But the guards were as vigilant as ever.

"Oy, miss, you can't go outside the city in this weather dressed like that – your parents will 'ave me for breakfast."

"Oh pleeease, I just want to see my uncle."

"Well you can look at him from here under the shelter of the lintel, then. He's right over there, talking to your mother and father." The guard pointed out through the gateway.

Tama looked out into the darkness and finally found three silhouettes –

shrouded in driving rain. She shivered, soaked to the skin, and rubbed the wetness out of her eyes.

"That's not Tris! Where's Tris? I want to see him. Has he left?" she cried in panic.

"He's right there; I can see him. Can't you see him miss?" The guard was pointing to the third member of the group.

Tama's breath caught in her throat. Now she saw straight through the black magick and could see that her parents were talking to an unearthly creature – a liche warrior! Its wicked eyes spied Tama and, knowing it had been caught out, it drew its blade and with two quick thrusts cut down the king and queen.

Tama screamed and rushed forward. The guard drew his own sword ready to fight, but the creature was already leaping onto its horse. It sheathed its cutlass, smirched with blood, and rode away into the darkness.

Tama ran down to where the crumpled bodies lay, and looked upon the pale, ghostly faces of her mother and father. She was desperate to change their state from dead to alive, but that was not going to happen. Not even Xylon's magick could fix this, the child knew. In a pool of blackness, King Husienna Marda and Queen Aislinn Temple lay slumped and gaunt. Their deaths had awoken the spiritual escort of the Plains, Salamar, who came wraithlike through the howling darkness to claim the king's and queen's souls into his custody.

Flashes of silver cracked against the ink-black clouds, and the distant, eastern mountains offered no shelter from the pounding wind and rain. In the background, the city lay subdued by the storm, except for the guards who looked on with desperate eyes from the rainbow-coloured turrets on all corners of the wall. The child's tears mingled with the downpour as she despaired over the enormity of this foul deed. The king and queen had been drawn from safety, against the better judgement of the guards, believing Tristane was calling them. In betrayal of their trust they had been struck down by this new evil, a liche warrior from Kye, city of the dead – once known as Barrakye.

Tama thought she was safe now, but the creature spun around to collect the spirits of its victims as they lifted from their bodies. She cried out as she watched the distant form, clad in shabby armour, ride back through the darkness to where she stood. Salamar, quick to recognise the enemy, collected the souls and retreated.

"Get away from them!" Tama screamed in fear as the liche scooped up the vacant bodies without dismounting, then snarled at Salamar for taking what he'd really wanted. He looked down at the helpless child and smiled horribly.

"It's only a matter of time before we take back what is ours," he rattled in a deathly tone. "I am Rakeem, first friend of universal darkness. Know my name, because it is your grandmother's curse that determined my allies and my purpose. And when I can, I will come for you, child." He leaned low towards her, his skeletal features menacing against the flashing of lightning, and Tama could smell death following him. She recoiled into the soft mud, afraid. "I will come, for your line must end to avenge the curse on my line." He sped off northwards into the dark.

She felt helpless and filled with despair, as Salamar had her parents' souls, and the liche had their bodies. Nothing remained but the fearsome memory of them being slain. She whispered two lines from an ancient poem she had not, until now, understood:

"The world might stop, and the heart within my chest:

But still this pain remembered would not rest."

"Murderer!" Tama screamed. "Murderer!" She fell to her knees, unaware of the mud sucking her into its coldness. Throughout the night her cries carried over the kingdom of Husienna. The intensity of her pain mingled with the strike of lightning and the call of thunder. Those that heard her cries covered their ears, and let the silent tears roll down their cheeks, sorrowing for their orphaned princess.

Through the foul, dank vapour a gush of warm air breathed across the child's face. Her eyes widened, it was the soft scent of the goddess Sriann, the mother of all flowers. For a moment the storm was set aside and peace lingered.

Sriann had come to collect her charge, the death spirit. Standing before Tama she commanded Salamar to return to his golden receptacle in her hands. Her voice, echoing splendour, spoke in an ethereal language. Tama understood the words since she was no longer of the earthly kind. A change had come over her on the fall of her parents, though she knew little of it yet.

Sriann spoke. "Tama, my child, your destiny awaits you. It has been foretold that you must fulfil a prophecy woven into the fate lines by the wyrd sisters."

"How can I be the heiress of prophecy? I am still a child."

"Not for long. The wyrd sisters have provided for your future since long in the past."

"I don't understand this. What does the prophecy mean?" Tama's voice was strained and panicked.

"A dark knight will soon be at your door. The one who would dry up the land and corrupt the world has come, freed by the hands of your grandmother, a plot, and a fate. He is ready to reveal himself openly with his new servant Rakeem by his side. To find the dark knight you must free the earth-bound spirit." Sriann looked across at the suspended storm and paused for several seconds.

"The dark hearts are coming again, aren't they?" Tama said, without the full knowledge of who or what the dark hearts truly were.

"Yes child, and you must be ready

for them."

"But how will I make myself ready?" Tama whimpered.

"Oh child, in three days you will be better ready for the world as it will become, and then you must follow the path to the Blue Hills. Xarjay can give you what you seek, and the sooner you decide to seek it the sooner you'll know what that is."

Riddles, thought Tama despairingly, and opened her mouth to ask the goddess what she meant. But she was too late. Sriann had drifted away and the storm came crashing down again, flooding the ground with muddy waters. The rain beat against Tama's fair face. Exhausted, she fell unconscious and was carried to her rooms by the guard she'd spoken to earlier.

*****

The rain fell for three days and nights, swelling the streams and gorges and giving the land no respite from its ferocity.

The child lay in her bed all this time, haunted by ugly visions; during her restlessness her body underwent a transformation, heaving unconsciously with the metamorphosis. Upon fully waking on the third day, no longer could she recognise herself as the child she had been. A stranger stared back at her from the great gilded mirror.

Tama looked deep into the mirror's aged haziness and gazed upon an unknown face. She saw for the first time the peach glow of adult cheeks. Tama let the strands of her long silvery white hair flow over her fingertips with velvet softness. The silken stream rained down her back, reflecting the light coming through the open window. Her eyes were now grey like the recent storm, and as large as silver coins. She wore a blue gown stitched with sterling silver thread, which coursed elegantly around her slight, newly curved figure. Black and white pearls clung to the high neckline and waist of her gown. She stared in wonder, lost to all that had preceded that moment, until a knock on the bedroom door drew her back to the present.

"Enter," she said. The lock undid itself and Tama smiled, savouring her new ability to move objects with her thoughts.

"My dear young lady, you're finally awake. We've been unable to get into your rooms these past three days. You've worried us all silly, espe..." Craven stopped in mid-sentence and rubbed his eyes. For a moment, in the filtered light, his vision had played tricks on him: he saw the image of Aleeah standing in full view. Impossible, he knew, because Aleeah had grown old, and besides she and Alden had been away on a diplomatic mission in the south for many months. When he looked again, he realised it wasn't the cousin he had adored since they were children, but a young woman of similar stature and elegant appearance. The resemblance amazed him and gave him hope, as he saw the strength of Aleeah glowing in the child-woman who stood before him.

"So it's true then. The fates were true

to their word, and they have given us an ally of such splendour that we should never again fear the unknown."

"Somehow, Craven, I never thought of you as someone who harboured fears." Tama smiled broadly and her voice melded with the multiple tones of the Zshar-pitsa, gathered on the window ledge to see her. The young woman's eyes were drawn towards these palace pets that needed no cage to keep them. These nocturnal birds, unusually awake in the freshness of the day, glistened in the sunlight. Tama's face was illuminated by the light reflected from their metallic-blue and green tails; a single feather from their long tails could awaken any darkness. They chortled, and black pearls fell from their golden beaks into a chalice below the windowsill. This once-off appearance would create a flurry of jewellery making, as craftsmen vied to honour the young princess, Craven thought, recalling that the same thing had happened before Aleeah's coronation, and again when

Husienna became king in his turn.

"They are not stupid birds, my dear. They would only have done that for a true heir." Craven bowed low as a gesture of respect, yet felt the void created by her instant adulthood and regal presence.

"Please Craven, I am still your family. Four days ago you played hide-and-seek with me, now you're acting as if I am a stranger. Please don't make this journey any lonelier than I fear it already is." She rushed towards him and threw her arms around his neck and he reciprocated the hug, momentarily relieved of the burden of higher duties and reverting to just plain old cousin Craven. Then he stepped back, sighing.

"I'll have to go and sort out your coronation. It will have to be tonight – you know how the council is a stickler for ceremony and paperwork."

Tama laughed nervously. No one had said anything about *that* in the prophecy, she thought.

"Why tonight, why so soon?"

"Because it is our way. The law says a crown must be crowned before it has time to fall down. Just about drove your grandmother to distraction, but order is important for the betterment of life, even when it is tedious that it be so."

"You are so wise, Craven."

"Devious, maybe. Wise? Well, I'm not so sure about that." He smiled back at her, still seeing an uncanny echo of Aleeah in her face and hoping that Aleeah and Alden had been found by his messengers and were even now on their way home. "I think you have a lot to do on your own while we prepare for tonight. Take a long look in your mirror. Xarjay insisted that it never leave your room, and that you were to look into it when your time came. I think this is what he meant. I'll leave you alone." As Craven turned and left the room, Tama's eyes were once again firmly fixed on Xarjay's mirror.

She sighed and shook her head as her reflection started to fade from view. A bluish mist covered the mirror's surface and another image formed. Slowly the outline of a man appeared before her. His blue aura glowed brightly, and in his hand he held a glowing orb with a small life inside. She could make out a baby, seemingly suspended between life and death. The image meant very little to her. She sat down to contemplate the puzzle. Only her mother knew how to comfort her, yet she was one of the reasons Tama needed comfort. The irony reached into Tama's heart and it splintered like glass on a hardened floor.

That night, all of the citizens of Tristany came to pay their respects to the new Queen, and whispers of Aleeah's hurried return spread through the crowd. The news of Tama's awakening had travelled fast, and the cobblestoned streets below her balcony bustled with sounds of anticipation, because no one had seen her new form except Craven.

Tama wandered out of her rooms into the hallway where her private gardens could be viewed. There she sat on a window seat to breathe the clear air and to bathe in the calmness of the scene. The sun had begun its descent, and she could see the night creeping over the horizon. She had hoped the peaceful evening would settle her churning stomach, but it had no effect. She felt herself to be lost in a lonely place – in charge, yet lacking the knowledge of authority.

Below, the marbled paths lay cool in the evening light, leading through to the gardens of remembrance. The view of the gardens brought Tama a moment's peace. She let her eyes wander through the main entrance, with creeper-covered stone walls either side, and paths leading to alternative entrances. The garden beds were filled with multitudes of flowers; there was even a blue-moon flower hidden beneath a bridge that traversed the sacred brook. A moss covered wall, illuminated by Zshar-pitsa tail feathers, sat at the far end where the names of the fallen were etched into the stone. She knew that it took constant work to keep the gardens in summer bloom, but the quiet peace was worth every laborious moment. Now she understood why her parents had spent so much time there, even doing some of the work themselves. For a moment she saw their image dancing in the filtered light; but they drifted away as her eyes tried to follow them. A faultless peace lingered alongside the quiet buzzing of bees, the soft calling of exotic birds, and the sight of gentle gossamer wings in the butterfly enclosure. A heady night perfume of boronia drifted through the House of March, into Tama's rooms, and down onto the street below – tantalising everyone who made their way up the avenue. Tama breathed deeply of the perfumed air, then turned away, knowing she must now prepare herself for the coming ceremony.

CHAPTER TWO:

Unwanted Guests

As the full moon rose high, all preparations for the crowning of the new princess were completed. Silence fell over Tristany: not even a bird sang. It had taken but a few hours to make ready for the short coronation in the April Hall, since the changeover of power needed to be swift in order to subdue the people's anxieties.

As Tama approached the hall, the soldiers drew back the solid silver doors, and bowed to her. Tama stepped quietly into the great hall and looked up in awe at her grandmother's statue, standing fifteen metres high and glistening in polished bronze. Garbed in her fighting costume with hair flowing in the wind of battle, she stood ready with sword in hand as protector of the city. The vision had come from Alden's description to the artisan who carved it. The plinth's inscription read, "I have no more to teach you, my daughter." Next to Queen Aleeah was placed the statue of Lord Alden, holding a lighted torch and his dragon emblem, and opposite stood Lord Guillian and the old King.

Tama felt the cold touch of the marbled floor through her slippers, even though it was covered in thick carpet. Deep inside the hall now, she felt dominated by its domed ceiling depicting paintings of the Virgin War, and the plague of the frozen sleep. At the end of the long aisle had been placed a rostrum, where Craven stood waiting for her.

He was not alone: Aleeah stood on his right and Alden on his left. The Rainbow City's trinity, thought Tama, relieved by their homecoming, and let out a small cry. She clenched her teeth to stifle any more unwitting noises, but her eyes welled with tears. Aleeah smiled down at her grand-daughter, recognising herself in the young woman. But Alden's memory flew back to the vision he had seen in the mountain springs so many years before. At last, he thought, she has come to end the reign of tyranny.

Walking with slow, deliberate steps, Tama made her way towards them. Her emerald gown of raw silk flowed behind her, like the mane of one of the great beasts of the woodlands, to a train carried by her lady in waiting. The gown was heavily encrusted with sparkling emeralds and ink-coloured pearls. The collar stood high around her neck, diminishing to meet a V-line bodice that enhanced her new womanly shape. Craven watched and held his breath, noticing once again her uncanny similarity to Aleeah as a young woman.

The people gasped at the beauty of this being and lowered their heads in customary fashion. Reaching the rostrum, Tama knelt and asked for the ceremony to begin. Flutes played, filling the hall with melodic tones, but a foreboding hung in the air. The music seemed filled with the bitterness of death instead of triumph.

"I, Craven, servant of the Marda family and secondary heir, do hereby commence the ceremony for the Throne of Tristany, our beloved Rainbow City," said the man at whose feet Tama knelt. His hands rested on a large book atop the rostrum, and he continued. "As is our custom, we will take a vow of truth from Princess Tama. This can only be read from the Book of the Gods by a true heir, and no other." He waved a warning finger at the audience, signalling for silence. Tama didn't find his words comforting, and wondered whether they had been designed to ease her nervousness.

Craven held up the leather-bound book with its golden inscription embossed into the cover for all to see:

By the power of Killan the giver of goodwill and A'shara the mother of our hearts, only the honourable will prevail.

It was the Book of the Gods, filled with ceremonies, duties and laws – a replica of the one true book held in sanctuary. Tama took it in both hands and it opened by itself to the page of the vow. Her hands trembled with the weight, and she read the vow to herself softly before speaking it aloud in a firm clear voice and asking for a sign of acceptance from the gods. A crack of lightning sparked high in the domed room, and the people gasped. Tama looked across at the trinity, but their warm faces reassured her that this was normal – they'd seen it before. She turned to the crowd, and Aleeah placed the silver crown on her head adorned with crystal flowers, then handed her the staff of longevity. Aleeah's hands trembled as she remembered the joy of giving these very items to Husienna, and the pain of him not being able to give them to Tama.

The diamond-cut silver of the staff glistened like the snow in winter, and at its crest shone the Blue Island Star of Celeron, a beautiful, thousand-point diamond, splintering the light into thousands of jewel-like shards around the room.

"All is well then," announced Craven to the waiting crowd.

Alden smiled broadly. "You have a new Queen! Through our tears for the loss of my son, Husienna, and his wife Aislinn, we will celebrate and hope that they are not lost to us forever." He'd seen stranger things happen than the return of the dead, he thought, and hoped for nothing less.

Tama led the way down to the cobbled streets outside, followed by her grandparents and Craven. Into the moonlight the new monarch led her guests to cheers of celebration. The crowds howled as she walked with a shy smile, greeting as many people as she could. A white woollen carpet had been laid for her to walk up the centre of the marquee to her seat at the head table, with Craven on her left, Aleeah and Alden on her right, and the council members on either side of them.

The night drew a heavy mist over Sky Crag as the party carried on into the early morning. The eastern mountains served as a backdrop to Tristany – ever echoing the festivities. The mountains were perilous to those inexperienced in the ways of mountain climbing, and only a few travellers were used to the pack route over the forbidding ranges. Deep crevices appeared and disappeared out of nowhere when the ground below moved and then settled itself to a new position. The surface of the Plains was still, after many ages, forming and re-forming. Lien was never satisfied with his work, and found comfort in re-creating the mountains of his beloved earlier time. His mind was a lonely one; even living as a Shaman, with all that this had given him, did not neutralise his craving for a human existence from the time before the restoration – before he was elevated to Shaman.

Some of the paths he had created were stable enough for a small pony and cart to negotiate, transporting goods to and from the trading cities on the other side; and then the ponies were stabled before the rougher ground was reached. At that point the traders would have to make many trips back and forth, over treacherous ground, to the waiting ponies on the other side of the mountain.

Travellers reported strange happenings whilst trekking over the mountain paths. Rumblings from deep in the earth could be heard at night when the sky was silent and dark. Lights sometimes glowed from the mountain's peaks, which could be seen through the heavy mists that regularly fell on the land below. People from Tristany feared these unknown things.

The only lights the Peliens cared for tonight, though, were those of the flaming griddles, which wafted their tantalising aromas through the air, mingling with other potent scents. The local fishing boats had returned from a week's trawling in the Kastrail Straits. They had moored off the western city of Alvah on the island domain of Moonara to take on fresh water, and had brought back a load of spices along with their varied catch of saltwater fish. It was a lush spread which tantalised the tastebuds, with its colour, taste and scent. Tama was famished; she'd not eaten properly that day, nor at all for the previous three, and sent Craven to fill her plate more than once – so no one would know she'd been back for seconds.

For the best part of the night the people simply enjoyed themselves, forgetting they were there for both a wake and a celebration. They were entertained by the angelic tones of Alima the bard, and conjuror Vamana's sleight-of-hand tricks. Though that would be little comfort, thought Tama, after she'd gone.

She had decided that after the entertainment finished she would have to speak – or rather, Aleeah had suggested it. Alden sat with his head heavy in his hands, then glanced up and nodded briefly to encourage her. Craven rose and struck his fork on the crystal wine glass, calling for quiet. Tama stood apprehensively at the middle of the long trestle table waiting until silence came. The main tent was filled with her court and officials; some she'd known before her change, but mostly the faces were new to her. Looking across at the tent openings she saw the city's guardians holding back a burgeoning crowd. It was hard for her to find the words to tell them that she would have to leave before Kalale next changed the moon for the sun, heeding Sriann's call to seek out Xarjay's help. Tama took several deep breaths before all in the tent ceased to speak; yet whispers persisted. Craven pounded the table, this time with a wooden gavel brought by the waiting staff, and called assertively for their attention.

Tama raised her hands slightly, looking briefly towards her grandmother for support. Aleeah nodded with an approving smile and Tama began to speak. "You've danced, you've eaten and drunk, forgetting the strangeness of the time, and I have held back what I need to tell you, not wanting to dampen your mood." She could feel the anticipation of the crowd and of her elders. "But time enough has passed for frivolities."

"I must leave tonight. Your leaders know this," she went on, gesturing towards her grandparents and Craven. "The council knows this, and many of you have expected it. I leave because about thirty years ago Aleeah the Retaliate, and her consort Alden of Ashfar, gave themselves to the lower-world spirits in order to prevent a tragedy."

Aleeah stiffened, as if unable to accept the honourable title.

"But that tragedy didn't end as it should have with the Virgin War, because the architect of our fates prevented it. He has revealed himself to the gods, and now I have, through the work of the fates, become a part of this, the Aldoran Saga." Tama paused for a moment in thought.

Glumness fell over the crowd of onlookers as Tama began to speak again, but suddenly the floor in front of her table opened up and fire leapt from its void. The fire spat and hissed, releasing the living-fire sprites to dance a ring of flames around the rim of the pit. From the midst of the flames rose a dreadful figure. His twisted grey beard hung in braids down to his waist. Foul vapours followed his image, drenching the sweet boronia-filled vases and choking the vibrant flowers. His long, bony fingers seemed to stretch out to anyone who dared to look his way. His flesh was yellowed and crawling with small snake-like creatures, creating the hissing sound of the sea. Aleeah clutched her chest, feeling the pressure of the being in her realm as her mind was dragged back to the time in the not-place where she had agreed to set him free in exchange for knowledge of the cithara's whereabouts.

Most of the watchers hid their faces in horror, because this was the first time they had seen the dark knight of legend. Nothing was known of him since he had turned

Xylon into a tree many years before.

Alden's memory stirred; he recognised this entity as one who took part in the terrifying events in the mage guild. He placed his hand on Aleeah's shoulder and whispered that this was Maris, the twin mage of Sera. It made no sense to her. How could he be two people?

Sriann's prediction was right, thought Tama; the dark knight had come to her door, though she was unsure whether this was spirit or flesh. The little she knew of him was common knowledge: that he existed because Aleeah had set him free, and that he had cast a spell on Xylon. But she was also aware he'd come to design a new future, and that she had been born for the purpose of undoing his design.

"So the gods send me a woman-child to do their work?" the creature began, glaring at Tama. "Perhaps they have run out of ideas; it is a wicked fate that makes a child the bearer of a god's will."

Then the apparition hissed at Aleeah,

letting her know he had not forgotten their transaction.

Maris had become gnarled and twisted in the time he had lain hidden among the tunnels of the mountains. "You are no match for me, heiress Tama. I have spent an eternity corrupting the gods' work. And as for the mighty A'shara – a charlatan with whom you think there is strength in love? Ha! She is no match for me – a mere woman who embodies the velvet love of a puppy." He spat out the words as if the very thought of this kind of love left a bad taste upon his tongue, then continued.

"I am older than the dawn of time and wider than the dimensions I've swallowed. I've lived in and out of the void and lain hidden in the maelstrom of time. I cannot be easily removed from the fabric of space, for I dwell in the heart of the Maker Eternal, your Celi Mawr. Grander plans are at work than this communion will ever comprehend. No child, prophecy or not, will dissolve *my* place among the stars!" His arrogant laugh was almost unbearable to ordinary ears.

"Vilest of all creatures, you have no authority here." Fear pulsed through Tama's veins as she raised her right hand, commanding words she had no knowledge of until now. Aleeah rose with her, holding her hand – anticipating the spell, willing it to her grandchild. The sounds of many voices, an angelic choir, sang softly in the background over the competing hiss of Maris's snakes as Tama spoke.

"Now cast him out,

Far beyond night:

Your soul be your torment,

The gods be your light."

Together the two women chanted these words over and over, as the apparition was shrouded in a grey mist rising from a prodigious swirling whirlwind. The old soul fought the spell tenaciously, but he had not estimated the potency of the women's response, and was ill prepared for the fight against two such powerful spirits. Still struggling, he was swallowed by his own hole in the ground. Finally all was quiet. A cool night breeze filtered in, bringing with it the goddess Sriann. Her aura filled the marquee with tremendous vibrancy. Tama was too exhausted from the ordeal to notice; she fell back against her chair with eyes closed, still chanting quietly as the older trio gathered around her.

"My lady, my lady, the goddess Sriann has come." Craven gently touched Tama on the shoulder as Aleeah stroked her head, then they helped her to her feet. The crowd bowed in awed silence as the goddess took the young queen by the hand.

"Sweet Tama, you have met your first test of power against our enemy with purity and with great strength. Together you have disabled him for a little while only; but at least it has bought you some time, of which you will have need. Maris underestimated you. He should have known better than to appear incorporeally. Now you have given yourself some time to seek out the mage Xarjay in the Blue Hills."

Sriann departed on a graceful breeze, her aura of gold filling the high tent with resplendent light which washed over the Tristanian people, left awestruck by such a presence. Her flowing golden locks cascaded to the hem of her shimmering garments as she floated away, leaving the scent of her only calling card, summer flowers in full bloom.

Aleeah sat back in her chair. "Who is this Maris, Alden? It felt like the one I freed from the not-place, when we were seeking the cithara."

"He is both the one you freed and Maris, Sera's twin. Remember when Jugger Short-Stop came to us for help with the ice-sickness, and we travelled south to seek help from the mages? When we were in the mage guild, Maris was scorned by the others for his uselessness, always wrecking projects and causing problems. But I found out that his soul was being consumed by another: the one you freed, the one who cursed our own Xylon. I was watching from a darkened hallway and saw him make a horrendous wolf out of Sera's apprentice, Baronna. The animal attacked us but I was able to fight it off. Maris bound my dragon spirit, and sent the wolf-man to the surface and our sons to a labyrinth he'd created. We barely escaped with our lives. That's how I ended up flailed across the rocks until Cullen found me and sent me home. My memory has been under a shroud ever since that time, and only when Maris turned up here did I remember. Ten years have passed since we went down the mage hole"

"I see, then we have a lot to worry about," Aleeah replied. "Do you remember what happened to Jugger? He never turned up at home like you and our sons did."

"No, his fate is yet to be revealed to me, if it ever will be."

Listening intently, Tama wondered if she was fit for the task ahead.

"Will you come with me?" Tama asked her grandparents. "I can't face this alone."

"We cannot. Now that the city is

under threat we must stay and protect it. You are the one to go in search of allies. Your time has come," Aleeah said in sorrow.

If she must go and resolve this problem, wondered Tama, who could she trust to go with her now she was in charge? She fought to hold back the floods of tears that were ready to break through her defences like a river in flood.

"Who will go with me on my journey?" she called, feigning her mightiest voice, though she felt within her the heart of a child. "Who will show their courage and ride at my side? I need the best sword, the best warrior and, most importantly, a guide." She paused briefly and looked down. "The outside world is mostly a stranger to me, beyond this locality. Who will come?"

"I will, my lady." A soldier stepped forward. "I am Caldor of Alvah, and I will go with you." The soldier bowed low before his young queen, awaiting her approval.

"Do you know the world at large, Caldor?" The soldier nodded.

"You are of the Aldora Adrian, are you not?" she asked sternly. "I think it would be improper if I were to take you as my guide and servant. We are not allies, Caldor. Your family is still threatening mine, as you well know."

Aleeah held her tongue.

"I understand your misgivings my lady, but many of our people served, and still do serve, in your guard because of the war of our ancestors. We gave our service to honour Queen Aleeah, after our own crown fell disgraced. It is out of loyalty that we remain." He bowed respectfully towards Aleeah and Alden. Goosebumps ran down Aleeah's arms and Alden wanted to breathe fire onto the captain. But that was not the way of the light hearts, he argued with himself, not to mention he'd been unable to transform since the confrontation with Maris.

Tama sighed in defeat. With no other takers, her choices were Caldor or nobody. "Maybe I will give you the benefit of the doubt, Caldor of Alvah, as proof of your loyalty is surely borne out in your service to us these long years." She felt a slight chill meander down her spine. She knew there were plenty of Adrian people living in Tristany, though she had had nothing much to do with them until now. Rakeem the liche, ruler of Kye, and now this soldier claiming to be a loyal subject, were her only contacts. For an old soldier, he certainly was young of face. Very few Peliens managed the art of staving off old age, though that capacity was in their blood.

"How far does your knowledge of the outside take you?" she asked.

"Extensively, ma'am," he replied.

"Good, then: as you seem to be my only volunteer, get yourself ready within the hour. We will leave quickly and quietly tonight." The crowd began to disperse and Tama found herself sitting in an almost vacant tent wondering about her new life.

Aleeah sat alone with her. "I've been where you're at. I know how you feel, but I also know you are a child of the fates. You can ask for nothing more." Aleeah left her to get ready for the journey.

Looking up at the tented ceiling, Tama sighed again, then rose with new determination. There was much to pack for her journey, and no doubt the trinity would take care of the city in her absence.

CHAPTER THREE:

Enemies Where Friends Hide

Tama waved her goodbyes and turned towards the south gate, with Caldor following.

Kalale, the god who watched over night and day, could be seen as a silhouette in the night sky with the moon on his shoulders. Tonight he shone a bright moon, casting long shadows over the land. The goddess Sriann had petitioned him for light to guide the two lonely figures as they left in the dead darkened silence.

At first Tama chose not to talk to her travelling companion, who rode dutifully beside her through stony streets. They trotted along the safety of the city's byways towards the southern gateway. Marbled columns stood intermittently along the city's walls. At the southern exit, two such posts of huge girth supported a wrought iron gate, its metal swirls linked together to create the kingdom's coat of arms. Only the tips of the gate could be seen as the rest had been drawn up into the chamber above the stone lintels. In front of the gateway, large, studded wooden doors sat open, leading to a drawbridge, and Xylon could be seen shimmering in the distant moonlight on the other side. Leaving such a fortress filled one with a sense of foreboding, thought Tama, hearing the clank of chains pulling the drawbridge back into its raised position after the inner gate had dropped and the doors clanged shut.

The road wound down the slope from the Rainbow City, passing directly by Xylon. Tama smiled as the eyes on the wise-old tree-face opened slightly.

"Xylon, I have missed you these past few days," she said warmly.

"Aye lass, I've missed thee also. Tha hast grown fuller than any mere mortal could've imagined – and I'm not even a mortal, I'm a tree!" He laughed at his own humour. "I see much in my solitude; and though I know tha's eyes, I could never have understood tha's magnificent new look till tha presented tha-self here and now." The old man laughed deeply with rich, timber echoes. His curious accent always ended a sentence low. "If only, lass, I could get out of this blasted tree and be at least thirty years younger. I would beg thee for tha's hand, indeed lass, I would. But, tha knows, tha should be aware, although I am old and perhaps a little senile, I know my own place, I do. There are those among thy future and the now that will not respect as much."

"You are wise, Xylon, but I have nothing to fear this early in my journey, surely. I am flattered by your sentiments, but I should think thirty years is one of your largest fibs yet when it comes to matters of age." They both laughed.

"Now, lass, you must head down t' road quick sharp, quietly and most vigilantly, tha must. Make no mistake, lass, a spy is a spy even if he or she doesn't know it yet, true also this is of jealousy." The old man's nose wrinkled. "The little green demon resides in all who walk, only the strength of the heart knows how to control this ugly part of our psyche." Xylon raised his woody eyebrows, and for a moment Tama became uneasily aware of her travelling companion. The sparkle returned to the old man's eyes and she left him with a smile.

Her thoughts turned ever to her parents, as old Xylon diminished from view. Their distorted bodies, lying still on the wet grounds outside the city's walls, puzzled and twisted her emotions. No answers had come of their deaths, except that Prince Rakeem was at the bottom of their fate, somehow. It was odd how the night guard had allowed her parents out of the city unaided, even at the request of her uncle. Though a stranger these days to the main city, yet this was not his way and the guards knew it. So did her parents.

Tama watched as the sun rose slowly, and night dissolved into daylight as Kalale gladly pushed the great fire-ball into the sky, to reveal countryside that could be seen only from the highest watch-tower in Tristany. Sweeping, rolling lands of lush green earth folded out to the horizon, made more magnificent by her ability to see the full spectrum at will – another gift from the Shamans to the Peliens. At will they were able to discern whatever colours and light they wanted to. Their pupils were able to widen to the full size of their irises, and like a predator's their pupils flashed bright silver in the dark.

Tama, still thoughtful, was filled with warmth and emotion from her lands. To her surprise and delight, the country was more beautiful than she had ever imagined, as a child looking out from the city's towers. The grass was greener after the previous storms, which had flooded the open plains and washed away the dead leaves of winter. Sriann's flowers were everywhere, in all the shades of the spectrum. Trees scattered sparingly far out to the horizon in all shapes and sizes. Some young seedlings swayed gently in the light wind over the Field of Chains, and Tama became restless.

"I want to stop here, Caldor, to smell the flowers and feel the grass, even if just for a moment. I see no evil yet, only the beauty of the gods, and the urge to play is still in my mind. I also want breakfast, how about you?" She looked at him alighting from his horse, his head slightly stooped to shield his eyes from the sun with the brim of his helmet. He looked like a troubled man, with the shadows cast across his eyes deepening them to a melancholy hue.

"The beauty of the gods comes in many forms, some not so pretty." Caldor had spoken before he realised his mistake. She'd wanted an answer about breakfast, not his philosophy. But he'd been in such deep thought he'd forgotten his place. Tama just stared at him curiously, wondering if he was mad. Worse than this look, he thought, he also felt her mistrust of him because of where he came from.

"If that is true, then I have not had the years to experience it yet," she replied sharply. She lacked skill in communicating with her servants, since she had not had time for the lessons normally given to one coming to the throne in an ordinary way. What Caldor perceived as mistrust and dislike was simply the words of a child in an adult's body.

The two dismounted by a stream that ran west, across the south of the virgin fields and out to the Sea of Kastrail. Its fast running crystal waters foamed and gushed in harmony with the sound of the birds merrily nesting in the trees, which on the southern horizon thickened into a mass of forests. The sun shone brightly, casting morning shadows and melting away the dew on the fine, feathery grass. Tama rubbed her feet through the greenery.

"My lady!" Caldor was agitated, persistently looking at the shadow lengths and observing the position of the sun. "Time really is not on our side, no matter what Sriann says. We must press on quickly. Our only hope of shelter is at least two days travel away, if we are to go direct to the Blue Hills."

"Enjoy the moment, my father used to say, for a moment will pass – and the next moment will come and it will deliver something else. It is pleasant enough here, and all the trouble I'm aware of is in the far north. I don't want to go yet, so eat up. I'm off for a paddle."

Caldor sat up straight; she was not listening to his warnings.

"Please forgive my anxieties. There is an uneasiness about this place: a remnant of its past lingers. I can feel it, and it takes all my strength to contain the emotion," he replied.

Tama balanced on the water's edge, tempting the cold crystal shallows to wash over her feet while she held her arms outstretched.

"I guess then we could discuss our plans. Maybe you'll be less worried if I tell you what we're going to do."

"I thought I knew. We're heading to the Blue Hills, yes?" Caldor responded.

"Yes and no. First we'll go to Ashfar to collect my uncle." She looked up at a distant place on the horizon, still balancing at the water's edge. "You do know the way, don't you?" she asked.

"The hidden city is not easy to find, my lady, hence its name – Ashfar, the black distance!"

"Oh I see. 'Extensively travelled' I believe you said?" Tama raised her brow and looked directly at Caldor.

"Yes, my lady, but I wasn't aware I had to know the secrets of the Plains also. I'll do my best to get you there, though I can't promise you. Your uncle has removed all signposts to his hidden corner of this world."

"Then let's hope that Tristane finds us. You would do well to remember we are now in his territory, with or without signposts," Tama snapped back.

She dried her feet, refreshed from the icy waters, whilst Caldor repacked their loads and watered their horses. The hazy day quivered over the horizon and Tama became enchanted at the rising heat. She watched it make the colours bleed into one another. There were shadows that seemed living to her eyes, and she became transfixed.

"What is that?"

"What is what? I can see only the horizon," Caldor replied, not even looking up from his packing. He had paused before answering, as if contemplating her question, but was aware only of the whispers in his ears. He hadn't got used to the whispers. He still foolishly believed he was different from his kinsfolk, and did not see himself as already a dark heart.

"Then look harder," Tama cried impatiently, unaware of his turmoil. She pointed at the shapes of beings shadowing across the plain. "They look like reflections of people, but what animal is casting them?"

"I told you we shouldn't linger, ma'am. If these are what I think they are, then we might be in some trouble." He was no longer concerned with packing and began to look around for shelter, but there was none. This was an open country, flat as a hotplate with nothing but the channel of the stream to hide in.

"What trouble, what are they?" Tama strained her eyes to get a good look at the flock coming towards them.

"Perytons. Half deer, half bird. They cast the shadow of dead spirits who have died far from their homes. Help me find a place to hide. They may not be fast but they are heading this way." His words were commanding and Tama didn't like it, she felt like a child again in her room, being told to go to sleep.

"I don't like your tone."

"And I'll apologise when we find somewhere to hide. So you can punish me later, just find a place to bloody hide, so I can be punished later."

"Why don't we kill them?" Tama asked. She still hadn't realised the gravity of her situation, unaware that Perytons killed beings like her and could not be stopped by any ordinary weapon.

Caldor looked around desperately. One of the creatures was close enough for him to see that its feathers were blue, indicating it was a female. It began to scream to the others, as high-pitched as a banshee. Caldor grabbed Tama by both arms and swung her into the stream, holding her and himself down below the water's surface. The Peryton landed at the water's edge above where Caldor and Tama were fighting to keep their heads beneath the water line. The horses were rearing frantically in complaint, but they were of no interest to the Perytons. The female pecked at them, then splashed the surface with its giant antlers. The movement of the water caused the submerged hostages to float back and forth. But that was not their only problem: Caldor was running out of air and the beasts were in no hurry to leave. He let Tama go and tried to reach the surface in a safe spot, but the five creatures followed his movement, stopping him from re-emerging.

Tama grabbed the dying man and pressed her lips to his, giving him her own air. In her new state, she knew instinctively that she could survive for long periods without oxygen. It was an unexpected kiss of life for Caldor, and for the first time he saw her through the eyes of love. Her kiss lasted for half an hour, keeping him breathing until the animals became bored and left.

She released him from the kiss and they emerged through the surface shivering and blue with cold. Tama drew in the longest breath she'd ever taken, replacing the air she'd given her escort. Caldor thanked her sheepishly. He was a stranger to this sense of love; yet this love was a falsehood and in his heart he was still a stranger. She had only given him air, not a true kiss, he thought. Still he couldn't help looking at her glistening in the sun with a new appreciation. Tama simply wanted them both to move on.

The Eastern Mountains peered down at the riders as they came closer. The sharp precipice of Mount Swali held fast to the surrounding rock, only to seem more menacing as the two neared the shadowy paths that lay creepily empty around the mountain's base.

"Well, Caldor, shall we head east towards the mount? If my geography serves me correct, then the opening to Ashfar is in that direction." She pointed.

He paused before answering, as if contemplating a move, but the whispers in his ears got louder, telling him which direction to take her in.

"Caldor, Caldor!" she called impatiently.

"Yes, I'm... I'm sorry" Feeling disoriented after the partial drowning. "We'll head a little north west. I believe that is the correct way from here."

Tama's heightened hearing was flooded with the sound of returning Perytons. "We'll have to run this time, Caldor. They're back!"

In a flash, Tama was travelling with the speed of the wind, cracking her whip and digging in her boots. Her horse grunted and snorted disapprovingly, taking the bit tightly in his jaws then unhappily obliging the rider. Quickly Caldor followed, straining to keep up, his horse not as lean as Tama's. They rode as fast as they could, with the Perytons' screeching getting louder and louder from the rear. But this noise only served to hide the new danger following them. The heavy hooves of riders galloping across the fields were smothered by squawks and squeals. Tama cried to her mount to be swifter, but still the horsemen and the Perytons came. Caldor knew now what was going on, he'd half-expected it when the Perytons arrived at the river. The riders, with cloaks of black and horned helmets, rode just as swiftly, their appearance threatening. It seemed clear that the dark riders were anything but friendly.

"Caldor!" Tama cried out over the tremendous noise. "We have to stop and fight, I can't drive my horse this hard any longer; it will surely kill him!"

Her horse reared to avoid a grass snake slithering across her path, and threw her to the ground. She landed with a crashing thud that knocked her out.

At first Caldor thought Tama was dead, she lay so still. He dropped to his knees and tried to rouse her, shaking her gently, but she didn't move or stir. After a few more moments, during which Caldor debated with himself whether he dared return to her the gift of breath she had so recently bestowed on him, Tama gasped and drew in air, coughing it back out, as her chest had over-tightened. Within seconds two riders and the five Perytons were standing over them.

"You'll not be popular with Rakeem and the dark knight if she's damaged in any way," said Gotlieb.

"You should tame your bloody beasts, you idiots. You're the reason we are in this predicament," Caldor snorted in reply.

"That's not how the masters will see it," Drugan interjected. "Your job was to kidnap her and bring her to the gate for processing. Instead you're off on some wild goose chase across this bastard of a field. Yeesh, I hate being 'ere!" Drugan shuddered from his memories of Caragh.

"That was my plan, fool. Had you not intervened I'd have had her walking towards the gate by now. Instead, she's unconscious."

"Well, perhaps it's not such a bad thing. We can transport her before she wakes up," Gotlieb said.

Gotlieb and Drugan were both on the path to liche-hood, preferring after many years of servitude to go the way of the dark hearts rather than remain as underdogs forever.

"'Ere, you fat lazy excuse for a bird, get yer butt over 'ere and pick her up. Take the lady back to the gate, you know the way," Drugan commanded, then slapped the beast on the rear. Drugan looked back around at Caldor. "Well, we'll be off then, loser."

"What about me? You can't just leave me here," Caldor protested.

"Yep, we can, and we will. As a relative of Tebore's, you are not well liked by your cousin Rakeem, who sends his regards – not! He says for you to get lost till the next time he needs ya," Gotlieb replied. The other four birds picked Gotlieb and Drugan off the ground and set off flying North West toward the mountain, leaving Caldor alone. He was a misfit with his own people, and now an outcast with the light hearts. Though, he thought cunningly, the light hearts knew nothing of his double-dealings yet. What a perfect opportunity to be a hero!

CHAPTER FOUR:

Lies, Lies, and more Lies

Tristane paced the floor. He'd grown restless with his new life as a Thane, missing the open roads and wild nights in the rain. He could barely contain himself waiting for Tama to arrive, though he wasn't entirely sure if she was coming to Ashfar at all. Craven's messengers had brought news of the terrible events in the Rainbow City, but said only that his niece was headed in search of Xarjay.

He had become more serious since he and his brother Husienna had found themselves back on the surface world, with little memory of the events at the mages' guild. On their return, Tristane had taken up the position of Thane of Ashfar, as Husienna had become king in his mother's stead. Dangerously ill after an attack by her old nemesis Lucinda while her husband and sons were absent, Aleeah had realised that she and Alden were past their prime. Ruling a new people was a job for someone younger, so they stepped into the role of diplomats, travelling through the country creating peace where they roamed.

"How long am I supposed to just sit and wait for her, Sera?" Tristane asked the mage sitting to his left in the shadows, reading the latest news in the *Aldoran Chronicle*. The long slim man, who appeared older once his head lifted from the flickering shadows cast by the candles, looked up knowingly at him.

"She'll come when she comes and go when she goes, and you shall be patient or wear out your toes," Sera said, smiling.

"Have you any idea how irritating it is when you rhyme your sentences like that?"

"Oh yes, quite aware. But we can't help it. All mages do it naturally. It breaks the monotony of waiting about for things to happen, just to rhyme a little."

"Sire, sire!" A man cried, running breathlessly into the room. Tristane turned sharply. "There's a fellow in the main chamber wanting to speak with you, Thane. He says there's news of your niece and it is of grave importance that he speak directly with you."

Tristane looked briefly over at Sera, then strode into the main hall. He scanned the small crowd of bystanders, and found the one face that stood out – Caldor, with his cropped dark hair and bony features. The soldier looked dirty and tired.

"Who are you?" Tristane asked.

"I was the escort of the young princess – no, I mean queen, as she is now – and she was kidnapped from under my nose by several Perytons and two liche servelings." Tristane went rigid upon hearing the news, while Caldor held out a shaking hand to complete the lie, and then clutched his heaving chest with the other. Tristane ordered some water be brought for him, then brought him into Sera's house of healing.

"Whatever you've been through, you must tell us everything," Tristane ordered, countering his instinct to dislike the man. "How did you escape the death birds? You are a long way from home, and that should have made you a prime target." Caldor hadn't anticipated his story being so flawed. He stuttered, and dropped to his knees, feigning weakness. Tristane lifted him to his feet and helped him walk towards Sera.

"Perhaps you can help him," he said to the mage.

"Hmm, perhaps I can. He is mostly in need of some water and a good rest, by the look of him. I'll give him something for that." The mage reached up to a high cupboard with a broad lock holding fast the doors, clicked his fingers, then whistled a short tune. The door sprang open and, pulling out a small brown bottle, he handed it to their exhausted visitor. Caldor consumed the liquid without protest, then stood upright and thanked the mage, seeming much refreshed by it.

"Now soldier, tell us about my niece, and don't leave any details out." Caldor recounted his tale of woe, only omitting the fact that he had known of the kidnappers' plans. Sera and Tristane listened intently, their faces serious. At the end of the story Tristane sighed uneasily. Already bereft by the loss of his brother, without having had a moment to mourn, he was now faced with the thought of his niece being kidnapped and at the mercy of an unknown force.

"I see," he said, considering. "Then you shall stay here for the night, Caldor, while we decide what the best way forward is. Come, I'll take you to your room."

He gave Sera a slight glance as he left the room with Caldor at his side.

"How shall you rescue your niece?" Caldor asked, curious about what the Thane would do with the news.

"I can't tell you yet. Sera and I need to talk about a strategy. As for you, you are our guest and shall be treated as such for bringing us the news of your escape and my niece's unfortunate kidnap."

Tristane gestured to Caldor to precede him through the doorway, and hiding his sorry heart. "Right Caldor, now we are about to amaze you with the wonders of our hidden city. See the lights in the dome at night," he added, pointing through the doorway. Since Caldor had arrived, night had fallen and shades of glistening grey fell around the chamber, with flickering candlelight giving off soft hues.

Caldor remained speechless for a few moments, taking in all that he could see, and becoming mesmerised by Ashfar's star-like quality. Its walls and the streets below were carved into the seams of gold which ran profusely through the mountain cavern. Moonlight poured in from a central skylight, diffusing upon the ore, and the people became shadows in the background.

They walked through a great chamber carved out of the rock. This vast area had huge sandstone pillars rising from the floor.

Each one had windows at regular intervals. Caldor could see faces looking through them, and realised they were some kind of dwelling. Portals could also be seen in the rock face, like a tower building, where more people peered out.

"It seems enchanted, doesn't it?" Tristane could see by the look on Caldor's face that he was overwhelmed by the view.

"Quite – absolutely, it does." Caldor replied.

"Good, I'm glad you like it. I'll show you to your rooms, where you can clean up and sleep. This way, soldier."

With that, Tristane led Caldor to an archway in the north wall which opened into another hallway with many steps, eventually leading up to the main palace. They passed a great hall, not unlike the April Hall in the Rainbow City: except for the sparkling walls and the polished metallic floors, the halls could have been duplicates of each other. A likeness of Princess Aleeah the Retaliate, in her ceremonial raiment, stood gesturing for visitors to enter. Behind her, the figures of Husienna and Aislinn were being carved into the walls, the gentle tapping cleansing the area of any other sound.

"The Century Hall fascinates you, I see," Tristane said. "It is our ceremonial place, and we decorate it with our leaders. See the old king, my grandfather over there, and his brother, before they split the territories." Caldor stretched his neck to see what the room had to offer as they passed.

"Aleeah is a fine woman," he said. "I remember her on the battlefield, but I was too young to fight and I just tagged along in secret. She was an unstoppable force. We were lucky that she did stop, or all of our kind would have been removed from this history. She seems so much more placid these days."

Tristane looked at Caldor suspiciously but didn't enter into his conjecture. "Enjoy what you see in passing. I shan't go in until the unveiling ceremony, but you can look for yourself later if you feel up to it." He smiled sadly.

With one more turn they arrived at the guest-room. "This is your room, an aide will be sent shortly with your belongings. Rest well," Tristane said, bowing to Caldor, then left him in the silence of his room, which was as resplendent as the rest of the palace.

The door clanged shut and Caldor shivered suddenly. What generosity had been given to him, a humble Aldora Adrian. He'd not dared to imagine his lot would bring him to the palace as a guest of the secret city. After all, if the throne of Husienna had been taken, he should have had some right to it as a son of Tebore and one of his many wives. The last to be born before Oraldo and Kerr, his breeding was considered far worse than the runt of the litter, and he resented that. The other members of Tebore's brood had succumbed to Aleeah's curse – save for Rakeem, who had taken the path to lichedom to avoid it.

Caldor knew it was only a matter of time before he too fell to the power of the Retaliate.

Leaning against the heavy bolted door, he took several deep breaths, believing his ruse had paid off, but it was less than satisfying. The walls jumped out at him, filled with pictures of the Marda clan members – Aleeah's family as they were before they separated. Caldor saw the old king and his brother, the king's wife and daughters, Aleeah herself, when she was younger, Craven with his cousins, and some others that he didn't recognise.

Two portraits in particular stood out. The first was entitled "The Saddest Boy", and hung left of his bed-head. To the right was a picture of a woman, entitled "The Loneliest Girl". Between these, Caldor saw the image of a cascading waterfall, iridescent against the golden hues of the backdrop. The three images were connected somehow, but by what he couldn't tell at first glance. The tears in the subjects' eyes dripped from hung heads and flowed towards the middle of the bed head. The flow from the top of the waterfall travelled from top left and right over a stony fall to a deep green lagoon, surrounded by the foliage of blue-moon creepers and tree-ferns. The pictures drew him closer into their dominion of desperation and loneliness. They wrenched at his heart as he stared longingly, wondering who or what they were about. As he came closer, he thought he could hear the sound of a sad and longing cry, the swirl of water down a fall, and a desperate whisper calling from an echoed place in time. He pulled back with heavy foreboding and collapsed on the bed, gasping for air.

The bed, the like of which he had never seen before, was big enough for three people to sleep in. Another room, carved into the rock to the right of the entrance and opposite the foot of the bed, had a continuous fountain of natural spring water spraying up through the floor for showering, and linen piled high for his use.

Washed by the light of the torches in the room, Caldor lay on his bed, subdued. The riches now ceased to impress him. His feelings were with Tama and her kiss of life, yet he knew in his heart that he was no longer needed, his task was complete. What would Tama want with a traitor anyway, he thought, bitterness seeping into his soul. He lay there uninspired by the ambience. Thoughts of never seeing Tama again tortured his mind, because no one came out of the gate room the same way they went in. He wept in silence, torn between two worlds.

***

"Well, what did you discern about our visitor? Is he telling us the truth?" Tristane asked as he re-entered Sera's room.

"In part I suppose he might be, but he wasn't suffering for it. I gave him liquid fresh-air, and it does absolutely nothing for fatigue, so he must have faked that. I think you should head into the mountain to find her – but take Caldor with you if you want to keep him close. I should think he knows more than he is letting on."

"But where to start looking...?"

"I'll try Calista's tuning fork, one of Xylon's toys that I picked up from King Bede a few years ago. It'll point you in the right direction, but then you're on your own."

"I'll take a small party with me."

"Aye, that's what you'll do. I'll see you in the morning, before you leave. Sleep well, good Thane."

Sera headed for his sleep chamber, but the mage's curiosity had been piqued by Caldor's visit. Only now was he realising that Maris was not dead, from the tales of his appearance in the Rainbow City. And few ordinary folks had the power to transcend into lichehood, yet Rakeem had, and there were others on that same path. This was in part the dark magick Cullen had taught them to avoid. This new Maris was so far removed from the man he'd known as a brother that he was confounded by the information. Briefly his memory flashed back to their last meeting, before Maris retreated to his chamber and the rest of the mages went out to rid the surface of the frozen sleep that had crept up from the south. He was pained not to be able to get back into the underground world where the lives of his brother and Cullen had been lost. The night drifted on while Sera meditated in his sleep chamber, contemplating his brother's new persona.

Tristane entered the hall at first light with his hand-picked search party, and a few minutes later Caldor joined them. Sera looked up from his study of the tuning fork.

"Well, now that you are all here, I should tell you that you will need to enter the trading route by the eastern pass. It can only be accessed from outside the mountain, but you may take the internal road as far as Quinlan if you wish to stay protected." He put the tuning fork down; it buzzed gently and spun of its own volition. Sera put his hand on it to keep it still.

"Where do we go after that?" asked

Tristane.

"As I told you yesterday, the fork is only a guide, and you will have to find your own way from there."

Caldor took a deep breath and Tristane turned to his men. His desire to go out into the world had been strong, but now it came to it he didn't want to go. Perhaps it was the type of journey he was wary of, he thought. They left through the eastern tunnel under the auspices of the morning glow that filtered through cracks in the rock face.

Nervous and wary of his companions, Caldor didn't speak for most of the journey east to the mountain's lowlands. They left the mountain proper at early evening. It would take at least a day more to reach the eastern pass, and Caldor wondered how well he could keep up his deceit.

The night was clear, and warm drafts of air swirled around them. The mountains loomed heavily over their path. Many eyes watched from the security of the rocky walls, but whenever the men looked for signs of life, they saw nothing. Tristane was used to this. He'd often travelled at night before his responsibilities took that freedom away from him. But Caldor was not used to night travel, and didn't much like it. Living in the Kye, city of the dead, from early in his life had made him very uncomfortable with the darkness of the world outside. Now these scampering feet and small, tumbling rocks about him made Caldor more nervous as Tristane grew more relaxed. There were many things that one didn't care to understand about the Plains, thought Caldor.

Cathal, Tristane's Captain and a close friend since he had wandered into Ashfar as a child, nudged Tristane as they watched Caldor slink further down into his riding saddle, then whispered, "Not much of a hero, that one."

Tristane grinned. "More like a snake in the grass, if you ask me."

"I reckon, and we'll watch him close

enough," Cathal replied.

He took the lead into another tunnel, at first just wide enough for the horses in single file but then opening out into a huge, torch-lit chamber. The bustle of rowdy life sounded from behind the entrance-way as they approached. Two guards appeared, gruff, unshaven and smelling of beer. They were dressed in blue shirts with silver breastplates, their helmets peaked above the crown of their heads and they clanked with the weight of their metallic leggings. Caldor peered around the side of the group to see which company they were from. Valaron, he thought, unhappy to see the uniforms again. They were an added reason for his family's downfall by coming to the aid of Aleeah, and he mistrusted them for it. Both men's faces were shielded by visors, leaving only room for the eyes to see. Though he couldn't tell from the masked eyes, Caldor felt their contempt for him.

"Say your business and ye shall enter. Silence will bring you your misfortune," shouted one of the men.

"It is Captain Cathal of the Ashfarian territories. Will you let us pass?"

"We will after your travelling companions state their business," said the other.

"I am Thane of the South Trist, and not in the mood for your nonsense," Tristane said sternly. "Let us in."

"Certainly sire," one of the guards quickly replied as they both leapt to attention.

The iron gate to the large chamber opened, moaning under its own weight. It dragged slowly along the stone floor to reveal the full height and enormous size of the chamber.

"I'll not be joining the men tonight," Tristane said to his Captain. "See you take care of our visitor. Perhaps he could do with a flagon of ale to help him tell a tale or two." Caldor watched Tristane leave, wondering what that remark meant, then turned to see the garrison.

He could see many doors in the flickering light, one in particular stood out because it was slightly ajar. Light poured through the gap into the dimly lit cavern, along with rowdy music and drunken cheers. Around the hall men and women soldiers sat in relaxed poses and chatted to each other. The women appeared handsome and statuesque. Caldor had never seen so many women in battle dress since the Virgin War. However, they were not of any Pelien race he had seen before, and he queried Cathal about their lineage.

"They are little known beyond the mountain and in the West where you come from. They came out of the Outlands far east of Valaron with stories of wild creatures plaguing their territories," said Cathal. It was only when Cathal removed his helm that Caldor realised Ashfar's captain looked just like them.

"They have come to fight what they call the devil. They are the children of Orion and have travelled a great distance to be close to their father. Orion is the name they give to Kalale and I am of the same kinship. They are my relatives, though I've had little to do with them since I was young. I prefer the company of Peliens." Caldor didn't know what to make of the news. He was walking now with the son of a Shaman, though it was obviously of little consequence to Cathal.

"You don't see yourself for what you really are."

"I could ask you what that actually meant, Caldor, but I won't because the reality is I am just a man, like you." Cathal quickly changed the subject. "This is Quinlan Garrison, if you haven't guessed by now, and it houses soldiers from Valaron as well as Ashfar. It's where we let our hair down – a popular spot and a day's ride from both cities. From here we can keep in touch with Ashfar, and a seasoned rider can make the journey to Valaron in less than a day with the right horse. But enough geography, there's not an ale house within a hundred miles that can soothe the soul of a weary soldier like this one can." Cathal pointed to the inn door that almost seemed to be jumping to the sounds of fluted music, and the smell of hot foods tantalised their tastebuds. Caldor was parched, but wanted to avoid such a place. Who knew what he might let on with a pint or two in him, he thought.

"A bed has been fixed for us here for the night, but I doubt if I'll make it out of the ale house," Cathal laughed, and his men smirked as if they all shared some wonderful secret. A common trait of the Ashfarians, thought Caldor. Not interested in socialising with Cathal, Caldor tried to excuse himself before they entered the inn, but Cathal wouldn't hear of it.

"Caldor, there are many hours of weary travel ahead of us. I cannot let you miss out on pleasures that will be few and far between once we leave here. Take a moment to look inside the door, have a mug of ale and if you still feel the need to retire then Durra will show you where your bed is; but until then, relax and enjoy the evening." Cathal was hurrying to tether his horse outside the inn. He called for a stable hand to look after their horses for the night, and then bowed in front of Caldor, directing him inside.

CHAPTER FIVE:

Burden of knowledge

At first the light blurred Caldor's vision, it was almost as bright as the sunlight. The music was loud, intimidating and haunting, mingling with the smell of smoke, potent ales, and body heat. In the far corner a woman danced to the music – her slender body gracefully swayed around the floor, enchanting the men with her curvaceous frame and slender legs. Her lily skin shimmered through the gossamer ruby gown, offering hints of her nakedness beneath, yet not yielding every secret. A rill of sweat formed in the valley of her breasts. The men drooled at her wicked taunting. Her long silvery curls, tossed from side to side around her face, hid the real beauty of her heritage. She was a nymph. Few had ever seen one: nymphs never dwelt in cities and towns; their beauty was too much for mere mortals to bear. Xarvia was not worried about her mesmerising beauty – all she ever wanted was to please, as was the will bestowed upon her, and that of all nymphs. She was the prize, though what that amounted to was overwhelming to most men, and they stayed away from winning it.

"So, Captain, do you still wish to retire, or are you brave enough to stay and be taunted by this creature of lust?" asked Cathal.

"I see now why you were so eager to spend your night at the inn; she tempts me to stay also. It's true, then, what the folks speak of? I thought the seven nymphs were a myth, alive only in the hearts of young men and disenchanted husbands. How did she come to be here?" Caldor asked.

"She wandered in here one night, lost, and has never wanted to leave. There's always an audience for Xarvia, but I doubt if she will ever find peace here," Cathal replied.

"It is said that they cannot bed down with any man unless the man be a virgin. If the man is not, his heart will turn to stone; but a virgin will reap the knowledge of the gods – if he be big enough to carry such a burden." Caldor's eyes never stopped watching the nymph swaying back and forth. She glanced his way and captured his heart with her eyes.

"That is, I believe, the story as it goes, but no man dares challenge the myth out of fear for the truth in it. All these men are brave and fearless with a sword, at least they think they are, but they are no match for the magick of a nymph. I see you are enthralled by her – don't stare too long at Xarvia's eyes, as she will burden you with her desire to be free of the bondage." Caldor, no longer listening to Cathal, continued to stare.

"Caldor! Caldor! Release your eyes from her, you are not the one to carry this burden." Cathal's expression grew more concerned as Caldor moved through the crowd, drawn by the nymph's deep, hematite-coloured eyes. He pulled Caldor back and shouted for him to break his stare, but the command fell on deaf ears. Caldor kept on moving towards the female, who was focused solely on him now, drawing him closer with her magical stare. The crowd parted to let him pass, not knowing what to do with the situation. As he came to her she felt that at last she was to be set free. Their fingertips touched and silence fell – save for a few mutters, and the last notes of music. The soldiers backed away from the dance area, unable to comprehend what was happening.

Cathal drew his sword, but the nymph threw him out of the way by thought alone. She was not going to be cheated of her freedom now. She stood, briefly waiting for another challenge, but Cathal lay stunned in the far corner amongst broken cutlery and smashed mugs of ale.

Xarvia spoke in her own tongue and asked Caldor if he would carry her burden.

The Captain made no attempt to pull away, and she had her answer. The crowd parted and allowed them passage out of the ale house into the main chamber. All activity ceased whilst the garrison watched them ascend to her rooms above the inn. The nymph held Caldor constantly in her gaze; moving as she moved, he was trapped in the passageway to her salvation.

In Caldor's mind, there was still sanity enough for him to break the spell at any time, but the prize was too great. Carrying the burden of the gods' knowledge would make him a powerful adversary; but it was more than wanting – it was an addiction. Even the kindest of souls cannot easily expel an addiction that is firmly fixed in place. Caldor was weak at best, and in terms of corruptibility he was driven by desire rather than by reason.

They entered her room, in which was a bed – laden with silk pillows and sheets that glistened in the same ruby red as her lips and gown. A red glow in the light filled the softly furnished area with tranquillity and warmth. They danced slowly as she hummed a tune. Caldor's spirit was completely lost in a subdued happiness that felt like real romance, though it was nothing more than an enchantment to snare him. Xarvia laid him down on her bed, then lay on top of him and breathed her final breath into his mouth, passing on the burden. The myth had been distorted: all it took was the air she breathed to be passed on to another. Caldor felt betrayed, but it was too late.

He felt the anguish of knowledge suffusing him – through his lungs, heart, and limbs. The exquisite suffering of a million thoughts and worries and wisdom entered his body like molten metal; rippling the muscles of his swollen body as each terrible and beautiful thought travelled its way through his veins, pulsing with the beat of his heart into his mind, and he knew for a fleeting moment that the consequences of his decision were beyond calculation.

Xarvia gave a final panting push of

air, emptying her lungs into Caldor's mouth before she dissipated into the atmosphere, leaving nothing more than a fine mist of her form, which lingered momentarily before Caldor lay alone, agonising with the new weight of woes, worries, and predictions. The pain seemed set to last forever, and stiffened his body as if it were a corpse that lay in wait for Salamar; but he was not dead. His emotions and senses were immobilised by the thoughts flashing in his mind – thousands of thoughts. He moaned and gasped in fear and enlightenment, not knowing what was real and what fantasy, and then the pain eased. He wept like a child and laughed like a jester; he pondered the possibilities of time and was angered at his own heart turning as black as the fires of the deepest pits. He basked in the glory of the creation of life itself, from the Plains to the five seas, but most of all, he revelled in the thoughts of his own glorified future, the future he craved.

The burden was more than any man

should have to endure, but it was now his for all eternity. Not even death could separate his mind from that of the gods. He had brought on his own purgatory. Caldor could never have imagined the size of the thoughts that had now entered his body, nor how to use them or how to know which were set in stone and which of those thoughts drifted like the ocean in a dance of mystery. He could not have known that all that was thought by the makers could change constantly; the book of the gods was always being written and re-written. He did not understand that the people of the Plains wrote their own destinies, yet the wyrd sisters could manipulate their choices, and the gods had their own designs too, creating a complex weaving of freedoms and fates.

Now, as he lay trembling like a small animal he understood his destiny. He was weary of his expanding mind, and drifted off into a restless night of sleep; but even there he could not escape from the constant babble of thoughts. Poor Caldor, a fool with knowledge lying helpless in the dimly lit room with no way back to the safety of his position in life, outcast and unreliable to all living things.

When he woke, the morning light from the garrison poured in through his window. All was quiet below. It was a strain to leave the bed and he struggled to the floor, at first falling on his hands and knees. His head pounded like a drum and the weight of his mind was too much for his neck to lift. Slowly regaining his strength and posture, he ventured out of the room to an audience that had gathered the night before, to wait for a result from his union with the nymph. He stood in the doorway naked and broken-looking, clinging onto the frame. The soldiers of the garrison gasped at his madness.

"What are you staring at, foolish Peliens?" he spat. "You have no idea of what is to come." His voice tapered off. "The world is changing and you can't stop it."

He turned slowly to the nymph's room

and dressed, feeling his muscles burning with fatigue. Gradually his strength returned as he adjusted to the new power and pondered his next move. It was written in so many ways; the pain was now ever in the choosing.

*****

Tristane had waited through the passing hours with a gathering crowd of men, having been brought from his bed before he'd had time to sleep in it. They had heard the groaning sounds of Caldor's pain, and the nymph's final breath as she ascended to the stars, passing through the solid rock as a red mist. Then female screams had echoed from all directions.

Some men dashed outside to see if Xarvia really had turned into a star, and were amazed by the several stars that now appeared in the sky. A formerly empty space had waited to embrace them. The seven sisters were joined to Kalale that night, the sky being his temple and all that dwelt in it his paramours. The panic-stricken soldiers ran back to tell their tale. The myth was no myth at all: the seven sister nymphs, who between them had carried the burden too large for one, had now all been released into the night by the one nymph determined enough to find her destiny in the house of her master. Each star had its own hue. One in particular stood out to the onlookers, twinkling ruby red; the others golden yellow, island-green, pale sapphire, sparkling silver, violet, and ivory.

Tristane spoke briefly to his captains whilst they waited for Caldor to reappear. They agreed to send word to Sera, and Ashfar's fastest rider was despatched through the internal caves, with another rider sent to warn King Bede of the evil that had befallen them that night. The young soldier rode as swiftly as his mare would allow, deep into the mountain's many highways. His horse tired quickly in the humid air of that part of the mountain, but the rider pushed his animal onwards. What would have been a day's casual ride was cut in half by the speed and talent of a great young horseman, with the wit to navigate each turn and gradient.

By the time he reached the hidden city morning had just broken, and Sera waited for him in the main city square. Sera had also seen the heavens glistening with the new stars, but awaited confirmation of what his mind already knew. The young soldier was weary from the journey and Sera eased his throat with spring waters. His horse was quickly whisked away to the stables where it could be cared for.

"My boy, your Thane did well to choose you for this job, but I have not the time to reward you. I know of what has happened by the night sky, but you must relate to me the details. Who carries the burden? You must tell me, quickly."

The soldier told the story to the mage. Sera sighed at what he heard. "This is by no means the worst news I have had all this long season," he muttered to himself, then dismissed the messenger and retired to his loft high in the city's walls. "It is time to assemble my guild," he muttered on reaching the last step to his room. The keys jingled as they unlocked the heavy brown door, then Sera waved his arm and it opened as if not burdened by any weight at all.

There he settled himself in a chair carved out of the great woodland oak tree, placed to have the best view of the sky through the open roof top. The seven sisters could still be seen, just barely, with the naked eye, as the sun was just breaking. He closed his eyes and began to chant incantations with arms folded across his chest, each hand holding the opposite shoulder. His voice was singular at first, and then it was joined by another, then two more – and four voices chanted the same words in harmony. His long, blue robes flickered in the cool mountain air that found its way in via the open roof, and his long beard flapped back and forth. The chanting stopped and the four minds were now joined.

"Xarjay, Mainheart, and Ranyel." Sera addressed them as if all were in the same room. "It is regrettable that we must speak on such a sombre matter."

"Oh, get on with it, you fool, and stop being so dramatic, because I only spoke with you last season about the failing crops. How much more sombre can you get! Now spit out your news, man, I'm in the middle of my breakfast," Xarjay interrupted.

"Hmm, yes, yes," responded Sera. "I will, if you promise to shut up and listen for once in your life."

"Gentlemen, please! This is no time for banter, there's time enough for that after we have discussed the urgent matters at hand," said Mainheart. "Now, I believe that you have called us in relation to the new heavenly bodies I observed from my tower last night. It was a beautiful night for observing the planets, and there they were, right in front of me, the seven sisters. My word! If this is what I think it is then we have a big, big problem on our hands."

"Yes, yes, yes! We do have a problem, don't we?" said Ranyel, soothingly. "Let's do try and get through this without all of your arguments. If we can put the situation in perspective using our logic and intelligence, then we have a place to begin."

"Intelligence, logic! Fottlewarts to both!" Xarjay expostulated. "Perhaps you would like to give us all spot tests before we begin, you studious creature."

"Studious is better than tedious, man. Now as I was saying – ahem – asking, who is carrying the burden? Logic tells me that the nymphs are freed, hence the seven sisters appearing in our night sky," said Ranyel.

"Yes, you are right, Ranyel, and the one who has achieved this is a blasted dark heart. He is the last in the line of Tebore's children not yet succumbed to the Retaliate's curse – if you don't include Prince Rakeem the new liche of Kye, or Oraldo and Kerr, still wanted for their role in Lucinda's attack on the Retaliate the last

time they reared their heads on Caragh –
present whereabouts unknown."

"Will this history lesson be ending
soon? I have things to do, objects to invent,
mead to brew, etc, etc." said Xarjay.

"I'm getting there, man," said Sera.

"Not before I'm getting old enough to
draw my last breath and my mind starts to
dither!"

"You say that as if it's not normal.
Now, as I was saying – Caldor was Queen
Tama's escort. But he turned up here two
days ago without her, claiming she'd been
kidnapped, which of course she has been.
Then there's the other matter – of Maris still
being alive. Yet there is still more to this
strange story. Yesterday morning, just
before the parties left the city, I was given
news of a sighting."

"A sighting? Of what?" Mainheart
demanded.

"The Order of the Ommers," replied
Sera.

"Really!" exclaimed Mainheart. "Then

we have to presume he truly is alive; but more importantly he is the vessel of the dark knight who Aleeah inadvertently set free."

"It was only a matter of time before this Pretender revealed himself. Now that the Ommers are here to recapture him, we must assume Maris is the one, all the signs are in" said Ranyel. "You know, Sera, there is still hope that your brother can be retrieved."

"I dare not hope it, for I was a fool not to see it in the first place, and without the advantage of surprise we have nothing."

"No one blames you for that. Your judgement was surely clouded by your relationship with him. But at least we know now that Cullen probably fell victim to this Pretender we assume is your twin, my dear friend," Mainheart replied.

"Indeed, the problems are much greater than any of us anticipated, Sera. Perhaps I should come to you and we can make plans to capture this Caldor," Ranyel urged gently.

"But what about Tama?" asked Mainheart.

"She is in the hands of her uncle... when he can find her – and find her he will, I'm sure of that. We know it is written that she be some kind of prodigy. Let's hope she can do what the wyrd sisters intended," said Sera.

"In that case, Sera, I shall definitely head north-west to you. Two heads are better than one," said Ranyel.

"That's settled then. We'll speak again as soon as I have any news, gentlemen." The mages said their goodbyes and Sera found himself staring through his open roof at the fading stars, waiting for fate to deal out its will.

*****

Caldor lay silent on the bed after dressing. His body temperature rose, and beads of sweat formed on his brow. The madness of his burden had already begun to shape his thoughts and desires. As he lay sifting through several millennia of dreams, ideas, hopes, and wants about times he could not remember and places he'd only thought of visiting, a whisper thread of Tama's ordeal while she awaited entry to the gate came into his mind, then disappeared. Quickly he tried to regain the thought, reaching out with a grabbing hand as if the images were floating in the air about him, but with little expertise of his new and heavy talent, it was like finding an ember amongst the stars. For an hour he lay searching for her, until finally, she was there in his head and he visualised keeping hold of the images in his hand.

"Now I have you, my lady." He spoke out loud. She was sheathed under the glass lid of a coffin, beating at it from the inside. Maris was busy preparing the gate for her entry. But that was old news. He had no desire to see Tama go into the gate room, so he turned his attention to the city of Kye. Caldor peered in on Prince Rakeem, who lay pampered and grotesque in his chambers, awaiting some order from his new ally Maris.

Jealousy enraged Caldor: it was he who should have the seat of power in the dead city, so he could take the Rainbow City and be king of the Plains. After all, that is what his father had wanted to do; it was his right to want the same. What flashed then before his eyes were the amulets that Sera and the other three mages wore about their necks.

"Yes, that's it. I'll bring chaos to the land and the land will become mine." He knew now that his first step would be to steal Sera's amulet, thereby throwing the elements into chaos. Then he thought to head south, to where he knew there were at least two other amulets he could get his hands on. Leaving the garrison would not prove difficult; he knew the soldiers' thoughts and how they planned to attack him on his exit. To know your enemy's mind was a great advantage, he thought. "These plebs think that they can take me now, but they are wrong."

As Caldor left the room he saw that the garrison had cleared a path for his exit, as he had foreseen. The marksmen were in place ready to shoot him when his back turned on them, but Caldor didn't go the way they expected. Rather he stayed close to the walls of the cave and melted into them, becoming a chameleon. He used his power to trick their minds and the soldiers shot blindly at what looked like an empty wall. He entered the cavern that led directly to the hidden city, with nothing more than a close call from a stray arrow brushing his ear, drawing a small amount of blood. He laughed at their foiled attempts to see him off. Nothing of Caldor was seen again in the chamber, but his deafeningly, bitter laughter chilled the garrison to the bone. His only challenge now was to navigate the correct turns along the tunnels to Ashfar.

Caldor stumbled along through the caverns, holding the walls for support. He grunted and laughed insanely as he staggered along. His mind was in a constant battle to remain focused. Knowing the minds of the Aldora became an assault of thoughts flashing in and out of his consciousness, creating an electrical storm that threw him in and out of spasms. His own thoughts were hard to contain in one place long enough for him to follow them. For the best part he was running on instinct – a gut feeling that was leading him to his reward.

By nightfall he had reached Ashfar, where Sera awaited his arrival. Sera watched as the madman staggered into the citadel's marketplace. Not a sound could be heard anywhere in this usually bustling place. Faces peeped through doors, but no one emerged. The people instinctively whispered through the halls, creating the sound of incoherent hissing down the winding tunnels.

"Sera! Nice of you to greet me. Frankly, I'm a little surprised, because I know your mind, yet you don't know mine," said Caldor in a mocking tone. His face became calm and calculating.

"You are mistaken, my young mad son. I wasn't born motherless and fatherless for no purpose at all," replied the mage.

"Yet you were not clever enough to see your own brother had become estranged to his own body, taken by the one who was freed. It is a strange time where circles are made in the lines of fate – where events meet on more than one occasion in more than one time."

"Perhaps my intuition was flawed to that occasion. But in the year of the Stolen Chalice, the best of us become cheated of our right thoughts. I am not under the spell of that constellation now, nor will be for a few more years, until it comes again; so there can be only one reason why you would come here."

"And that is...?"

"You are a failure in your own body, so you want mine, and you want my place in the world so you can save your sorry soul from the Retaliate's curse and become Maris's new equal."

Caldor crossed his arms as if it wasn't such a bad thing. "Well, not a bad idea, but body-snatching is so uncouth." Then he lowered his tone, becoming darker in vision than any of his relatives could have been. "So I'll settle for your head and that shiny amulet hanging below it!"

With a flash of his blade he quickly turned and decapitated an innocent bystander who had foolishly stepped out into the open. With another flash he had sunk his sword deep into the heart of a pet dog. The villagers, startled behind their doors, began to scream and run wildly away from cover. Sera was floored by the ferocity of Caldor's attack, and Caldor knew it, taking the opportunity within seconds to kill another and another. Before Sera could compose himself, several victims lay dead or dying in pools of blood. There was confusion and screaming, no one knowing what to do. For so long no blood had been shed in the light of the golden caverns; it was senseless and malevolent.

Sera, his senses now restored, cast his right arm forth, expelling a fiery ball of lightning towards Caldor, who dived for cover behind a barrel of ale. His senses too had become heightened in his moment of directed rage. Caldor's adrenaline had taken effect upon his mind, for the first time that day he had become centred on his own mind and the mind of Sera. It was enough for Caldor to outrun the fiery assault, and a battle of wits began. All the villagers had again hidden themselves inside their homes and the city streets were silent, except for the sounds of fire crashing against the solid rock walls.

Caldor dodged in and out of the onslaught, biding his time, as he knew Sera would eventually grow weak. Sera turned furiously, trying to find his nemesis, but when his back was turned Caldor lunged with his sword, deeply penetrating Sera's heart. The mage gulped as his blood gurgled up into his throat and a tear of defeat rolled down his face.

Sera breathed his last breath and whispered his final words – words which echoed through the whispering walls, transcending the darkness that lay about like a blanket of dust. "My young, mad son, remember this day as our last free day. Evermore my journey will be on the tail of yours." With his last remaining strength Sera grabbed Caldor's forehead and burned a bloody hand print into his brow, reminding him of Sera's promise to hunt him down. The stench of death drifted into the chamber as Salamar's hands reached out of the air to take his new prizes to the afterlife. Sriann waited in the background for Salamar to finish his work, then she called him back to his receptacle. Her scented gracefulness brought calm to the chaos and eased the mourning coming from behind closed doors. Caldor thought for a moment he could hear the voices of a chorus singing a lamenting melody.

Sriann spoke, casting her serenity across the fouled air. "Caldor, you have much to answer for when you finally meet the Maker Eternal. We each write our own destinies. Yours is now forged beyond the wyrd and golden threads of fate. No more will they undo what is done, or open other doorways, because your choices cannot be invalidated. There is no hell for you to be bonded to; but you will know hell because of your choices here today. You wear the mark of a mage, the keeper of the water elemental talisman. He owns your soul, it is his last right. Killing the guardians of the Plains will ensure a severed soul." Sriann, as always, spoke softly and steadily. Her words of dread should have brought fear to Caldor's heart, yet he was at peace whilst in her presence. She left as quietly as she had come, and Caldor finally fell to his knees, realising his first triumph as he searched Sera's limp body for the talisman. Ashfar was his!

Caldor watched as the exodus of

civilians began. He looked on with a keen eye, reading their thoughts, but he was unable to match a face to each one. He smiled privately, not making any attempt to stop them. The people were glad of this and used the moment to gather their families and head out toward the garrison.

His thoughts now turned to the other mages. He would need at least two amulets to cause the havoc he wanted, he thought, and looked around for the stables.

"Finally!" he said as he came upon them. His horse showed discomfort at being used against its will, but sensed its own death was close should it do otherwise. Caldor left by the south tunnel, feeling triumphant in the shadows of the whispering caverns which flickered lightly with candles and torches. He knew that Xarjay lived in the Blue Hills, and that was his next appointment.

By night he travelled under the glowing full moon and a sky full of sparkling stars. But Kalale was watching intently from a lonely cloud in the troposphere, and blew his heart out in search of a cloud to cover the light of the moon. A storm wafted in and swirled across the night, covering the moon's glow and making the horse's journey difficult. Driving rain further hampered Caldor's animal, which slipped constantly until his weight gave way on loose rocks and he tumbled. The horse snorted and snuffled as he tried to regain a foothold, but it was no use; his back legs had become lame and he could no longer be of use to his master.

Caldor, quick to anger, leapt off the horse and hacked off its head in a fit of rage. The Captain fell to the ground under his own swing, cursing and swearing revenge on Kalale for blocking the moonlight and sending the storm, but determined not to be beaten by it. He travelled on foot, still muttering obscenities to the sky. Kalale heard but did not respond, the clouds drifted away of their own accord and once again the moon shone brightly, guiding his path as an eagle glided high overhead, watching him – or so his paranoid mind believed.

He plunged down the mountainous track, heading further and further south, not anticipating any more problems. But Kalale was not finished yet. The night air grew cold as the Shaman drove a southerly wind in his direction. Noises in the dark rose in volume and unhinged the already tumultuous mind of the Captain. Now, filled with fear, his heart pounded, eyes darted and ears twitched at every whispery blade of grass that moved. Caldor clutched his coat tightly around him, partly in fear and partly against the southerly wind. Kalale stirred the air to create willy-willies which crossed Caldor's path, kicking up dust and flinging debris into his face, causing him to dash for cover in a nearby cave.

Increasingly, Kalale was happy with his efforts to slow down Caldor's travel plans, and continued to whip up a dry storm. Caldor held out in a small cave, almost at the bottom of the mountain, and could hear the wind howling. Thinking he was safe for the moment and wanting peace from his babbling mind, he closed his eyes. The sleep he craved came as desired; his mind was as silent as the ancient pools of mercury that sat below the poles. He slept for the first time since the night before his journey to Ashfar. Sweet, beautiful dreams blanketed his mind – no whirling maelstrom of thoughts to hinder his restful slumber. The strangeness of the gods' thoughts did not come to taunt him; yet he dreamed, and the dreams were pleasant and beautiful. Several hours later, Caldor awoke: warm and happy, snuggled up tight, with his head on a pillow of supplies. The waking took several moments, but when he had come to full sanity Caldor realised that he was not simply tucked up in a cosy cave. He was bound like a wild beast, unable to move either limb or muscle. He sensed another mind in the cave besides his, but was unable to read it or explain to himself how his thoughts were no longer plagued by the gods. Fear tentatively grasped his being until his companion showed himself in the light of the cave entrance.

"Well then, I see we have caught ourselves a captain, and a sane one at that. I knew my spell would work. It's just a matter of formulating the right mantras. Have a lovely rest, did you? Yes, of course you did. I created it, and I never do anything that isn't good," said the man. "You know, Captain, you weren't as difficult to capture as I had anticipated. Sera and I had grave fears about you after you did what you did. Such a man should be locked away for even thinking he could court such a woman. My, my: Sera will be pleased when I take you back to the city and lock you away."

"For the gods' sake, don't you ever stop talking? For the first time in two moons I've had mental peace and quiet, only to be captured by the Plains' most babbling fool. Anyway, you shouldn't worry too much about Sera. I have this vague memory of killing him," Caldor curtly replied.

Ranyel, startled by the thought, rubbed his hand across his chin, which sprouted a day's growth of red hair. "Oh dear, that is a catastrophe. Well, I guess that explains why you have a blotchy red hand print on your forehead. Hmm! You should be happy to know that a mage doesn't die permanently. It's rather confusing compared to the old world, where things were cut and dried. If you were dead you were dead, and that was that. This world, well you just aren't dead till you're *really* dead, and even then you may not be. If you're lucky Sera will be on his way back again. Then again he may not; could be more fun waiting till you get to where he is so he can carry out his promise to you. Done it once or twice myself, you know." Ranyel twitched with a small measure of dissatisfaction, inconvenienced by the passing of his friend, yet not mournful.

"Well now, it's time to eat breakfast and make our way back to Ashfar. Unfortunately I can't untie your legs; just one arm will have to do for now, so you can eat. My napkin is laden with berries and the like. Hungry? Yes, of course you are," Ranyel answered his own question as he untied Caldor's right arm without touching the rope.

"I'm curious. How did you make my burden disappear so easily? I feel like my mind has been cleansed," asked Caldor, lightly. He felt that this incarceration was only a short intermission, and as soon as Ranyel looked the other way he would escape.

"Well, sir, if you've been around as long as I have, you tend to pick up a trick or two. It's simple, really. I have created an illusion; however, I have not fixed your dilemma, rather put a kind of bandage over the top of it and recalled your sanity and your own mind back from the depths of whence you sent it. I can switch it off at any given moment if I choose. So be a good soldier, eat and follow orders, because I can also turn up the pain and turn your brains into semolina pudding. Eat, boy, eat!" Ranyel dismissed the Captain with a swish of his hand and ate heartily.

The travellers set off in the light of day. Caldor was strapped hanging beneath a broom like a pig on a spit, gliding through the air with Ranyel walking by its side guiding it back up the mountain. They travelled in silence for the best part of the journey. Ranyel, not needing to chat openly with Caldor any more than he already had, was relieved when they finally reached the city's sanctum. The whispering caves had been a bustle of gentle verbal activity whilst the twosome passed through. The few who had dared to remain rejoiced at the sight of Ranyel. Ranyel found his way up to Sera's lair and safely locked the Captain in a small corner of the room, secured with bars of steel.

CHAPTER SIX:

Stuck in Hell

"What would you have us do in this new situation, Thane?" Cathal asked as Tristane raged.

"Perhaps I should have you cut off your own heads, because there seems to be a large degree of incompetence. Would you like to just knock on the door of the dark hearts and say, "Here, we're too stupid to look after ourselves: we'd rather 'hell and servitude' for our master!" Cathal looked down. Blood had slowly dripped from the wound on his head since he'd been thrown several hours before and the bandage was stained heavily. He had pain enough for ten sore heads without being berated by the Thane, his long-standing friend.

"It was completely unforgivable of me. I should've been more careful with one of those people," Cathal said dejectedly, trying hard to concentrate through the headache.

Tristane took several deep breaths and calmed himself, realising that anger would not solve this huge problem. "Perhaps you should have, perhaps not. There seems to be no end to this saga against my family."

"Then, coming back to my question," Cathal moved forward and placed a hand on Tristane's shoulder, "what would you have us do next?"

"Tama is the key to the undoing of all this. I don't know how, but we've got to get on and find her."

"What about Caldor? Shouldn't we go after him?"

"We've lost the element of surprise on that front – he knows all that the gods know now, so we are no match for him. No, I'll leave him to Sera and the other mages, they'll know what to do, I hope... I think." Tristane threw his hands in the air. This event had completely thrown him off balance, as if he wasn't already in no man's land, he thought. "We'll go as planned to get my niece. Assemble everyone out in the foyer – including the Orions, I think," he pondered aloud. "If I were the self-proclaimed enemy of my family, such as the dark hearts are, then I'd prepare for some kind of an attack; we need Tama back in our hands to fight it."

"It's not unreasonable that an attack will happen. They've done it before." Cathal scratched his head, realising he'd stated the obvious. "I mean, that's what kind of people they are, the dark hearts."

"Yes, and now they have a liche in charge, not to mention Maris egging them on." Tristane shook his head – every time he said the name Maris, a flash of his own history in the mage guild came into his mind, though splintered out of all coherence. He remembered running continuously through a basement with his brother Husienna while being chased by an unknown beast created by Maris's hand – Cullen coming to send them home, and

Craven waiting there to give them the news of Aleeah being seriously wounded.

"You can go now," he said, as his mind snapped back to the present.

Cathal bowed politely and left Tristane to gather his thoughts while he called the garrison to order.

"There's no point in beating about the bush, you all know what's happened. We are wholly unprepared for what is going to happen, so the rest will be made up of guesswork. We hear the stories of Rakeem's zombie army, we know he takes our living and turns them into something undead – and he himself is one of them, so we've heard. The heir to the throne of Husienna has been kidnapped by his henchmen, and a malevolent spirit has come as the image of Maris – perhaps it is Maris, I don't know – and now there is a dark heart with the power of forethought roaming about the underbelly of the mountain. The times are dark, I cannot recall any history when the people of the Plains have faced so many enemies – yet we are not lost. We have many strengths and I believe these strengths lie in our will to be free, and our given right to be free. So, if our common destiny now is to fight to the last breath, then so shall it be." Cathal paused for breath.

"Then what do you propose?" asked the Orion female, her accent strong and sharp. A tall woman with dark eyes, she stepped out of the dimly lit background, pushing her way forward. "I've heard your pretty words, Orion son. For months now we have been fighting against many in the Outlands that we have no quarrel with, yet they come and steal our people. They are the dead ones, with no soul, as you say. They come, our people die, our children have disappeared, and now we talk. What is this? A battle plan is what we need." Her voice strained from too much beer and talk as she threw her hands open. "All we have done since we came is talk, talk, talk."

"You know as well as any, Orion daughter – that we've been preoccupied watching and waiting for Rakeem to show his hand. Well, now he has. The image that came to Tristany was that of a dead mage, at least supposed dead – and perhaps he is, except for a new driver in the body's seat. None of us know for sure." Cathal was not pleased with her attitude: one rebuke in a morning was quite enough, he thought.

"Then give me an occupation, Orion son, as I am the leader of our people. It is only fitting I lead the Orions, since you chose not to live with us," she snapped back.

"I don't have time for family feuds, Orion daughter: save it for the enemy and you will be the first to have your orders!" said Cathal sharply, turning back to the gathering.

Tristane walked through the crowd. He normally left the "doing" to his captains, but a revelation had hit him in the last hour – he was in charge! There was no one else, no parents to rely on, only to be replaced by a brother now dead, and the child of the fates had been stolen from under his nose.

"Perhaps it is unreasonable to let Cathal do all the work here today," he said loudly, and the audience turned as one to look at him. "I am all that is left to direct what comes before us, whatever that may be." The garrison stood to attention. Tristane was not usually commanding, but this was different, now he had no choice.

"You should all head out to the city of Valaron, where Bede awaits news. From there you should assume you are going to be attacked, because Valaron lacks protection. At least the Rainbow City still has Aleeah, as old as she feels she is. As for myself, I will go and get my niece back, because she's the key to the door – so to speak."

Cathal looked around, but no one moved, they were waiting for more talk. The very idea that they would find themselves a second time in battle was quite extraordinary for them.

"You heard the Thane, get your bony

arses off to Valaron!" The men and women moved out slowly. Tristane, Cathal, and a small band of men remained behind.

"You should go with them, Cathal."

"They've got enough leaders among them, we'll go with you," said his captain. Tristane smiled, knowing there was no one he'd rather have with him than such a true friend.

"Now, Thane, what is the direction we should find ourselves travelling to?" Cathal asked.

Tristane pointed to the northern pass.

"That's the trading route. Where she could be beyond that is not clear, but it's a start," he said.

"Then we'll take what we need and head out as soon as we can. We'll be there within a few hours if we take our swiftest animals," Cathal replied.

The small band of highly skilled soldiers packed their horses, and Tristane took his team out of the garrison, leaving the cavern almost empty but for a few staff.

They trotted on horseback northwards up the side of the mountain, where Sera had foreseen Tama's whereabouts. Tristane forged ahead, picking up speed to a slow gallop and disappearing over the horizon and into the shadows of the mountains. His group struggled to keep up.

Tristane's eyes widened at the sight of the northern mountains. Today they appeared more ominous than usual; suspended in time and encased in low, black smoke rings. His mind was on many things, but most of all how to enter the realm of Maris without being detected. Looking around at the quiet faces of his men, he realised the desperation of his situation. No general or thane would send his cavalry and arms into battle without their trusted leadership. Yet that's what he'd just done, if indeed there was going to be an attack of the minions and dark hearts as he'd guessed. The conjecture frustrated him and he sighed several times. Cathal noticed his behaviour and felt for him, but no words were there to settle his leader's mind.

"Come, let's pick up the pace. The path to the mountain is clear – at least we have that much going for us," Tristane ordered. The small company galloped quickly into the looming shadows of Mount Swan's eastern face to search for an entry point. Tristane tried to remain hopeful for their sakes.

"I can see some creature has passed through the foliage off the path," said his tracker.

"Then that is what we must do, too." Tristane motioned for the men to walk their animals through the thicket. "I'd never have seen this myself," he nodded in thanks to the tracker.

"I have a keen eye, but I don't recognise these prints. They look like a horse, but how many two-legged horses have you seen?"

"Perhaps I shouldn't speculate on the answer to that, tracker. I think the men are going to have enough problems to deal with when we enter this place. Keep these tracks to yourself." The tracker nodded again and returned to his duty. Cathal strained to overhear the conversation, but the air was strangely carrying their voices upwards and away from his ears. He turned to look at the men behind him, and felt their apprehension. The smell of dust drifted up past Cadfer's nostrils and he began to sneeze.

"You should've had that seen to," said Cathal. Cadfer acknowledged him through watery eyes. He was a veteran of the Virgin War, which had left him with an over-anxious immune system.

The tracker finally relocated the hoof-prints, which swung to the left, far from the main trail. The group moved slowly, carefully negotiating the steep terrain. They had dismounted, but the horses were struggling to find secure footing on the narrow pathway. One slip from the horse and the rider could be dragged down with it into the black chasm that gaped to their left.

Autumn was not yet halfway through anywhere else on the Plains, yet here the temperature had dropped considerably and the breath of winter was upon them. Tristane shivered. The cold didn't bother him usually, but this was worse than the polar cold he'd trekked through in his youth, he thought. Looking back, he saw his followers had reached into their supplies and wrapped blankets around themselves. Ice had formed casings around trees, now naked of leaf. The water crystals sparkled with the feeble sun bouncing rays off them, adding a magical feel to a dangerous place. The ground was black, icy, and precarious. Tristane felt his perception of danger increase as the trail steepened, making the journey almost impossible for the horses.

"Tracker, take the animals back to safety. We're sure to lose one of them if they keep going. You can go on your way after that because we can't wait for you. We'll have to make do without you from here. Go safely, you have served us well."

Now a group of five, they pushed higher into the gorge.

"This gorge has been hand-carved," Tristane said to Cathal. "What do you make of it?"

"I don't know what to make of it, sire. It belongs to no architecture that I'm aware of. It's none of ours, and by ours I mean Pelien."

"I'm inclined to agree. Frankly, I wish I had the time to study it. Those swirls in the rock alone must have taken half a lifetime to achieve, and the spires and finials... I'd say they were designed for the water to run off the mountain and drip from their ends to create those giant ice spikes. I'm overwhelmed by the sheer energy of it. It looks as if the artist was in a state of cathexis when they achieved this vision."

"I'd probably agree, if I knew what 'cathexis' meant," Cathal replied, grinning.

"It means, my friend, the investment

of emotional significance in an object, activity, or idea. So what I'm saying is that the artist was so involved with their work that this became a manifestation of their emotions. In short, this place is some kind of sacred domain, at least to its creator."

They continued up the gorge until it widened onto a plateau, with more icy trees lining the path. Tristane spent much of his time slowly absorbing the carved mountainside, before spotting a cave entrance. He took a deep breath and headed towards it, closely followed by Cathal. Both men hoped the other three wouldn't notice their reluctance to be there.

The cave was lit by torches of softly flickering firelight that danced to their own shadows. Stalactites and stalagmites seemed to form a pattern on the roof and floor, menacing the company as they passed through the darkened, rounded entrance. Their feet slid on the icy floor, and each held fast to nodules on the walls. The room was empty, save for an apparent exit at the other side.

"Well now, where do you think this goes, Tris? That floor looks incredibly slippery to me." Cathal hovered about the edge, not wanting to take a further step inside.

"Slippery or not, it's our only way forward," replied Tristane. "Hold on as best you can and to whatever you can – all of you." Tristane turned to speak to each of them. They all stepped inside, but the mountain appeared to be unstable, gently shaking them further and further into the cave. By the time they decided to retreat, it was too late, the mountain had them all in its grasp. Tristane slipped to the ground and the others tumbled after him.

"It seems we are to descend into the mountain without choice!" shouted Tristane as he tried to cling to the icy ground. It was no use, there was nothing but a skating rink to hang on to, and the cold went burning through his hands as they clung. Tristane slipped from the room first, with the other four careering after him. Just past the opening, an ice tunnel appeared. It ran steeply and deep into the heart of the mountain. Faster and faster the men slid, with twists and turns enough to make them ill. Their screams were rolled into one as they accelerated downwards.

After several minutes or so, each man had an aching back and bruised elbows, and was cold beyond belief. The tunnel widened at last and they began to slow, slipping from side to side and finally coming to an abrupt halt against a wall of silvery ferns. The noise they had made during the descent and on their crash landing was enough to wake the dead, Tristane thought as it echoed about them, removing any chance they might have had of covering their presence. For several moments they sat silently and without movement, resting, catching their breath and preparing for more surprises.

Slowly they became aware of the sound of wings beating rhythmically in the air above them. Tristane looked up. The creature hovering over them had violet-coloured flowing locks that curled into ringlets over pale white skin. A soft olive gown floated about her curvaceous body and the long, slender arms reaching out towards them ended with sharp claws. Four gossamer wings flapped gracefully, holding her suspended above them. Her face wore a bemused smile.

"Are you a gift?" asked the creature, floating around the room. "My larder is empty, as you can see I am not in the dark one's favour. So why are you here? Are you my supper?" She spoke with a scratchy whisper.

The soldiers, none too keen to find out more about the creature's dietary preferences, moved closer together, their hands on their swords. Tristane dragged himself upright, cautiously watching her every jerky movement.

"We are not gifts of food from anyone. Rather, we are travellers looking for our friend; and we have stumbled into your larder by mistake. Please, we are not here on purpose. We just need help to find our way out. Would a beautiful lady like you care to assist us?"

"Why should I help you when I have been starved of good food for so long? I can't even remember the last meal I had that wasn't more than a rat or a scrawny bird. I like creatures such as you. You look very tasty... mmm... juicy. I could do many wonderful things with the flesh off your bones. Why should I help you?"

"Because we want to be your friends. Friends don't eat friends, do they?" replied Tristane optimistically.

"Friends," she whispered as if the word was an alien one.

"What name is borne by such a beautiful being?" he asked warily, hoping to appeal to her womanly vanity – if indeed she had any, or *was* a woman, he thought.

The creature smiled. "Oh, I am Mesha, and I am hungry." She swayed in the air like a snake with wings, her movements were so fluid.

"I don't have any friends. I used to – lots of them – before I was captured. But now my master grows weary of me and leaves me alone without proper food. I am hungry, and I need my children to wake up too. They just won't hatch out of their sacs, and that makes me sad – and very hungry! Without food my children will never grow. You are lots of food, tasty, and I can store you for many months here in my larder." Mesha's eyes grew larger every time she mentioned food.

The other soldiers stood and hugged the frozen walls. Each one slowly edged away from the flying temptress and towards what appeared to be another cave exit. Tristane also eased his way along the wall, wondering what he could possibly say to dissuade the creature from devouring him and his men.

"Our flesh is not tender for the eating. We are tough from exercise; our muscles aren't for the likes of your children. Why don't you fly out of the tunnel, the way we came in, and hunt yourself a nice rabbit off the mountain, or a goat or a fresh young lamb? There's a lot choicer to be hunted outside. Why don't you fly away?"

"But I am forbidden to go outside. Maris will be angry at me and chain me up."

Tristane shivered as the name stirred more vague memories of his terror in the mages' underworld, but he knew he couldn't allow the creature to sense his fear. "Not if he doesn't catch you," he said firmly. "Maris has much bigger plans than you flying away right now. You said it yourself: he has grown tired of you. Why should you stay where you are not wanted? It's easy, just flap your wings and fly into the light. Fly away. Beautiful Mesha should not be hidden from view. The world needs to enjoy your splendour."

"Yes, yes, I am splendid and beautiful, indeed I am. Can I really have fresh lamb and rabbit to eat, as much as I want?" she asked with a whisper-soft voice, looking longingly towards the icy tunnel, obviously pining for freedom.

"Yes, you can have it all. As much as you want, whenever you want, and Maris will not know for ages that you have gone," said Tristane enthusiastically.

"Then I will go. But not before I have tasted at least one of you!" She cackled like an old witch as her snake-like tongue unravelled from her mouth like a whip and lassoed the nearest of the soldiers. He screamed as his body was wrenched upwards and the thick wiry tongue wrapped around his midriff snapped his back with a loud crack. The soldier's cry was choked off as the life was squeezed from him, until he drew no more breath. Tristane drew his sword and slashed vainly at the cunning and agile creature. She danced on the air, carrying the man adeptly as if his weight meant nothing. The other men joined in, but Mesha was quicker than even their battle-hardened reflexes. She dropped the semi-lifeless body to the ground and dived in to attack, hissing and spitting at them until Tristane called for a hasty retreat. The soldiers bolted into another icy chute, to the sound of their companion's bones being crunched.

They quietly slid further into the belly of the mountain. Tristane felt growing anger but knew he must remain focused – if this was just the beginning, he thought, what on the Plains could he expect next? He'd better be ready.

After sliding deeper and deeper, they landed in a chasm that had a domed ceiling carved with odious beasts looking down at them from the highest points. Gargoyles, thought Cathal. The four men stood up gingerly, and viewed the room with an uneasy sense of longing. Their swords were drawn and they stood ready for a fight, confronted by the sound of scuffling feet – but from where, Tristane and his men could not tell. Cathal felt the chill through his heavy leather cuirass and frowned, still feeling the loss of his companion. He touched Tristane's shoulder.

"I fear this place, Tris. Let us go as quickly as we can."

"I know, I've been in caves before, but this one is uninviting to say the least," replied Tristane. He sighed.

"What is it?" asked Cathal as the other two soldiers walked around eyeing off their surroundings. "I can tell you've got more on your mind than you'll let on."

"My memory is coming back about the mage guild. Most of it was lost until now. I remember Jugger Short-Stop going missing in one of those mage visions and getting lost in the living towers. Every time I hear the name Maris another piece of the puzzle reveals itself."

"I'm not sure now is a good time to be learning of such things."

"Well, who knows why it's happening now, but it is and I can't remember it fast enough."

"What about the man we've just lost?"

Cathal asked. "I'll not forget that. He may not have seen service, but there's no one who could aim an arrow like Durra."

"I understand. Durra was like a brother to many of the men, but we have to hold it together. I need a unified group; and if you lose it, I'm done for – because they answer to you, not me." Tristane paused in mid-sentence. "Did you hear that... kind of shuffling noise again?"

"No, I was listening to you."

"Shh! Listen."

"No need to listen," cried Cadfer as he tapped Tristane on the shoulder. "Look, we're surrounded by these ugly rodents." Cadfer drew his sword again and waved it in front of the animals like a torch. Tristane and Cathal turned to look at what Cadfer was seeing. The biggest of the rodents daringly moved closer, but Cadfer jabbed his sword so the animal jumped back. It stared upwards longingly at the men's faces, each one in turn, studying their expressions. The creatures' eyes seemed to be without soul, but sadness and loneliness began to project from them. Tristane looked hard into the eyes of the nearest one; he sensed the being that was trapped inside it.

"They are children. Can you feel it?" Tristane said. He sheathed his own sword, knelt down and the animal came up close and rested its head on his bended knee.

"Careful." said Cadfer. "They have to be more than children: just look at them! I've seen better looking faces on dead cattle." Tristane frowned at his companion.

"Have a heart, will you. They didn't come into the world packaged like this, I can assure you. This is the work of Maris. It's all coming back to me now. This is what he does. He makes things – creatures – out of Peliens so he can control them and take over their will. That's what he did in the mage guild with Baronna the apprentice mage. The wolf-man: you know him like we all do. This is the work of the demon Maris."

The rodent continued to rest his snout on Tristane's knee and a tear rolled down its matted, furry face. The animals all started to scratch madly at the dirt floor with black claws, forming the words 'help us' many times over.

"We have to help them, though I'm not sure how," said Naret.

"I don't know either. Look, the little one is clawing at that stream of gooey liquid coming out of the wall over there. It looks putrid and sour." Cathal moved towards the fluid; but as he drew closer, the smell repulsed him and he recoiled. "It's repugnant, whatever it is. Maybe they've been drinking that to survive. Get your flasks out and we'll see if there's enough to go around. There must be thirty of them; give it sparingly just to make sure it will last."

They followed Cathal's lead, dripping water into the mouths of all the rodents, who drank willingly all that was offered them. By the time they had shared the last drop of water, the animals who had drunk first began to morph back into bipedal form.

One by one, children appeared where there had been small ugly rats, and they ran around jumping with joy.

"Quiet!" shouted Tristane, as the other men clapped their hands to bring some order to the chaos. "Quiet, please!" he shouted again. The children turned with smiling faces and thanked them all for their help.

"How long have you been down here, like this?" asked Tristane. The oldest of the children spoke.

"We have no idea. But there have been many, many moons and seasons since we became trapped here. Our eyes don't see the light down here. Please, will you help us to get out? The Wobutter usually comes for her nightly feed about now, and we have lost so many of our friends to her hunger."

"What's a Wobutter?" Tristane asked, but realised after he'd said it that the child was talking about the creature that had attacked them in the upper level. "Oh, I see. She eats your friends too. Well I'm sorry to hear that." With his softest voice.

"I don't think you need worry about her any longer," said Naret.

"Did you kill her?" the boy asked.

"No, but we tried and she took one of our men. If she comes back again tonight, then I do believe there are enough of us here to finish her off. Don't you think?" Naret replied, reassuringly. The boy smiled.

"I think we should stay here for the night," Tristane said.

"Is that wise, knowing who our closest neighbour is?" asked Cathal, who had realised these were the missing children of the Orion.

"She'll be full for tonight, I'm sure," Tristane's stomach churned as the words left his lips, "or she'll have left for better prey. It's as safe a place as any. So let's just rest; it's been a long day. The children can scout around for their clothes while they have a chance. Otherwise, they'll die of exposure down here."

Cathal nodded, seeing reason in his

friend's words. The party set up camp for the night with a small fire, using the tinder each of them carried, and shared their meagre supplies with the children. Afterwards the children slept, but there was no comfort for the men in the bowels of a cold rock.

*****

Tristane yawned. He'd managed a couple of hours sleep here and there, but nothing like being in the comfort of his own bed. Yet it took the sounds of many hooves, feet, claws, and winged creatures moving about to bring him back into the moment. He could hear them through the cave's acoustics, but from where exactly was not clear. He got up and stretched, listening cautiously and hoping the footsteps were not close. He could feel every muscle protesting with stiffness from the sparse bedding and hard floor. The noises of footsteps were joined by the sounds of chains clanking and armour grinding, it was disjointed and incoherent. It sounded like a host on the move. Tristane shuddered: he was trapped with thirty children and three soldiers in an icy dungeon with only one way forward – further into the deep – and no way to stop what was happening on the surface.

"Right," he said, as cheerfully as he could. "Everybody up! Let's get a plan of action going."

"I guess we could see this as a lucky break. I mean, if the halls are empty of... whatever these things are," Naret said, "then we could find her ladyship without bumping into too many of them."

"That's the spirit." Tristane slapped the soldier on the back and glanced at Cathal, who gave him a grim look in return. Minding children wasn't a contingency they had planned for; and Cathal was aware of Tristane's real mood under the cheerful façade. Cadfer sat alone, gracefully stroking his blade's edge with a sharpening stone as if hypnotised. The sound sheared off as his stroke neared the end of the blade – then he began again immediately.

"Are you ready, Cadfer?" Tristane knelt down by the man, who looked up.

"If I'm out there it is with them, those things, coming to get me, and if I'm in here it is with the evil and this insufferable cold. And as I can't get out there with them, then yes, I'm ready when you are."

"Good." Tristane turned and asked the children if they knew how to navigate the tunnels to find another way out apart from the one that led back up the ice chute. One of the older children nodded and said he knew them in part, but was not aware of the way out. The child beckoned the men to follow. At least he could show them a way to somewhere, thought Tristane.

They found the air getting warmer, and realised they were looking at the mountain's thick grey rock rather than ice-covered walls; the noise of trampling feet grew fainter. It was dark, and the smell was bitter. In fact, apart from a few lit torches they had salvaged, it was pitch-black, and there was little else they could do but trust the children's sense of direction. The children walked complacently through the familiar caverns and deeper into the mountain, but no longer downwards. Twists and turns foiled Tristane's ability to remember his way back, but that no longer mattered: he just wanted to find Tama.

The walk was long and the smell in the air became more acrid. Tristane recognised the emanation from his time on the roads before he became Thane. It was the smell of a bloated dead carcass left to burst open and spill rotting matter everywhere. It made walking hazardous – and most unpleasant. "The smell of the dead could not be easily removed," he found himself thinking in an analytical way, his thoughts taking him back to his carefree wandering days. Then he felt the distant rumbling of the mountain's belly that repeatedly sent tremors through rock and men. The ice was gone, and the air was humid – warm and unwholesome.

They came upon a hidden spring of

crystal-clear, trickling water. Dehydrated and desperate for a drink, their mouths begged for its cool sparkling relief. Naret stepped forward and cautiously tested the liquid, placing his glove into it to see if it had an acidic reaction. The glove caught fire in an explosion of incandescent orange and yellow light. Naret dropped it and tried to stamp out the fire before it could harm anyone, but the flame was alive and moved too quickly for his foot. It danced a merry dance around Naret's legs and set them on fire, before leaping up his body, hissing, crackling, spitting black embers in every direction.

Tristane tried desperately to smother the flame with his cloak, then the others came with their blankets and wrapped Naret's fire riddled body in them. They rolled him about the ground, but the flame knew their trickery and jumped onto the outside of the blankets. Soon, Naret's cocooned body was fully alight like a funeral pyre and no amount of frantic effort by the others could stop the deathly mischief. Naret screamed as the fire tore into his body, burning away at his flesh and ultimately his life.

Naret's screams waned into silence and all his friends could do was watch the flames die away slowly, leaving only a pile of smouldering, blackened bones and ashes. The living flame leapt back into the deceptive spring from which it had come.

Cadfer dropped to his knees and wept for his friend, and for the man's family, swearing revenge on the cursed Pretender. He threw his arms in the air and screamed several chants of hatred towards the villain that had brought them there. "We are being picked off, sire. Can't you feel the evil in this place? Who will be next?" he shouted, dragging himself back to his feet. His voice expressed the pain Tristane was feeling.

"Why didn't you children warn us about the water?" Cadfer said, vengeful and suspicious of their new friends. He started towards them with hatred in his eyes and sword raised in anger, but Tristane pulled him back.

"They didn't know, Cadfer. Look at their faces: the horror is in their eyes also. They are our only link with the tunnels inside this forsaken hole, and without them we are completely lost. Don't let your judgement be clouded by what you have seen. We will take revenge when revenge wants to be taken. Let it be." Tristane was horrified by what had happened as well, but Cadfer barely noticed in his anger.

Cathal held his head low and said nothing. Thoughts of his beloved home came to him in this dark hour and gave him the strength to move on.

Again they followed the children deeper and deeper into the heart of the mountain, as stealthily as they could. Heavier lay the air on their drooping shoulders as they trudged through what seemed like claggy dirt on the floor, as thick as mud but drier. The soft, dense earth coated their shoes and stuck – making walking in the heat intolerable, without water to drink.the walls were lit by sparkles of blue light, pretty, these little luminous yet tiny amoeba began to light their way in patches through the dankness.

The oldest of the children stepped back several paces to walk with Tristane, trying to warn him of the coming dangers. The ground that they walked was not just a pathway, he whispered, but the earth of a garden. However, it didn't house pretty flowers and shrubs, the boy cautioned. Tristane eyed him suspiciously, though he wanted to trust the boy. All the same, Cadfer's words had got to him.

"We should go quickly through here," said the boy, anxiously. "There's no telling where the mushrooms might be, and they are very protective of their soil: it houses their young that have not risen to the surface yet. We can't afford to upset them by standing on their spores."

"Mushrooms, you say!" said Tristane, with slight disbelief, but perhaps not as disbelieving as he would have been at the beginning of the journey. "What, pray tell, can mushrooms do to hurt us?"

"They are not like normal mushrooms, sir. They have names, for one thing, although we can't pronounce them in our tongue; and they can move through the dirt as if they had legs, yet they have only long creamy-white stems. They are as tall as you and... well, it's hard to describe, sir, but they sort of look like their caps have been sliced clean off to reveal the black veins on their underside. They also drip black slime wherever they have trodden. If you step in their trails, you are too close and will surely be speared by one of them, sir," said the boy.

"Then we shan't linger, my son. Tell me, how are these spears lethal when they attack?"

"When they have attacked us in the past, sir, they've spat sharp black spores that were tiny enough to fit under one's fingernails. These are their young. They embed themselves in the ground usually, but they will also burrow into flesh and take root if that's what's available. We've lost several of our friends this way. It's a slow and painful death, as they don't sprout instantly; but over time the young will grow roots into a person's body and gradually use the flesh and blood as their own food supply. Eventually the person becomes the earth, and part of the garden." The boy sighed.

Tristane looked down in growing unease, imagining that he was walking through the decomposed bodies of children. He groaned in frustration and despair. "How I loathe this journey to hell. Though there is not such a place that I know of, yet here it is, the very manifestation of such a name." The boy looked at him with soulful eyes. "Go back to your place at the front, and thank you. My companions will try and protect you from these... these mushrooms."

The boy shuffled quickly back to the head of the line, prouder and taller for his own leadership.

"Cathal, Cadfer, we must move very quickly. We are, so my young friend informs me, in a lot of danger. There is yet another one of Maris's beasts for us to deal with. This time we have forewarning and must make use of this knowledge to avert any attack. Take flanking positions up ahead and protect the children. I will stay at the rear. Draw your swords and take down anything that moves," said Tristane. His eyes flashed with a passionate hatred toward the host of this dungeon.

The two men headed forward and to the sides of the children, their drawn blades flashing in the dimly filtered blue light. The only sound that could be heard in the tunnel was the swishing of feet shuffling through the mud.

Cadfer could hear the sound of his own heart, and the release of breath from his nostrils sounded like a dragon's swishing wings in his ears. His pulse raced, and his senses were heightened until his eyes became sharpened through the full range of the spectrum, so he could see fully without the torch. Now that his adrenalin had given him his animalistic senses, the world seemed to slow, and he drew breaths deep and audible only to himself. Instinctively, he held his sword with both hands clenched around the gilded hilt, and stalked into the darkened abyss.

Cadfer could hear every sound that his companions made as their feet squelched into the muddy floor. He looked across at Cathal; he too, was in a position of defence, searching the darkness with keen eyes. Cadfer paused as he stepped into an unfamiliar substance, which sucked hard at his foot. He became caught in the glue-like material, and focused on freeing his captured limb. The others stopped immediately to help, but the distraction became fatal. Out of the shadows of the walls emerged several large, black-headed mushrooms, exactly as the boy had described. From circular mouths placed high on their stems they spat millions of spores in a violent attack. The projectiles came through the air in black clouds and homed in on their targets like heat-seeking missiles, only stopping on impact.

Cadfer panicked, he was helpless to avoid being the triggering target. A flurry of children began running and screaming in all directions to escape the clouds, the spores only seeking those who were stuck in the goo. Several children got caught and became direct targets for the spores.

The three men slashed their brilliant swords at the soft, sticky creatures. Tristane rapidly removed the heads from three of the deadly mushrooms in one swoop, and they dropped to the floor with piercing screams. Cathal stabbed at anything that moved, and split two mushrooms in half. Cadfer could do little to defend himself in his captured state, yet he held his sword up and swung in any direction his restricted body would allow. But in the instant of attack he had been hit more times than one could count.

The first onslaught was over and the others turned back to rescue their companion. Cadfer had been covered from head to toe by small black spear-like spores. His pain was evident. His body started to swell instantly and he struggled for each breath. Cadfer fell to the floor, gasping. He reached out to his companions who came to hold his hands in frustration.

"Hold on man," cried Tristane. "We'll get you out of this mess. Cathal, help me cut him free so we can get him back to the chamber. We must remove these stings."

"No, sire. It's too late; I have not the strength to lift myself up." Cadfer's voice strained through an almost airless channel, swollen by the reaction. "I am dying. You must leave me here and go on. Without the histaweed, I have no chance. I can feel every cell in my body swelling. Please go. Do not witness my end this way – go!" whispered Cadfer as he struggled for air. After a few more moments, Cadfer's features became so swollen he was unrecognisable. His throat puffed up and gradually deprived him of his breath.

"You have served us well; may the death spirit take you to the other side where there is a transcendent freedom waiting for you," Tristane said gently, but it was too late for Cadfer to hear. The group fell silent. Children returned from the shadows wailing and sobbing as several of their friends lay in the mud, doomed to a slower death than Cadfer was granted. Tristane and Cathal looked at each other and then to the children. Nothing could be done for so many fallen in such a manner. Tristane raged inside, but he knew his only hope now was to escape as quickly as possible. Up ahead a light could be seen.

"Sir! Sir!" shouted the excited boy as they all dragged themselves through the gloom. "That is where they are taken – the bodies of the stolen ones, but the light only lasts a short time. We've tried to get through because we think there is an opening to the other side of the mountain. But we've never made it before it has closed and it's always been too dangerous to stay and wait for the next opening."

"But you don't know for sure what's there...?" Tristane said.

"No sir, but we've seen people in there until the light goes out, and then the pathway closes."

"Okay, then we'll charge like a cornered dragon. Let's go. Move it, everyone!" shouted Tristane. Hurriedly Cathal guided the children forward, gesturing for them to move quickly. They ran as fast as they could, but the light was already starting to fade. Behind them another host of the terrible mushrooms came swiftly from behind them, gliding on the surface of the mud. As they ran, Tristane and Cadfal swept up two of the smaller children who couldn't keep up the pace, and lifted them to their shoulders. Tristane's passion for freedom carried him on with the extra load. The light was still fading, but as they drew nearer the shape of the doorway became clearer.

The door was already halfway closed, and Tristane stretched out his long arm to prevent it from shutting any further. He threw himself forward as if tackling an opponent on the playing field. His fingers made contact with the heavy wood, and then the weight of his entire body was thrown upon it, flinging it fully open. The impact threw his body sideways, and the child he carried swung around his neck like a drop on a chain and slid to the floor. He hung onto the handle for stability and swivelled around on his heels, skidding down to his rear as two dozen children and Cathal swiftly followed. Their momentum sent them all crashing against the wall on the other side of the room. Glass vials spilt and crashed; wooden stools flew through the air and bounced off the benches, as twenty-odd children and two men fell into the room at high speed.

As Tristane composed himself, supporting the child he had carried with his free arm, he looked out into the tunnel. Several of the great marauding mushrooms were almost upon them. He heaved at the door and shouted to Cathal to help him close it. They both pushed as hard as they could, but the door had been twisted on its hinges and it didn't want to budge. They heaved harder and harder as the mushrooms drew closer, almost to the door's opening.

The two men shouted for the children to get behind them and help. The mushrooms were gaining, and with only inches to spare the door finally moved – slowly at first, but then it gained momentum from the new force applied to it. It slammed shut, locking the creatures out. The group fell in a heap with a sigh of relief, hearing thudding sounds as several large bodies made contact with the other side, then a swishing sound as if the soft bodies had squashed on impact and smeared down the wood, and then an eerie silence.

"Welcome, welcome! So many willing

guests to the gate room: my master will be pleased," came an unknown voice. They looked up, and saw that where they had come to at the end of their journey was not freedom, but capture.

CHAPTER SEVEN:

The Gate Room

Tristane turned to look at the being who was talking to him. She was without flesh, a bony apparition of a former Pelien. She wore several coloured layers made from hessian and draped as cloaking, with a hood partially hiding her skull. Under the hood she wore several linked chains draped down her forehead, ending with a diamond drop. The light caught it and drew his eye.

"Who are you?" he asked, cautiously getting to his feet.

"You don't recognise me, do you, uncle Tris? It's no wonder: I was a child the last time we met, then I was a mistress of the gods, and now I am perfect."

"Tama!"

"Yes, that was my name, but I prefer to be called Owena now. It means 'well-born', and I truly am well-born to this new life." She turned to the other liches waiting in the wings of a darkened doorway. "Drugan, Gotlieb, take them into the prep area and feed them through the gate."

The two liches came forward with long dirty forks and grabbed the men, then ordered the children to walk before them into the gate room, jabbing at them with their weapons. Tristane was struck by disbelief – there was something wrong, something didn't fit in this jumble of good and evil. He stared at Tama, or the new Owena, but she gave him no reason to think any of this was a lie.

Being strapped into a see-through coffin didn't help Tristane's disbelief of the situation. He looked at Cathal under the next one, and several of the children they'd just rescued lined up in more coffins to his right while the rest of the children sat scared and motionless, awaiting their fate. Tama came to watch. At the far end of this room a large gateway dominated their view.

Its twisted configuration mimicked the pain and suffering it caused, as the innocent were taken and transformed into something unwholesome – something deadly, a pawn of the Pretender's spawn.

Cathal's coffin moved first along its tracks. The entire network of tracks merged at the gate's entrance. As with the tracks of an ordinary train, the operator had to change the points for each carriage, and this was Gotlieb's job. Tristane watched out of curiosity and morbid fascination as his friend disappeared through the cavernous hole in the wall. He thought it a giant creature swallowing whole his dear friend. The coffin completely disappeared in the darkness and the gates closed behind it. Tristane struggled with the restraints, but they were far too strong for him, his yells fell upon deaf ears, and all he achieved was bloodied wrists. Finally he calmed down and accepted his fate.

It appeared to take an age before the gates opened again, and out of the opening emerged a new being – Cathal: now a skeletal creature with disjointed movements, gaping mouth, bleak eye sockets, and pale skin lying like dry flakes over his bones. The gate had made him a wight – a leader of soldiers in life and now a leader of zombies in death. Tristane had heard of these creatures with a foot in both worlds, but he'd never anticipated becoming one or seeing how they were made. Cathal stood by his new mistress and watched Tristane become the gate's next victim.

"So it's over – and this is how it ends," Tristane said to himself. His coffin began to move towards the gate as Drugan pulled back on the brake lever, releasing the tracks beneath while Gotlieb aligned them. The iron-gate was blackened and coated with thick fire-dust. It creaked, groaning under its own weight, and drew apart. Beyond, there was no light, so no chance to see what was on the other side. From the corner of his eye Tristane caught sight of Tama's lips moving slightly, and felt completely betrayed

– wasn't it enough that she'd become one of them, without casting spells on him to finish the job, he thought? Now closer to the yawning hole where the gate had been, he could make out the shapes of beings moving against the blackness. Nothing but their eyes flickered light. Once inside he disappeared from the view of the gates and heard them swing shut; through the crystal-domed coffin they sent their vibratory message of doom. His breath shortened... why didn't he fight, why did he allow Drugan and Gotlieb to push him around? He thought. Now it was too late; all he could do was go with whatever they had in store for him and his companions.

Cathal watched as Tristane emerged a new being: he'd become another wight like him, it seemed, and he smiled in gruesome welcome.

"Well done, boys," Tama exclaimed. "But now the gate is dirty again. You need to go in and clean it before these children go in, or we'll end up with some gnarled and no-good excuse for foot soldiers."

"But, but... argh, I did it yesterday," Gotlieb grumbled.

"Yeah, and it only takes one skivvy to do the job," added Drugan.

"Well, I say it takes two, and I say it takes two right now," Tama ordered. "So get your bony-liche backsides in there or I'll call the master, because he's put me in charge and warned you not to disobey me! Hasn't he?"

The two bowed their heads, so used to taking orders that they had no thought of disobeying. Shoulders slumped, they marched off towards the gate and waited unhappily for it to open. Tama pressed a button and once again activated the mechanism that pulled the iron door open. Gotlieb and Drugan walked in, the gates closed, and she ran to them, pulling down a huge iron clasp that sealed the gate room tight with the two liches inside.

Tama shook herself vigorously, and her outward image fell in splintered shards about the floor then turned to dust, revealing her true self underneath. Tristane and Cathal's new images also fell to the ground, and Tama smiled at her uncle then apologised for the deceit. Tristane and Cathal took several breaths of relief, and began to laugh out loud. The children clambered out of their crystal prisons and rushed their freedom-fighter friends to join in the celebration. But Tama cautioned that they should not linger, since Maris was a frequent visitor to the room.

"Let's go then," said Tristane, gazing at his niece. Deep in her eyes he saw the girl he remembered, now in the form of a grown woman and looking uncannily like Aleeah. In the background the screams of Gotlieb and Drugan could be heard, shouting and banging to be set free.

"What will happen to them in there if they've already been changed into something?" Cathal asked.

"I've no idea, but they haven't gone through the gate room yet. The gate would have made them zombie foot soldiers, not liches, because they are not magick by nature. The gate chooses your fate. A mage becomes necromancer or liche, a captain becomes wight, and so on," Tama explained. "Whatever's happening to them now doesn't sound good; I'd rather not stick around to find out what that could be. Come on, I know the way out: it's just down this hallway." She quickly beckoned them back to the room they'd fallen into such a short time before, then led them through a narrow opening in the opposite wall. She turned sharply left into a narrow hallway that led uphill for several hundred metres, and out through a doorway that placed them midway up the mountainside.

The relief of seeing the setting sun, and feeling its warmth on their bodies, was like a rebirth after the horrors of the darkness they had left.

"We should wedge the door shut," Tristane said. "It's far too easy to follow our escape route."

"There are many escape routes around this place," Tama replied. "I didn't come in this way, but I know it's here because I can sometimes see direction since the prophecy was enacted. I didn't know it until it was too late, though, and that charlatan Caldor had led me to the claws of the Perytons."

"Will that skill find rocks big enough to jam this doorway shut?" Tristane asked as he looked around for a piece of rock that wasn't still attached to the mountain.

"Over here!" shouted Cathal. He and the children were rolling a large boulder up a short rise.

"That's no way to work," Tama said. She motioned them away from the rock, then pointed at it and it lifted from the ground, levitated it through the air and plonked it down in front of the doorway.

Cathal looked at Tristane and smiled. "Not bad, these relatives of yours!" He clapped his hands together to remove the dust.

"Too right, too right indeed," Tristane agreed. "So if you think that'll hold, then we'd better be off." Cathal and Tama nodded, and they set off down the mountain accompanied by the children.

"So, when are you going to tell me how you managed to stave off your transformation back there – and mine too, come to that?" Tristane asked as they followed a narrow path between the rocks.

Tama laughed. "You know, I'm not sure how I do it, but the words just come to me. I thought if I could trick the gate into doing the opposite of evil by applying a reversal spell on me, then all I'd have to do would be to include an image spell to make them all think the gate had worked. When I came out, I'd been in there for about three hours and Maris was so impressed by what he saw he put me in charge of the gate. I've kept those two busy cleaning it since so it couldn't be used, because I'd heard that you had entered the realm. I thought it would be a good opportunity to save you, get rid of those two lugs and escape in one fell swoop."

"You had me convinced, though I was supposed to save you," Tristane replied. Tama smiled at her uncle, and walked in silence as the long but foggy memory of her ordeal came into her thoughts:

She felt the air rush past her ears, but the pain in her head made opening her eyes difficult. She realised that she was being transported above the ground but her mind drifted in and out of consciousness, feeling no motivation to investigate the situation when lucid enough to do so. Finally, the creature thumped to the ground, with several other thuds close by. Tama flicked her eyes open briefly and saw the shadow of a person, but that must have been an illusion, she thought. Gently, the creature placed her on the ground and she slumped over groggily.

Gotlieb looked down at her and a remnant of his history taunted his altered mind. Once he had been a moral man, he thought, but the idea drifted away as his transformation into the liche was almost complete. And with each deadly deed he performed, the more complete his liche-hood would become, alongside that of his companion, Drugan.

"We'll have to carry her from here if she doesn't get up." Gotlieb said.

"Aye, Maris will be pretty offset and left of centre if she is brain-damaged," replied Drugan.

"Offset and left of centre! You're reading too many of the master's black books. Any more educated and you'll be thinking that you are better than me," Gotlieb jeered.

"What d'ya mean, thinking I will be? I already am."

"Keep dreaming, bone-man."

"Who are you calling bone-man – sap for brains!"

"Just shut up and lift."

They carried Tama's limp and semiconscious body through the tunnel and into the gate room, where Maris was waiting.

"Quickly, put her down there." He pointed to a stone slab with a glass-domed lid that was open and awaiting its next victim. Tama became increasingly aware of her surroundings; she opened her eyes and watched the crystal lid shut over her. There was no room to sit up under it, she was entombed in a crystal coffin. Her heart pounded as the three creatures came closer and looked down at her, and she stared back at them.

Tama clenched her fists and began to thump the lid, demanding to be set free, but her words were muted by the surroundings. Not that it would have made a difference, she thought, as Maris stood and watched her panic. Nothing pleased him more than a helpless being, and ignoring her cries he turned and told the liches to prepare the gate for her arrival.

Tama soon gave up, realising her actions were not going to save her. "Okay, what would Xylon do in this situation?" she said to herself, careful to look away from her captors so they could not read her lips. She forced her body to relax, and chanted herself into a state of meditation.

"Whatever bad they plan for me,
Make it a goodness they can't see,
Deceive them, betray them,
Send forces to sway them
To think my mind's theirs,
Though this is not so.
Let me be, let me go!"

She repeated the chant under her breath as the coffin began to glide towards the open gate. The slight whisper and the movement of her lips could have given her away, but fortunately her captors were too busy with their preparations to notice. When at last she re-emerged, to all appearance she was transformed just as Maris had intended.

"Niece, are you still with us?" Tristane asked anxiously, jolting her out of her reverie.

"Oh, yes, I'm sorry. I was just thinking, that's all."

"Well, your 'just thinking' has got you all the way here in silence," Tristane said, as the group reached the city of Ashfar. They were weary from the long walk but in good spirits, though the lack of activity around them made them wary. There should have been hustle and bustle, thought Tristane as he looked about, but nothing more than the cry of a cat shattered the silence.

Tama breathed deep, feeling all was not well. At the same time, she was happy to be finally back on the journey she had set out on.

"So, then, do you think that Caldor has had something to do with the quiet?" Cathal asked Tristane.

"Yes," said an unexpected voice from a distant point under the dome. The group turned to see who spoke. Tristane recognised the face immediately and ran over to greet Ranyel.

"Thanks for coming. It's good to see you again." They shook hands vigorously.

"It's not as bad as you think," the mage said reassuringly.

"What, what's not as bad as I think? I don't think much of late, Ranyel. Where is everyone? The quiet, no markets... what's going on?"

"Like I said, it's not as bad as you think, but bad enough for us to be worried. I mean, Sera... that is, he's gone, he went in the fight and most of the dwellers here scattered, but some have returned. Yes, there's quite a few now – now they know it's safe again," Ranyel explained, but his listeners looked even more confused than before.

Tristane focused on the word "gone". "You said Sera's gone. Gone where?" He became suspicious, not understanding Ranyel's euphemism.

"To the otherworld... well, not the one you'd go to, but he's gone all the same, though you shouldn't worry. Mages have a habit of coming back," Ranyel said with a shrug. Tama placed her hand on Tristane's shoulder. Tristane and Sera had become good friends while he'd been Thane, and it was another loss he'd not anticipated.

"I'm just about done with all this death and dying! I never signed up for this," Tristane exclaimed, turning on his heel and pacing the floor in frustration at not being able to put his feelings into words. Tama turned to Ranyel. "We all liked Sera a lot, and he was funny when he had a moment to be so. Everyone loved him."

"Yes, perhaps you knew him that way, but you shouldn't worry so, he'll be back when he's ready," the mage assured her, then spoiled the effect by adding, "If indeed he ever is."

"Then you must also have some idea of Caldor's whereabouts. I need to get square with him and fix his... his sorry excuse for a rear end!" She folded her arms and huffed. Ranyel smirked. He'd met her grandmother, and this was Aleeah manifesting herself all over again.

"Well, I did know where he was, up until last night. He found a weak spot in the cage and escaped. He'll be climbing down the mountain or squirming his way across the top of it by now, I suspect."

"And... and what, you're just going to let him?" demanded Cathal, speaking up for Tristane who, having heard this extra news, threw his hands in the air and cursed the gods under his breath.

"Well, yes, but his impatience to get out has cost him the spell I used to keep him from insanity. It could take him years to get down from there. And what do I look like, a bloody spider monkey? Not to mention the cold air up there..." Ranyel shuddered.

"So you lost him, then," Cathal insisted.

"Well, no, I know where he is. He's not lost, just... difficult to find, if you know what I mean."

"There's nothing like a mage to muddy

the waters," Tama said, with a slight smile. Even under these circumstances she held onto her sense of humour. "So, then, if he's not an immediate danger to us, we'll get some rest and then sort out our next move." She and Cathal turned away and began to organise the children, but stopped when Ranyel reluctantly spoke again. "Well, that's not quite the end of his... that is... Caldor's story." They turned back on hearing the old man's tone, anticipating more bad news. Ranyel went on.

"Caldor took Sera's talisman. It's not just any old good luck charm. Come, let us sit." He waited until they were comfortable, then continued. "After Caldor caused the untimely passing of Sera, he took the talisman from his neck. We each have one that we must guard. I now hold my own as well as Sera's, which I took back from that despicable blackguard and excuse for a Pelien. We are the guardians of the spiritual gateways where the spirits sleep. Without the sleeping spirits, time becomes tumultuous and the elements become uncontrollable. I wasn't aware of his light fingers for several hours after his escape, when I found the talisman lying on the floor of the cage he occupied."

"What does this mean to us, Ranyel?" asked Tristane cautiously.

"Because Sera has left his post, so to speak, the ancestors will awaken, called to duty – unless they are reunited in the spiritual centre of the Plains. The spiritual centre lies directly beneath Kye, the city of the dead. The awakening has already begun: seas have whipped up in frenzy over the coastal regions. This started when the water elemental talisman became separated from Sera. When I give you mine to carry, fire will begin to spit and hiss until it grows out of control and all matter will desire to burn. You will have to travel back to the Blue Hills and collect Xarjay's talisman."

"And that would be – which?" Cathal interrupted.

"Earth – his is earth."

"So then, we may expect...?"

Ranyel sighed in reply. "The quaking of the ground, a great deal of fire and tumultuous tidal forces." For a moment Ranyel appeared defeated. "You will then have to quickly go to Mainheart. He holds the air talisman."

"The weather will become unstable – surely the god over night and day can take care of that," Cathal protested.

"Yes, I guess it will, and no, unfortunately, he can't. Kalale, your father, well – he controls that which is without chaos."

"Why can't you all just come with us – you know, keep them on, then we only have to deal with one elemental?" asked Tama.

"I wish it were that easy. But there are some places we simply cannot go to as corporeal beings, and one of them is the spiritual centre. We could go after death, but then there's not much point, I suppose. We are the keepers, and in order to prevent us from meddling with the affairs of gods, we must not be allowed to tread their physical paths. I'm sorry, it's a universal premise – and I'm too young to get vaporised beyond where our dear friend Sera now resides."

"Yet we are expected to do just that – walk right into the arms of the enemy and ask if we can borrow his basement?" Tama said sarcastically.

"Well, when you put it like that, it seems quite unreasonable, yet give me a moment and I'll give you hope. There is one of us who *is* able to take you with him safely. In fact, it is his job to do this very act I ask of you now – a safeguard, you could say. Unfortunately he's become somewhat… indisposed, and it will take a great power to reverse his indisposition."

"Surely you don't mean who I'm thinking of? Everyone I know would see him turned on a spit before they rescued him from his ugly prison," said Tristane emphatically.

"Who, Tris? Who does he mean?"

asked Tama.

"Baronna. The wolf-man."

"I thought as much," Cathal joined in. "That skulking beast never relents, never rests, never stops looking for his next victim."

"I guess my parents didn't think to tell me this bedtime story. Who is the wolf-man?" Tama asked again.

"Baronna was once a wizard in training, Sera's apprentice, in fact. He came to the surface world as a ferocious wolf." Ranyel paused and looked at Tristane then back at Tama.

"I'll fill in the blanks, now that my memory has returned," said Tristane. "He was changed by Maris into the wolf-man, but only now has it come to light. Even our mage brethren here had no idea how he got that way until recent times, but I've remembered the unholy details well enough since being down in Maris's domain."

"Freeing him is very important – you will understand why later. But do not forget why you began this journey. In order for us to give you our amulets, you must complete the reanimation of Cailean White Stone, the earthbound spirit, because no one else can hold back the elementals long enough for you to even get to the spiritual centre," Ranyel said.

"I was to seek her out before I was kidnapped, before the talisman was stolen. Sriann said she was important," said Tama, wonderingly.

"That she is, young prodigy, in more ways than I can tell you."

"You are all tired," Ranyel went on. "When you've all slept, with only the oceans up in arms, we may have a few days to spare. Then I'll show you what your powers can help you to do, my child. Tired or not, you are far stronger than you realise."

Cathal had become increasingly restless during this talk of Baronna the wolf-man. All too aware of Tama's presence, he was unsure of his place and felt it was the wrong time to make any advance.

Choosing to return to his outpost at Delgare, he said his goodbyes.

It was clear Ranyel wouldn't be persuaded to part with any more knowledge there and then, so Tama retired. Saying goodnight to Tristane, she headed up into their private residence.

Tama felt the immediate warmth of home in her heart. She closed her eyes as she breathed in the aromas of fresh herbs and spices wafting up the airshafts from the kitchens. Considering the city had exhaled its population, with only about half returning, she was surprised to hear the clatter of dishes echoing down the hallway, and to smell food cooking. At any other time the clanking would, by its loudness, have been annoying – but Tama wallowed in the familiar noise. The moon hung low in the sky that night, dimming the surrounding lands of light. She drifted into sleep as if on a wave. Awakening at last to the sound of Tristane knocking vigorously on her door, she realised that morning had come.

"Come on lazy, you're missing the spectacle in the foyer," he shouted.

"Aw, what spectacle? I'm too tired, go away!"

"Come on down quickly and you'll find out."

Tama rolled over and shielded her eyes under the pillow, but it was no use trying to get back to sleep now – there was a spectacle, her uncle had said, and she was awake to know about it. She rolled out of bed, dressed, and ran down to the foyer to see flecks of red light passing in and out of the walls accompanied by repetitive chanting.

"What are they?" Tama cried.

"They are the Order of Ommers. We shouldn't try to hinder them: just stand still and they will pass by," replied Ranyel.

"But what are they? I've never heard of, um, what... the Ommers, did you say? What do they want?" she replied.

"They are looking for Maris, I have no doubt. Sera told me of them being sighted, another sign that the Pretender is well and truly established. They are his keepers and have come to claim him. Watch as they glide about – they have no mind or form beyond the tiny light. I never thought I would live to see this day. What a treat!" Ranyel delighted at the presence of the glowing-red particles.

"I wonder what their chanting means. It's so rhythmic." Tama listened intently to the sound and it became clear that they were making the noise by which they were named. "Ommer, ommer, ommer, ommer" drifted across the hall as they passed through solid walls and around Ashfarians. She watched them travelling in pairs, featureless, nothing more than bright specks of floating orbs. Six in total glided through the city. But their presence enlightened Tama. Mesmerised by the beautiful lights, she began to speak.

"Maris is the dark from the light, as he said when he entered our city: 'I am older than the dawn of time and wider than the dimensions I've swallowed. I've lived in and out of the void and lain hidden in the maelstrom of time. I cannot easily be removed from the fabric of space for I dwell in the heart of the Maker Eternal'," she quoted her adversary. "Now I understand, Ranyel. We are conscious only because the Maker Eternal is conscious and lonely for an answer to why it is so. We are the solid matter that binds a formless thought; we prevent implosion. When solid matter came to be, it was the birth of a thought, greater than the gods Killan and A'shara, and greater than the communal gods we know that grace the Plains. When we die we become that which first projected us." Tama took a deep breath, whilst Ranyel and Tristane stared at her in wonder.

"Yes, my dear, I believe you have it," Ranyel said softly. "There is no beginning and no end, and very little that could comfort the Maker Eternal but us, so it – I say 'it' because the Maker is genderless – creates us. Maris is the bad thoughts one has on a bad day, but when you're the

Maker – or I could say 'Celi Mawr' – then your bad thoughts become manifest as the likes of the Pretender. So you create thoughts that have but one purpose – the Ommers. For you, child of the wyrd, they are the source of the inspiration you are now having because you dare to look into the truth of what they are," Ranyel continued. Tristane was clearly dazzled by her expression of their spiritualism and smiled, feeling comforted by her new-found maturity.

"They are not beings then?" he asked Ranyel.

"That is correct, my friend. They are but a thought of a being, and nothing more, sent by that which we are, in thought, to rein in its own reckless mind."

"The Celi Mawr is complicated." Tristane rubbed his forehead, wondering if he'd truly understood the conversation. Ranyel smiled silently at Tristane's unwitting half-truth. Only the *explanation* was complicated.

The Ommers left and Ranyel pulled out a long document to give to Tama. "I spent the night writing this down. It is all the instruction you need for now; study it along the way because I want you to leave as soon as you can, now that I have seen the Ommers."

"I thought you'd say that," said Tristane. He clapped his hands and their horses were brought out.

"Nyara," Tama cried happily. She patted the horse's underbelly. "I hope that big breakfast will not slow you down."

"He'll work it off. Come on, you're on my turf now!" Tristane had jumped on his horse and was trotting off quickly before Tama could get her feet off the ground. Ranyel shrugged his shoulders and graciously bowed her away. She finally caught up with Tristane halfway down the south tunnel.

"Thanks for waiting, then," she said.

He laughed. "May I never have to wait for a woman, especially one who is as beautiful as you; should I not end up with a yearning of the heart? I want the wind in my hair and the open ground beneath my feet – to hell with all this leadership."

"If only Aleeah could hear you now!"

"Yeah, she'd give me one upside the head and then agree with me. It's why she fell in love with my dad. I had Alden's life until the South Trist became my home."

On both sides of the tunnel, lit by open torchlight, Tama could see pictures etched into the rock depicting life in Ashfar.

"Do they interest you?" Tristane asked.

"They always did, but not for the same reason. As a child I just liked them, but now I know they are this city's history."

Tristane put his hand up to his ear. "Shh! Listen." Tama attended to the musical whispers that hissed in soft velvet tones – like gentle waves washing the beach with the wind joining the chorus. To focus her concentration she half-closed her eyes and relied on the horse to carry her off to some distant place. The sound was hypnotic, drowning out the mind's endless chatter. Ashfar's whispering walls were another feature of the city that she enjoyed. A full voice never carried, but whispers travelled for miles.

"They are returning home," Tristane said, sounding both happy and sad. As much as he had fought the idea of being in charge of anyone or anything other than himself, he felt the needs of the Ashfarians more than he cared to let on.

CHAPTER EIGHT:

In Search of the Wolf

It was mid-morning when they finally hit the open road. They felt the southern wind beat against their bodies, a brisk flush of air gusting up the mountain's slope. It was not obvious from inside, but the citadel was quite high inside the mountain, and the view of the land from the mouth of the tunnel was breathtaking. Tama could see for miles down the winding pathways that would take her into little-known territories. They needed no maps for the time being; for as long as they followed the mountain's base to the river and passed the Boulders Gorge, all would be well.

"It's about a day's ride to the river from here," said Tristane. "But I am not happy about having to pass the great boulders – even knowing that we have to –

to find that beast of a wolf. He spends his nights in the forest and his days prowling the boulders. We're sure to find him lurking there"

"You make him sound very frightening."

"That's because he is – well, he was when I met him. He almost swallowed the three of us – me, Alden, and Husienna – in one gulp. Were it not for my father's abilities, I'd be dead for sure."

"I see. So my father and grandfather were there with you," said Tama, looking at Tristane with sympathy. He was obviously unhappy about saving a wolf that would probably want to kill them, and that had already tried.

"Not much of a choice you've been given – sorry – *we've* been given," Tristane muttered, giving his mount a couple of sharp jabs with his heels. The horse responded immediately with a trot, then broke into a gallop. Tama swiftly followed down the steep slope of the rocky trail. They forged on through the day, finally reaching the northerly edge of the Boulders Gorge. The sun was low in the sky, and cast a deep red light over the lands ahead of them. The mountains began to cast heavy shadows, stretching like long fingers across the slopes and lowlands and drawing the heat from the land. The rising moon cast a chill silver light.

Tama felt the wind drop as she and her uncle slowed their pace. She shuddered and, for the first time since being home in Tristany, she felt lonely. Tristane looked back to see her eyes darken. He pulled up his horse and suggested that they camp in the lowlands, amongst the rocks to keep themselves hidden. They dismounted and walked their animals to a stream that bustled and sparkled in the splintered moonlight.

"I'll get the fire going, Tama, if you would help bring some food from the saddlebags. I don't know what has been packed for us to eat or whether we have to cook it or not, but I can assure you it will be the best of whatever Ashfar has to offer us."

"Great, I'm famished," she replied.

In Tristane's bag a flask of wine bulged. She wondered how he had ridden with such an item protruding so. Although Ashfar was known as the hidden city, it was well known to the traders and stocked the best wines that money could buy – mostly from the Aldora Alvis, the raven-skinned Peliens.

"Isn't Delgare around here somewhere?" she asked as they sat down to their meal.

"It is. How did you know? Oh, your sense of direction, I remember now," Tristane replied between mouthfuls of beef strips and gulps of red wine, spilling it down his chin in an effort to get it all in fast enough. "Why do you ask?" He wiped his mouth clean with his forearm as Tama frowned over his lack of etiquette.

"Well, I was wondering why we are camping out here in the frosty night air –

with little comfort, and a wolf on the loose. Shouldn't we stay hidden until we want to meet the beast, and, more importantly, shouldn't we have access to the facilities I just know are inside such a dwelling? You don't post a Pelien out here without comforts, do you?"

Tristane laughed. "You're getting too smart for your own good. I wasn't going to bother Cathal any further. He's usually such a loner, and it was only by chance he was in the city at all when Caldor arrived. But I guess he wouldn't mind us visiting if you've finished eating. He does have hot springs in his utility room." Tristane lifted an eyebrow inquiringly.

"Well, I'm exhuasted, and cold," said Tama. "That warm bath is starting to sound pretty good about now."

Tristane jumped up and, as usual, she had to run to catch him as he led the way out of their rocky seclusion and down into a hidden cave. It seemed to go deep into the earth, with the stream directly above.

The darkness was lit only by a bright moon until they were fully inside the cave, which they found gently bathed in flickering candlelight. They came to a left turn and were faced with a slatted timber door, arched and coated with old age. The wood grain was stained deep ebony-red and had pictures of Ashfar chiselled into its surface. Tristane gave four rhythmic taps, two short and two long, then stood back. The rhythm was repeated from the inside of the door, and Tristane replied in the same fashion. This time the door was unlocked and opened.

Tama could not believe her eyes at the sight of the man filling the width of the doorway with his broad shoulders, slightly bent to see under the door's height. Cathal was in his best white shirt and leather britches, his face clean of the grime she'd seen him in before, and he had no helmet hiding his velvety black hair. How could she not have seen him, really seen him, before this, she thought?

He leant his right hand on the top of the door frame as if to stop it falling over. His hair flowed below his neckline, his eyes were wide and kindly but within their depths Tama felt the chill of his heart. Never had she seen a man with such dark hair, even in comparison to the Aldora Adrian, the dark ones of Moonara. Her own people, the Aldora Argentum, and those in the hidden city were fair. Even the brown-skinned Alvis had not the hair colour of Cathal. His unusual colouring mesmerised her; the two locked eyes and became lost in each other's fire for several moments, until she realised her position. An uncomfortable moment followed, until Tristane broke the silence, a little awkwardly.

"Well then, there's no need for introductions. You obviously remember each other," he said, keeping an eye on his niece. She met Cathal's eyes again, but knowing Tristane was watching she looked towards the ground, hoping he'd not noticed the attraction. Cathal bowed to her and took her hand, gently kissing the back of it as if it was a treasure. Tama felt the warmth of the kiss long after it was over, and cradled her hand secretly.

Cathal had known how he felt before he left Ashfar, but this meeting was so fresh to his eyes that he was unnerved. Tristane's niece was surely off limits to any man.

"I was expecting you both much sooner. Where have you been?" Cathal spoke softly, but not so softly for the whispers to carry along the passageway to the next outpost. The two men shook hands vigorously.

"It was not my intention to bother you after our recent excursion, because I know how much you like your solitude. So we've eaten comfortably at our camp in the outcrops and the horses are still tethered there. We'll not stay long, but Tama would like the comfort of your hot springs – and I can't say I blame her. I'll probably need them next: my rear-end is numb with all the riding we've done today," Tristane replied.

"Well that's easily solved. Step this way, Lady Tama." Cathal smiled and showed her to his private room, then bowed politely and left with Tristane. She could hear the two of them talking and laughing for a few minutes, but then the sound was gone.

She undressed in the carved ante chamber and stepped down into a rock pool with mineral waters bubbling up from the ground. The warm water soaked through her every limb as she lay there, while cooler water trickling out of the rock walls mixed with the ground pool. Her aching back enjoyed the massaging effect of the water rippling around her body, and she closed her eyes from exhaustion. Slowly she drifted into a peaceful sleep for an hour or so, until the voices of Tristane and Cathal returned. Their voices drifted into her sleep, waking her slowly and comfortingly. The torches flickered on the walls around the chamber and Tama began to open her eyes. She dressed and entered the small room that was Cathal's lounge and dining area. Both men arose from their seats and bowed politely.

"I thought you were out of action for the night. The springs will do that to you," Tristane said.

"Yes, they did do that to me, but now all I want is a bed. My skin is waterlogged from bathing so long. Any longer in there and I would be as wrinkly as an elder," she replied.

"A bed it shall be, then," said Cathal. "You can both stay here instead of shivering out in the rocks."

Tristane nodded his agreement and excused himself to enjoy the springs, leaving them alone. Cathal handed Tama a goblet of wine. She wasn't used to drinking, and felt a little like a child stealing from her mother's cup at a celebration. It was hard to lose such feelings, she thought, having only been an adult for about a week.

"I don't ordinarily drink, having come of age very quickly: but this is quite good. I could get used to it," she said, happy to find herself in the realms of adulthood. She took several large gulps and found out very quickly that it made her dizzy. Tristane hadn't offered her any with their dinner, forgetting her new age. "I don't think I should drink any more, though," she said, worried by its effects, and put the goblet down a little unsteadily.

She looked around at the sparse room: an old wooden table with two chairs and a sofa, a fireplace carved up into the wall and roof, and a stone mantel with a few odd trinkets. Among them was a beautiful golden chain with a star diamond, dangling off the mantel's edge as if it had been carelessly slung there with no thought to how it lay. Disappointed that there was a woman in his life, she asked about it. "Will we meet the lady of that necklace tonight?" she said.

"No, my partner is long deceased." Cathal became melancholy. "She loved to walk in the evening by the forest, taking no regard of my warnings about the wolf-man. I lost her to him one night as he ventured home hungry. That is why I came here permanently: I keep my eye on the sly wolf and one day he will be weary from travelling, and I will have him as my trophy. It is my intent to rid the south Trist of his mangy body so we can again walk without fear. Where he wanders is no place for any other living soul. He has a ferocious appetite and cares nothing for who he feeds off. I wish to travel with you. I know you want to – have to – turn him to our side, but just give me a chance..."

"Killing him would have dire consequences – you heard what Ranyel said. We need Baronna. Without him we cannot enter the spiritual centre of the Plains," Tama said softly. "I know now why you want to kill him, but it is a turn of fate that we should need the help of a turned man."

"Then I'll go with you anyway. He might be unstoppable by any means other than the sword."

"If you come, come for me and not for the past. It's the future we need to save now."

Cathal nodded, though disappointed with what they had to do, and excused himself in favour of sleep.

The night felt to Tama as if it had been cut short when she woke cramped in her makeshift bed. The night howls of the wolf-man had awoken her several times and she could feel his pain in every screeching breath, as if her senses had come alive beyond ordinary mortality. With each passing hour she was becoming more like a sorceress and less like the child she had been such a short time before.

With the sunrise they were once again on their way south.

CHAPTER NINE:

The Taming of Baronna

Rakeem wore a crown of eyeballs, like a string of bloated bloodshot pearls, about his head as he entered Maris's dwelling below the northern mountain and below the pony trade route. Maris sat in the darkness of a corner, his face half-covered with a hood and the shadows from the dimness making his eye sockets seem blacker than night. Rakeem feared him: in part, for his mysterious coming, the powers he exuded, and his contempt for all the living things in the world, but more for the unknown quantity of force behind the so-called man. Yet, thought Rakeem as he sauntered towards his ally, he was fearsome enough himself now he'd become the vessel for Maris the Pretender's wants and needs. Were it not for Aleeah's confounded curse, he'd be as righteous and normal as the next Pelien – though just what normal might actually mean to a dark heart was a question Rakeem did not attempt to answer.

"All your kind are failures! Look at what I've done for you, yet you let me down in so many ways. I cannot begin to describe the disappointment," snarled the Pretender.

"I understand your disappointment, darkest of the dark hearts, but my men underestimated the prodigy. No one could have foreseen how she would deceive the gate. She deceived even you, master." Rakeem bowed low, wondering if the Pretender would notice his back chat.

"You slimy amoeba, you are a wart on the end of your own society, no less. I should cut you off, watch you fall, and then stamp on you to make sure you're dead. But that will wait for another day. I didn't expend my abilities to save your worthless backside from the curse just so I could end it. Give me your report so you can leave me!"

Rakeem hesitated, knowing his news would not be welcomed, then handed over the report. Maris appeared to study it.

"So, the Retaliate's son has no darkness in his veins still, and refuses to go through the gate. He's a fool!"

"He is also sick and getting sicker. Oraldo has only a few days to live before her curse finally finishes him off, yet he insists that he deserves redemption from it. He believes it will come, or he did while he was still lucid. I should think he is beyond that now – like my other family members till you came and saved us, my lord of the darkest lords," said Rakeem.

"Fat chance the Retaliate will come to redeem him," Maris laughed bitterly. Somewhere in his inscrutable mind Maris admired Aleeah the Retaliate, but showed only clenched fists while he turned back to the rest of Rakeem's report. "Your two, foot soldiers ended up as soup at the bottom of my gate, then. What a mess. Still, a fitting punishment for letting go of my prize."

Maris then pointed to the table where he kept his instruments. "Over there." Rakeem stretched his bony neck to see. On the table rested two large bloodied eyeballs with big black pupils set against dark brown irises.

"The eyes of the wolf-man. I've given him mine so I can see what he sees."

Rakeem crept closer – eyeballs were his favourite ornament. As he moved across the dimly lit room the pupils followed and watched him. These were fresh, still working, he thought. He looked back towards the Pretender, who stood up slowly and revealed his face, his eye sockets empty and bloody. Slowly he walked over to the table and pushed Baronna's eyeballs into the empty spaces.

"Ahh, that's better. I can tolerate some light now." He twitched a finger at the gas lamp and it brightened.

"But how did you read?"

"I don't need eyeballs to read or to know what has gone on in my own domain.

But I do need them to watch over our enemies on their walkabout."

Rakeem smiled. "That is truly devious."

"As am I." He put a gnarled hand on Rakeem's shoulder, squeezing it tightly. "That'll be all for now, so go home to your city and wait for me to tell you when and where to move next."

Rakeem turned to walk out, but was stopped by a parting shot from Maris. "By the way, what happened to that relative of yours, Caldor? We've not heard from him since he hid under Ashfar's cloak. I heard he joined with the one who dwelt in Quinlan. That makes him dangerous to all of us. Find him!" Rakeem nodded and left.

*****

Still weary, Tama gazed with concern at the sky's colourful robe; it reminded her of how life had been before it became complicated. The dewy grass glistened down through to the valley floor, with the blue hues of the hills drifting over a harmless looking forest.

"I can hardly bear our task," she said, breaking the silence.

"I know. It is so much to take in, isn't it?" Tristane replied.

"Tell me about Baronna before he was changed," she asked.

"A simple mage in training, polite, hopeful even. He was abandoned at the mage guild as a baby and Sera took him in. That's all I know. I didn't get to know him at all really. We met just before he explained how the guild grew its towers and that the rooms contained the visions of their creators. That was how we lost Jugger, your grandad's friend. He disappeared into one and became a memory of Cullen, the guild-master. Cullen said he couldn't be brought back as the same person, so he wouldn't try."

"Do you think Baronna will definitely be there in the forest?"

"He'll be there all right – lurking in the shadows and skulking about for fresh meat. It's what he does now. You can't compare the man we met to the wolf he now is."

"This is his home, my lady!" exclaimed Cathal. "We can be sure he will sniff out our presence under the canopy of that dark place. Don't let the picture of tranquillity deceive you. He is death incarnate." Cathal practically hissed his comments. Clearly his mind had festered over the beast and its dire behaviour.

"I hope that his mind is not completely lost after all this time. For my part I cannot see how we'll need him, but then I'm not a mage," Tristane said, stretching out his arms, neck and back to rid himself of riding stiffness.

"You could've been though, couldn't you?" Tama replied.

"Maybe I could a long time ago, but it's too late now. I am my father's son, and my longing to explore the world is far greater than toying with things I can't understand." He smiled at her, and they headed down the path into the shadows of the forest. It did not take them long to understand why the forest was named Fornay, a local word describing vast darkness. The canopy of fig and pine trees engulfed the air space, stretching out to sunlight like arching columns of stone; wiry vines hung from their upper bowers. Great figs rained down their curtains of root from thick and twisted branches, some so old and splayed out they joined with the other trees, completing huge girths to navigate around with temple-like archways through which the light filtered softly. The old forestry road that they were following disappeared soon after they were inside the forest, with no one left to tend to it since Baronna had moved into the neighbourhood.

"The air seems dead in here. And there's a musty odour – but I can't place the smell," Tristane said.

"I can," Cathal said. "It's rotting flesh after it's been hanging for a while. Just like in the Wobutter's cavern, but here it's disguised by the scent of the forest."

Tristane lifted his head to sniff the air, then agreed. Tama had not noticed the smell; rather, the hairs were sticking up on the back of her neck. She felt an unfamiliar presence. She reached over and tapped Tristane on the shoulder.

"We're being stalked." She pressed a finger to her lips. "Shh. I want to listen to his movements."

The three of them tensed, then slowly moved on through the dim light, seeing every shadow as a wolf crouched ready to spring. An hour passed and their cautious exploration had taken them into the heart of the forest.

"How long are we to keep this up?" whispered Tristane.

"I don't know, because he's gone." Tama sighed. "He disappeared from my thoughts about ten minutes ago. I've been trying to find him again, but I can't."

Cathal breathed a sigh of relief and slung his bow back over his shoulder, then jumped down from his horse to rest. Tama swung round at a sharp crackle of breaking branches, and saw the wolf bolt out of the shadows and lunge at Cathal, knocking him to the ground. It growled deep – and saliva dripped over Cathal's face. The soldier, his heart thumping in panic, struggled to get out of Baronna's grip, grabbing at the animal's snout to force it away from his face. Baronna's gaping jaws revealed a mouth full of stained jagged teeth. Tristane gathered himself, reached for his bow and arrow and shot the animal, but it made no difference; his hide was thick and Tristane's arrows were too light for such a job. He made another attempt and this time the arrow pierced the beast's right eye. Baronna let out a roar that rattled the trees, and somewhere far to the north echoed another faint scream of pain, felt rather than heard. Tama raised her palms and willed the animal to cease. Baronna slowed, then stilled and slumped on top of Cathal as if he'd fallen into a deep slumber. The air left Cathal's lungs as the weight of the body bore down on him. "Get it off!" he croaked. "Get it off before it wakes up!"

Tristane reached across the animal's broad chest and attempted to haul it off but it wouldn't move. He looked across at Tama, but she was still holding the beast in its sleep-state. "Damn it!" he said, looking back at his friend. "You'll have to help. Do what you can but I can't shift him alone, Cathal. On the count of three, push up." Cathal was turning blue, he barely had a push in him, but Tristane counted all the same, it at least gave him a moment to focus his own strength. With a last mighty heave they rolled Baronna to the ground. Cathal lay gulping air back into his lungs, dizzy and unable to stand, as Tristane struggled to secure ropes around the great beast.

"Don't tie him, kill him!" Cathal said with venom, still gasping for breath.

"I can't, you know that."

"Your ropes won't hold him for long, he's too powerful."

"He's hog-tied, and tied to the tree:

he's going nowhere in a hurry," Tristane said and dropped down beside Cathal, feeling almost as out of breath as his friend. Tama, relieved of the spell she'd cast, opened her eyes and slid down next to them. They sat for half an hour, waiting for the beast to wake and for each of them to regain stamina. Finally the animal stirred. As Baronna awoke from the coma she'd sent him to, Tama looked at him tied and alone and felt sorry for him.

"It's not his fault!" she blurted out. The other two looked at her with some surprise. "It's not his fault," she repeated. "He was a man once, and a good one. This corruption is not who he is. Please let there be someone left inside to save," she said, to no one and everyone, as she got up and walked over to him.

Baronna's curiosity had taken his mind off food for the moment, and he lay quietly as she approached him, letting her eyes roam across his huge body. She could see his shoulders were broad, with lean powerful muscles. His snout was black, and the fur that covered him was matted and unwashed. Both men jumped up and anxiously called her back, as Baronna's mouth was not tied. He could still bite. Though they recoiled in the gust of wind that brought to them his pungent odour, their swords remained poised to strike.

"What did you think he was going to smell like, clean washing?" Tama responded, annoyed at their interruption.

Baronna uncharacteristically cowered. He dimly recalled when he'd been captured before by the Pretender, and felt some of the same helplessness and terror of that other time; yet, in what remained of his real mind, he sensed that this being was different, and meant him no harm. He looked long and hard at the swords pointing towards him, as their owners covered their faces to avoid his scent.

Tama edged closer to him, kneeling to reduce her height to a less imposing level. She felt his wet nose sniffing gently against her soft white skin, and could feel all the anger within him disperse as if it had never been. Baronna dropped his head at her feet, his nose resting against her ankle. She stroked his neck, breathing heavily, cautious of being this close; calm or not, he was still able to kill her if his mood changed. Placing a hand under Baronna's chin she lifted the heavy head to look inside his one good eye. If there was hope, she would find it there, she thought.

"By the knowledge of the lower world, let the gods see what I see." She stepped back and turned to Tristane and Cathal as if startled.

"What is it?" asked Tristane, but she didn't answer. Turning back to the animal she threw her stiletto, blinding its other eye. Baronna howled in pain, and again Tama heard the answering screams in her mind.

"What are you doing?" Surprised by her action Tristane rushed forward and grabbed her by the shoulders.

"It was him! Maris! The eyes – they

were his eyes, not Baronna's. I could see his reflection in them. If we'd saved the animal then he would have been an unwitting spy. He might be blind now, among other things, but he should be a safer companion for it."

"If you can't save him you've doomed him to death from starvation. A predator can't hunt without its sight," Tristane said. He pitied the creature now that it was disabled.

"If she can't save him, I'll kill him," said Cathal.

"Then I'd better get on with it. Take off the ropes – he won't run away, he's too afraid of the nothingness he now sees." She looked at Baronna in his pitiful state, blind and trapped, then took several deep breaths while a spell came to mind. Deep in her thoughts the notes of a tune rang, and she found the words that went with it:

> *"A child of the eternal I*
> *bring back his body,*
> *Filled with the spirit of*

what he once was.
Call forward his heart,
the one that is good,
For it shall be bigger than
he once thought it could.
Give him his conscience,
for conscience will make
him,
And distance the
memories that once made
us hate him.
Let him keep his
strength, the strength of
his flesh,
For it can be turned to
the good.
Give him the wealth of
his current stealth – let
nothing be lost
Lest it blacken his heart,
then it shall part
With the man I call forth
from this hell."

Tama sang the words softly but clearly, then sank down into an exhausted slumber. Too much of her strength had been used to make the spells to subdue Baronna and to change him. Tristane knelt down to see if she was okay: her breathing was shallow but it was clear she was not in danger.

"Look at him! The spell hasn't worked, and now she's in some kind of state for trying to save him. This creature is not worth the trouble he causes," said Cathal, raising his bow. His arrows were heavier than Tristane's, and he was a trained huntsman. He took aim at the animal's head as it lay limp against the soft mossy ground. Cathal pulled his bowstring taut and, as it reached the point of no return, a voice shouted, "No! Stop! Don't kill me!"

Cathal's startled reaction sent the arrow spinning up towards the canopy as he stepped back, showering them in falling leaves. The two men stared at the mouth of the wolf which had just spoken to them its desperate plea.

"By the gods, you can talk!" said Cathal.

"Yes, yes, I can talk, it would seem. Yet I am still a wolf, but I feel free. She has freed me, in mind at least. I can talk, and you can hear me and understand me. It's like I have been pulled from the trap I was living in for so long." Baronna sniffed the air, his wolf instincts still powerful, and recoiled at the stench.

"Ugh, that smell – I guess it's me." He ran off towards a nearby stream and the two men stood and stared in amazement as the man-wolf dived under the water, still babbling to himself.

Tama stirred as she regained consciousness.

"How are you feeling?" asked Cathal.

"I'm fine, I think, Cathal; but what about Baronna, is he changed?"

"It's hard to answer that question accurately. I'll let you judge for yourself," Tristane said. "As you can hear, he sounds like a man, but when he returns from having a bath you will see that it's a wolf who likes the sound of his own voice."

Tama looked puzzled by the men's expressions and decided to take a look for herself. She stood up and headed off towards the sounds of flowing water and endless chatter. She was disappointed with the result and sighed deeply at her apparent failure after expending so much energy into the last spell. Baronna heard her light footsteps coming over the grassy rise. Unable to see her, all he knew came from nose and ears.

"I'd recognise those light footsteps anywhere now, they're imprinted in my mind; though I have not my eyes to see you any more I can feel your glow across my heart." She smiled. This was better than nothing, and the words that she'd chosen so carefully had obviously preserved his efficient wolf attributes, even though she was hoping it would be as a man not as an animal. He listened to her slight sigh and judged her feelings with unerring accuracy.

"Oh my lady, don't be so disappointed. You have given me so much to live for, yes, live for. I feel, though I may not look, like the man I was. I am no longer trapped inside this body: rather I feel like it's mine. Yes, that's it, I've finally claimed this body instead of being trapped in it. But above all else, I'm free. And as for my appetite, I never want to see raw meat again as long as I live. My lady, dear honourable lady, I thank you from every inch of my being." Tama touched his snout gently to stop the endless flow of words long enough for her to talk.

"In a day or two I can try again, Baronna, and we may get a little better result." He licked her hand, it was the closest thing to a kiss he could give right now, to show he didn't care if she never tried again.

The new party gathered on the bank while Baronna shook the water from his huge body, splashing anything within a three metre radius.

"I don't know what to say, Tama. You have proved us both wrong, yet he is neither a man nor a beast," Tristane said.

"I was hopeful that I could do more for him." Tama sighed again, feeling defeated.

"You shouldn't feel down on yourself, my lady," said Cathal. "He is conscious, as I am conscious – he is no longer the enemy's tool of death. I can live with that."

A strange sight to behold now, as the trio turned foursome headed south. Baronna led the way, still constantly mumbling to himself. He knew the woodlands like a mother knows her own child, and quickly led the group into the daylight, needing no visual markers to set them free of Fornay. The day was slowly starting to dissipate in the lull of the afternoon light. Twelve hours or so had been spent inside the canopy of the woods without any rest, and now that the wolf seemed as harmless as a puppy they felt at ease camping nearby.

Baronna led them through Boulders Gorge, a short cut to the forest further south to help catch up some time. Huge grey rocks, perfectly round, sat peacefully on the landscape lining several gorges, which provided suitable hiding places for the party. Tristane found a sheltered place to set up camp: though they were now a full day behind schedule, the rest was important, he thought. Tama stood alone and watched the two men perform their tasks. Baronna was sitting close to his rescuer and imagined she was blinking her eyes against the cool wind from the south that wafted through the air, bringing with it a lingering aroma of Sriann's full winter blooms and filling Tama with beautiful thoughts. Baronna followed Tama everywhere she went, like a faithful pet – one that could talk back. Indeed, his behaviour amused her.

Cathal, still a little wary of the beast, sat back from the fire's glow so only a flicker of light passed across his handsome face.

He stared at the unusual couple enjoying an aeon of words in just a few short hours. The two had much in common, both experiencing change beyond the normal course of growing up or old. Cathal could see it, but reason was not with him when it came to emotions that unsettled him – and she did unsettle him, he thought. Never had he imagined that he could possibly want to love another woman again, yet he felt her strength and beauty on the surface and her tender soul beneath. He wanted to reach out and hold her, stroke her hair and enjoy her company. But the timing was impossible; he lay back against a rock, listening to the strange chatter, with a large mug of wine for comfort instead.

"This is my favourite place around here, my lady," said Baronna. "The running water calmed my unhappy soul and I could find some peace. It's where I came to sleep."

"It's an irony that you found peace by a river named for its lies."

"Yes, it is. As calm as the surface

looks, there is a rip running below the full length of the river. You can't see it, but it's there and those who don't know are pulled down. So the river lies."

They were close enough to hear the gentle swishing of water against the rocks at the river's edge. The water, glistening in the moonlight, could be seen through a break in the trees. The woodland sounds, the running water and the splashing of fish, coupled with the flow of wine, set the companions fully at ease with the beast that was now their companion.

Mienna, the river guardian, silhouetted against the brightness of the full moon, watched the party of four curiously from her perch high in a golden-barked tree. She was watching with eagle eyes – her favourite form, as it allowed her to soar in the sky and enjoy the splendour of the first Plains. She was a harmless but mischievous Shaman for Killan and A'shara. Killan gave her the freedom to choose the forms which pleased her most while on the Plains; in return she would watch over the river and warn Manna the priestly caretaker of potential dangers heading south toward his sanctuary.

She watched curiously, knowing one of the party well. Baronna, whom she had befriended during his moments of mental torment, had anticipated her arrival. He was not sure in what form she would appear, as she had only ever addressed him as a wolf of equal stature. These were the times he had reached his lowest point and spent the night howling into the wind. She would join him in his grief and howl alongside him until his anguish had passed. She had imparted much wisdom to him, though until now he could not have put it to any good use.

She stretched out her wings and cried out in the native eagle cry, then swooped down to the party camped among the rocks and landed next to Baronna, greeting him with a squawk. Baronna knew immediately who she was and licked her eagle face in his excitement.

For the first time, he was able to speak to her in his native tongue: no howls, whimpers or barks. The words poured from his lips and Mienna listened intently. Her dainty, feathered brow tilted to the left, enjoying her friend's renewed passion for the spoken word. After several nonsensical but happy sentences, Baronna finally took a breath and she greeted him with a word or two of her own in her bird language; and he nodded in acknowledgement.

"Are you going to introduce your friend, Baronna?" asked Tama.

"Oh, of course, my lady. You see, this is the first time my friend and I have communicated other than as wolves, and it's all thanks to you. You see, this is – or was before you found me – my only friend."

At that moment, Mienna found it more befitting to change her form. Her feathery wings, splayed out to their full extent, transcended into delicate arms and hands; the ivory talons, sharp as the point of a needle, became graceful feet, and her feathers were replaced by a blue gown concealing soft flesh. Her aura glowed pale blue as she levitated away from terra firma. She tossed her long, black, flowing mane from side to side with a childish giggle, then looked directly at Tama.

"I am Mienna. I watch all that cross the river, and today I am watching – you! I've been expecting you for some time. This is your time. You know what you have to do and where you have to go; you go with my blessings and Manna awaits you if you dare to cross the land that is."

"I dare, the sacred ground will choose for me life or death because my choice is to go where the sacred land is. There's nothing I can do about that."

"Aha, loyal to the will of the wyrd sisters, are you? Perhaps you should be asking if they are loyal to you, before you go any further. They have far too much control over things, you know."

"No I didn't know. But I'm told this is

the way of the wyrd, and I must take it regardless of the consequences." Mienna was jealous of the wyrd sisters, for her own powers were far less than theirs.

"Did you know there is a stray relative on your tail, something the wyrd sisters have chosen to ignite and ignore?"

"Do you mean Caldor?"

"Oh, you are clever; clever, clever girl Tama, with untapped powers of unimaginable variety. Poor child, your heart breaks every time you have to use them, because of how you came by them. The Aldoran Saga is but a slow and painful one."

"What is it you want?" Tristane said, feeling the Shaman was taunting his niece.

Mienna took a deep breath. "Nothing, I want nothing at all – just to tell you of what I can see from the clouds. Caldor is coming and you can't stop him. There is the fate that you can see and the fate you can't. Who'd have thought the seven sisters would ever have ended up shining down on the world they helped to destroy. Ah well, that's the way it goes, I suppose."

Tama looked up at the seven starry sisters, then spoke again. "We're not dead yet, and just what kind of a goddess speaks like you do, with such negativity?"

"One who has better things to do than sit talking to you," Mienna retorted sharply. Baronna was surprised: he hadn't heard her use that tone before.

"Why do you speak like this?" he asked.

"Because when she crosses the river, my job will be over. I will no longer have to watch the path to Go-shifa, for it will be empty of anything needing watching. Then maybe my usefulness will be at an end."

"There's no end, just new beginnings to old paths," he replied.

"Perhaps you're right, old fellow. In the meantime there is a mage healer waiting in the blue hills; without his help you will never make it to the holygrounds. The paths therein are without mercy. A young sorceress like yourself could make it easily;

however, your companions cannot. You should leave at first light." She turned directly to the wolf. "Baronna, in the morning you will wake as a man. Tama's magick works just fine, if a little slowly for my taste. But then, I'm a goddess! Good-bye!" With a laugh she changed back into an eagle and soared high into the night, expelling several loud squawks.

"So then, Caldor has found his way down from the mountain," said Tristane, and Tama shuddered.

"Should we go on in the night, or stay and finish resting, Tris?" Cathal asked, and Tristane looked around. Baronna had settled down for the night hoping to bring in the morning faster, and Tama was patting her pillow ready for the night's sleep. Cathal watched as she yawned and stretched out, with Baronna lying at the foot of her swag.

"Perhaps I don't need the answer then. Sleep it is."

"Yep, you take the first watch – I'll take the second, and we'll let them rest,"

Tristane said. Cathal nodded and Tristane climbed into his swag, leaving the duty of their safety with his trusted friend.

*****

"Sleep soundly while you can, son of Aleeah. Your time is short, because my strength grows greater day by day. You may have destroyed my eyes, but I have other ways of seeing, and a long memory for those who cause me pain." Maris's hissing words seemed to be carried by the wind as it whistled through the rocky gorge. Though the Pretender was far to the north and deep underground, the words still reached Tristane's ears and sped his already quick-beating heart.

CHAPTER TEN:

Xarjay's Boat

Stirring quietly, Baronna stretched out his long arms and stiff body and breathed a sigh of relief at the moment he knew his dream was now a reality. He rose as a man from his night's repose, tall in stature but proportionately set. His body having been his tool of survival for more years than he cared to remember, the strong exaggerated muscles had remained with him. His face was slightly grim, but handsome, and a five o'clock shadow lingered around his lower jaw. He seemed to be in his middle years, yet he had lived a lifetime. His hair, golden brown, flowed to just past his shoulders – a further inheritance of the wolf. There was still fire in his will, but no longer the violence of his animal nature.

Tama watched in awe: the new

reflection from his aura entranced her as he strolled around the spent campfire wearing nothing more than a sheet, which clung precariously to his naked hips. Baronna was clearly enjoying his regained upright stance, smelling the air for its beauty and not for a highway to the next meal. His blindness did not seem to bother him at all since he still had his perfect hearing to guide his movements. Tama was hopeful that she had thought of everything in giving him the attributes to compensate for the loss of his eyes.

She was intensely fascinated by the change in physical appearance as well as the obvious change in nature. He no longer babbled on endlessly, as he had the day before, but had become thoughtful. She was intrigued by his bodily form and his obvious strength, though she found this unnerved her. Not in the same way Cathal had – this was purely physical, a new and wondrous feeling that tingled in every part of her adult figure; yet she felt shy of it.

Tristane, still awake after being last on watch, also held his gaze intently on their new companion. His disposition had taken on many forms on the several occasions Tristane had met Baronna: the shy apprentice, the violent wolf and now the mature but melancholy man.

"Would you be interested in some tea, friend, now that you can hold a cup to your lips?" he asked.

"I would dearly love one, Thane. The gods only know how long it's been since I could drink one. Here, let me boil some more water," Baronna replied in a soft and friendly tone.

"I don't know how you do it, but you move with the sight of a sharp-eyed tail fish. If I didn't see the bandages or know your history I would not guess you were blind."

"I have my other attributes, and they are sharp. I cannot believe how I've been blessed with my original body, yet it's not me at all: now I am built like a fighter." Baronna bent his right arm, feeling the muscles flex though he could not see them, then smiled. "Tama was kind to me in her work." His soft velvety voice carried across the mossy ground.

"Yes, she was," Tristane agreed. "I can't deny we were apprehensive when we were told we needed you."

"Needed me? How?" Baronna tilted his head, animal-like, to listen carefully.

"We're on a journey to the spiritual centre so that we can reset the course of events that are now in motion," Tama joined in. "We had motivation for your release, but it was such a long shot, and you were not the most popular of beasts to rescue."

"No doubt I wasn't, but the memories are a little shaky." He tilted his head the opposite way. "Blurry, more like."

"That is as I intended them to be. You should not carry the guilt of your oppressor if it can be set aside."

Baronna nodded his head in gratitude, drawn to her as a patient to the tender help of a healer. Perhaps he was misplaced in his feelings, he thought, and resisted the aroma of attraction. Then Cathal stirred, and Baronna became aware of Cathal's scent of ownership over Tama rising to replace the other. He turned his head skyward, heeding the call of Mienna as her shadow floated above. Cathal also looked up, shading his eyes. Mienna gave several harsh cries, then moved on.

"We'd better go," shouted Cathal, as he gathered up all their belongings and started packing the saddlebags. "Baronna, you ride with me." He threw him a pair of leather pants. "My horse is the strongest and she carries the extra weight well."

The others watched in amusement as Baronna struggled to fit into leather pants several sizes too small. "Never mind," said Tristane, "they'll stretch with wear."

Following the river's deepening gorge south-west, they drew close to the mountains by midday, and were glad of it. They were hungry and tired, but eager to reach their destination. As the mountains' beauty loomed up towards them on the other side of the river, they saw a shadow appear from a cave on the lower slopes and beckon to them. To reach the cave they had to cross a deep river chasm by a long timber-slatted bridge, precariously suspended by ropes at either end. It creaked ominously as they crossed one at a time, not daring to look at the breathtaking view below. The bridge was guarded by two huge birds that watched their every step. Unnerving though this was, they knew they were safe because Tristane and Baronna had recognised the shadowy figure waving to them to hurry.

Once inside the confines of the mountain, they dismounted and, leaving water and food for the horses, tagged quickly behind Xarjay, who led them up into the heart of his quiet domain. Tristane thought it funny how mages loved their high points and towers. It was as if the height was some kind of security for them, but perhaps it just gave a good vantage point.

Either way he felt he understood, as it was in his blood. Though he'd denied it for so long, his own will to follow the mark of magick was still there, stirring at moments of curiosity.

The mountain caverns were damp and smelled of musty soil. Baronna didn't mind the smell so much, but shivered as the cold air met his naked chest, no longer protected by a shaggy coat. The cave system was poorly lit, adding to the sensations of damp and cold now surrounding them. Tama tried to keep her eyes firmly fixed on Xarjay as he disappeared through an empty room and towards the bright light of his home. She became increasingly uncomfortable with her surroundings, wondering why there was such foreboding in her heart when the room was empty. It was an unsettled place, and her skin tingled with discernible energy as if being touched by something invisible.

Tama walked around the room listening to its peculiar resonance. She heard whispers and sighs that didn't come from her companions, coupled and mingled with their thoughts, and began to breathe nervously. A light wind brushed past her face and she felt more than her own soul in the room. Tristane and her friends she could see, but there were other spirits she felt. A sharp cold jab of a finger poked Tama from behind and she jumped aside, then another and another touched her. Her heart raced as she became completely overwhelmed by them.

"Help us," they repeatedly said to her, several whispers overlaying each other and followed by more. "Help us." Tama spun about as if taunted by the noises. Again and again the words mingled into her mind; and as they repeated, visions of ancient beings appeared and called to her. She was moved by their pleas for help, but powerless to do what they wanted.

Xarjay rushed back quickly and clapped his hands loudly. The voices stopped immediately and the shadowy figures retreated into the walls. Tama's expression showed her discomfort and strained emotions.

"Come, come," Xarjay said. "We must keep moving. This locality is no place for the sensitive of mind such as you, my dear child of prophecy. There are darker secrets that none of us need ever know in this world, and this cave houses but a few. Let's go before you become completely enraptured."

Within a few moments they entered another room which was friendly, warm and dry. Artificial light hung inside a glass teardrop. In the left-hand corner of the room stood a cylindrical object with a turning handle on one side, mounted to a large, heavy-looking wooden box, and to the right were many objects of contrivance that had no meaning or use obvious to the Peliens.

"Welcome to my humble abode, friends. I was beginning to wonder if you would ever get here. I am Xarjay: but of course you know that. I should say I'm the healer of the bunch." He reached out to grab the wolf-man, shaking his hand vigorously.

"Baronna, my dear friend! What a delight it is to see you again after all these years, and out of costume at last. I don't doubt that the hand of Tama brought about your release."

"Master Xarjay, I think you have changed little since our last meeting. It is my honour to be within your fine company after such a sorry farewell. Yet now I'm here it seems only a day or two since the last meeting with Cullen and the others," Baronna greeted the mage, pulling him into a bear hug, squeezing the breath out of him. Xarjay coughed in Baronna's grip.

"Well, I can see your strength has improved somewhat. You can put me down now, old fellow," spluttered Xarjay. "Perhaps we can talk later of your journey, and if you wish to come back to the order then we can talk about that too, though you know the guild is gone – crushed by the same hand that changed you." Baronna nodded in agreement, pleased to be accepted back into the fellowship of the mages.

Tama looked into Xarjay's eyes: they

sparkled with each smile. He was dressed in an unusual fashion, intriguing the group except Baronna, who'd seen it before. Xarjay wore striped cloth pants, a striped jacket in white and yellow, and a white shirt. A golden pair of round-rimmed glasses fitted snugly on the end of his nose so that he peered over the top of them all the time; Xarjay's eyesight was perfect, but he felt they made him look more of a scholar. Though his appearance was eccentric to the travellers, Tama sensed his friendly and welcoming nature.

"My Lady Tama and Thane Tris, you are rare treasures in these uneasy times. Now come, you must all rest. We have a great deal to do if we are to prepare you for the rest of your journey. Not least of all, we can sink a few drinks of friendship. Mienna has informed me of the tragedies that have struck so far," said the mage, looking dire for the temporary loss of one of his kind.

"Do you know of all the problems? I mean, has Ranyel contacted you about your amulet?" asked Tama. She held out her hand and Xarjay kissed it ceremoniously.

"Indeed he has, and when you have for a travelling partner the earth-bound spirit you seek, you shall take my amulet to its necessary home."

"Good, then that makes our job a little easier," she replied.

"What is easy, prodigy, with Sera's amulet gone from its master? All the coastal regions have been thrashed by high tides. The river you followed is swelling and will eventually break its banks, as will they all. The coastal people are displaced and without homes. Easier? I wonder if they think it so." Tama felt he was berating her, but that was not Xarjay's intent. Realising, he changed the subject. "Lady Tama, you have become the essence of your grandmother's beauty. You will make the most prolific leader in her stead. She was the fire and you are the light it produced. Perhaps you will even give us an heir, if we are worthy." Tama blushed as Cathal tossed her a helpless look.

Xarjay turned to greet Cathal. "Ah now, last but not least, the reluctant warrior. How is your father? I haven't spoken with him lately, but you are in his image."

Cathal shrugged. "He's fine, I guess. We have little to talk about, him being so busy with his work."

"That is the truth for any Shaman, and nothing we can do will change that about him," Xarjay reassured him.

Tama looked up, startled. She'd forgotten this about Cathal – it was only a vague rumour that he was descended from a god.

"You're a little worse for wear I see, Cathal," Xarjay added. "Why don't you sit down and have a drink of my special brew. The 'nectar of the gods' I call it." Out of a long, flexible pipe dripped a golden brown fluid with an unusual, pungent smell. Cathal sniffed the drink cautiously. Unable to determine its content, he pulled back.

"Drink, drink, it will help put the colour back into those pale cheeks of yours. Yes, let's all do that." Xarjay promptly filled another four cups.

Tama's curiosity now stretched to examine each corner of this intriguing room, filled with trinkets and gadgets that didn't appear to do much of anything but collect dust. Xarjay's bookcases were stocked with books of strange origin and rolled up parchments lay strewn upon every surface. Sketches of flying objects and war machines were pinned to the walls, and some had even been made, in part, as miniatures.

"What are we drinking, Xarjay?" asked Tristane.

"Dearest laird of the hidden city, we used to call it mead back in the old days. You can call it whatever you like."

"I see. The favoured drink of the mage," said Tristane, happy to be filling his own belly with such a brew.

Xarjay gulped his way through another cup. "More, my friends, drink,

drink. It will help you sleep." The mage poured another cup for his guests. "Yes, now that's better. You'll feel quite relaxed by the time I'm done with you." Tama hiccupped and fell back in her chair. "There, it's working, you see! Now come, you shall all have a place to sleep for the night."

"But I can't feel my legs." Tama complained.

"Yes, well, it is a little strong this batch, but when you're used to it like I am, then you don't worry too much about that. Cathal, will you give Lady Tama a hand?" The soldier stood up to help but Tristane intervened.

"Up you come with me, niece. You're drunk," he said, lifting Tama to her feet. He followed Xarjay up the stairs to the sleeping quarters, and Cathal bowed out gracefully, pouring himself and Baronna another drink.

"Well, I guess it's you and me, Wolf."

"Wolf!" exclaimed Baronna. "I think you have also had too much to drink, Cathal."

"Not nearly enough to end this day, friend," Cathal sighed.

Baronna let his head sink back, relieved to be warm and at ease; behind his tough exterior his mournful mind was comforted to be part of a team again. However he couldn't help his thoughts drifting towards Tama, much more than the gratitude of a patient to his carer, it seemed. He fought the attachment for her, but it was impossible. Baronna contemplated these feelings warily; he knew he would put everything at risk, but he couldn't hold back the tide of desire. He listened as his new companion dozed off and all else was quiet in Xarjay's house, then he crept upstairs, using his heightened senses to find his way to Tama's room. His stealthy feet were heard by no one except Tama. She'd woken from the alcohol-induced sleep and lay quiet and alone, as Tristane had gone straight to bed after putting Tama into hers. She opened the door when Baronna knocked; then he was inside, pushing her up against the door as it closed, with his lips pressed to hers and both hands planted firmly on her shoulders.

"What are you doing?" she gasped, trying to wriggle free of his grasp.

"I can't stop thinking about you," Baronna whispered; even aware of the bond between Tama and Cathal, he had to tell her.

"And I you," Tama admitted, "But you are not the one."

"I know where my place is; I'm not looking for a wife. But you will be looking for a lover, and I am he," persisted Baronna. "Everybody needs a lover. Even one as amazing as you will need someone else in times of heartbreak, and marriage will break your heart even if it is only temporary and you awake anew each time it happens."

"You speak of marriage break-ups as they are always a fact; you speak of needing lovers as if that is therapeutic. Is this the way of love, truly? I haven't the will to cheat on my future husband, though that husband has not yet set his hands on me nor asked for my hand to marry. I know it is a truth, but for time keeping us apart."

"Then perhaps you will not be cheating at all. You think me cynical, but no one else will understand your pain as I do. For we carry the same ill will towards the one who has done us both more harm than one should have faced in a lifetime."

Tama stared at the white cloth covering his eye sockets and wished she could see his real eyes, because he was beginning to make sense.

"I have carried more from my wolf days than you know; so perhaps, yes, I am cynical," Baronna continued. "But it is also true that you want me no matter what you say. Keeping secrets will make you stronger."

"Are you trying to convince me or yourself that it would be right?"

"Neither. Just choose to be with me now while we have a chance, rather than tomorrow when we do not. Cathal is not sworn to you yet, as much as you think it a fact that he will be."

"Perhaps," Tama replied with a sigh; then she let go of rational thought and yielded to his strength. They fell into an ardent embrace upon the bed, until the wee hours were stretched beyond the time they could share. Then Baronna quietly departed as if nothing had happened, leaving her with a strange notion that she had changed her fate by giving herself to him – but whether for good or ill she had no idea.

CHAPTER ELEVEN:

Ascendance

Baronna returned to the room downstairs and sat back in his chair, putting his feet up on a small foot-rest and picking up a pipe along with his glass of warm mead. Cathal still slept blissfully, only waking to the sound of the cheerful mage preparing their breakfast, and humming merrily to some gentle music that filled the room. Before dawn, Tama and Tristane arose from their beds and rejoined the others in the mage's main chamber, feeling groggy and hungry. As they sat down at the table, Xarjay appeared with a large platter of sandwiches and fruits.

"Ah, all awake at last. Sleep well, Baronna and Tama?" He paused. "Tris and Cathal, I hope you did too. Now, let's get on. You, prodigy, will need this." The mage produced a small carving of an ivory coloured ship and placed it in Tama's hands. She held it up to the light and turned it this way and that, seeing different shades of pearly light reflecting from its surface.

"This I have been keeping for you since you were a small child. Killan has blessed it and only you can make use of it. When you reach the gates of the holy grounds, you must use your powers to make the ship large enough for the four of you to travel in. The sails will lift you above the earth by the wind of Kalale and take you safely to your destiny. When you have retrieved Killan's earthbound spirit, the ship will carry you in safety to your next destination. Nothing will stop you, the hands of Killan are the sails and he will protect you at all costs. Now, you cannot spend any more time here. Eat as much as you can and let us get on. I will guide you to the edge of the caverns, but I can take you no further than that. You must go on foot from here: horses will be no use to you where you are headed. Don't worry, I'll take good care of them until... you are free to use them once more."

With Mienna's warning in mind, Tama asked the mage about the dangers that might lie ahead. He reassured her that now she had the pearly boat they would not need to touch Go-shifa's sacred soils and face judgement. "As Mienna well knew," he chuckled. "She does love to tease, that one."

They left Xarjay at the mouth of the cave. Full-bellied, well rested and newly supplied with food, they set off down through another tunnel, then headed eastwards with the walls of the holy grounds in distant sight. Xarjay waved them on until his shadow was too small to see and Tama gave up turning back to look for him.

By nightfall, the great grey walls of the holy grounds loomed above them. Tama looked up at their grey imposition and shivered, feeling the very fear of judgement that Mienna had spoken of oozing from the hardened stone. But now she had the travel implement, Mienna's words of warning were no longer so dire, she thought, and smiled to herself that she should have doubted there would be a way other than on foot.

Tama pulled the small ship out of her pack and placed it on the dry ground in front of her, concentrating her thoughts on its size, then she stepped back and the object began to grow. Its silken sails flapped gently in the breeze as its girth spread. The ghostly vessel was soon large enough for several passengers and sat hovering slightly above the ground. Tama gave a cry of delight.

Her companions were much less enthusiastic; they worried about the safety of the boat, despite knowing they had no option but to journey in it. Baronna felt it with his hands, because it carried no scent and offered no sound, while Tristane and Cathal walked about its ivory walls suspiciously, their faces unmoved by its shining glory.

"I've travelled in some contraptions over ground, but I'm none too keen on getting in this 'ere boat-thing," said Baronna, scratching his head.

"I don't think it will be so bad, have a little faith – you might just get to like it," replied Cathal, obviously amused by the big man's nervousness. "We have to look down; at least for you that is an advantage because you can't." "Not much of one," thought Baronna, as he managed his way up the ramp and onto the boat's deck. He found himself what felt like a secure corner and sat stony faced, prepared to endure the flight.

"So, a flying boat; it couldn't be worse than being on the back of a dragon, and I've survived that," said Tristane, attempting to be optimistic. Tama sensed his reluctance, but that was his way, she thought. Cathal waited for her to go first, stealing a touch of her hand as she walked by; she stopped to look at him, but found herself thinking of

Baronna and withdrew.

They rose up over the giant walls of the holy grounds to find a scorched earth below in the shape of a large hand. According to the stories Tama had heard as a child, A'shara's imprinted hand had been left behind when the goddess was ending the reign of Maris, before he came to be imprisoned in the void outside of time. This ground was so pure that trespassing was almost impossible.

"It's far enough away to kill, you know. The ground, that is. I wish you would sit down. You're making me nervous," Tristane admonished. Tama smiled at him but kept her place at the helm. She found herself controlling the ship's speed and direction with little thought. This was a tiny pull on her powers compared to those that had come before.

"This from the 'I've flown on the dragon's back' man!" she teased.

"Yes, well, at least I had the sense to sit down," he retorted.

Now the gardens of the inner temple were below them. The sweet-smelling and familiar fragrance of the Sriann blossom filled the air, permeating every nostril and saturating the ether with heady aromas. In the centre of the scorched print Tama could see a temple-like building, adorned by arches and spires. It was nestled in an unscorched spot where the middle of A'shara's hand had not touched the earth, thereby created a divine haven, safe from any approach except by air.

"Wow! Come look at this, come on." She looked back at the others, thinking how silly they all looked clinging onto the sides of the ship and refusing to budge. "Well, if that is the strength of leadership, we are in trouble."

"Okay, okay, I'll look at your view, niece. But don't blame me if the boat tips me out." Tristane got up and cautiously edged forward to the bow. The air flowing past felt seductive, pulling at him to let go, to feel its power. So many times he had felt this call, but then pulled back reminding himself of his place – master, not mage, he thought. "Right, I'm here," he said as he steadied himself, and then looked out below. "Oh yes, the view is worthy of my rattling nerves."

Five spires threw themselves up into the wind, standing proud against a sultry blue sky. Each spire was clad in knotted and twining platinum, skilfully curling upward to its pinnacle then spewing out in serpent-heads that seemed ready to attack any daring assailant. Tama examined the building carefully; she saw that the spires were linked halfway up their height by buildings roofed with slate shingles. The temple from the air formed an open pentagram, with the spires at the points of the shape. In the centre the ground was covered with white flagstones – flat, and without doubt their only possible landing place.

"Let's drop down there," she said, pointing at the flagstones, and Tristane agreed.

As Tama landed the ship gently, she saw a man standing in the courtyard watching them.

"Who is this? I have seen none like him," Tama whispered to Tristane.

"I guess he could be from the Aldora Raven, yet he is darker skinned than any of the traders we have come across from the Barragotha region."

They approached the watcher cautiously. He stood proud, with a wide smile and arms open in welcome. "Queen Tama, Thane Tristane and company, I am the guardian of the gateway. I am created in the image of the great priest, Manna. I have waited here for an eternity, protecting the sanctum you are about to enter. I have prayed for your souls," he said solemnly, and bowed his head lightly. "Delaying will cost you your future, so go inside and take Cailean White Stone to her destiny. Manna is waiting." The large, black-skinned man opened the great doors to reveal a hallway of many paths.

Baronna scented the flow of air from the various openings. "Which way must we travel?" he asked uncertainly. This place made him uneasy. He felt the wave of purity from outside the pentagram penetrating his mind in spite of the surrounding walls. Though he was no longer the vessel of evil, the imprint of evil that followed him unwittingly controlled this emotion.

"Only the traveller can answer that question. All the tunnels will yield the same outcome, so choose for the sake of choosing," replied the dark-skinned guardian unhelpfully, as he bowed to them and bade them to enter again. Tama watched Baronna struggling with anxiety. Their secret was still intact, but it was another burden to carry, she thought, and not one to make her stronger as Baronna had insisted.

Cathal broke the impasse. "I see; an existential choice, then. Do you remember what Xylon used to tell us as children, Tris?

All roads lead to home, he said – especially when we had been in trouble. I think I understand now what he meant. Each of us will walk our own destiny here today, but we will all end up in the same place, or at least our own place. Well, I for one know my path. I'll see you at the end." With a flash of his woollen cloak he was gone.

"Okay," said Tristane, reluctantly. "I suppose this means we are all on our own until we arrive at the other end. This, then, is my path." He pointed directly ahead, then kissed his niece on the cheek and left her standing with Baronna at her side.

"Well, Baronna, it looks like we are on our own. I believe this is my journey. Do you think you can find the one that is right for you?" Tama asked, concern in her voice.

"Of course," said Baronna, with more confidence than he was feeling. "Go ahead. I'll be fine."

Tama turned to enter her chosen tunnel, glad to be away from Baronna at last, because he created a storm under her skin.

Baronna, forlorn and alone, hesitated before feeling his way into the darkened tunnel he believed to be his providence. His shoes made no sound and the darkness pressed down on him; he began to feel true fear for the first time in a long while. No sensation to guide him: no scent, sound, or instinct. Touch was all that remained momentarily of his senses. He hesitated and asked for help, but none came his way. The bravest of men, with a wolf's attributes, was now stripped of everything he had learned to depend on. In fear he edged gingerly forward and the darkness penetrated him; each breath he drew became shorter and shorter until, panic-stricken, he yelled out for help.

No answer came to Baronna's plea. Gradually it entered his mind he was alone, and that his senses were about to be removed as punishment for a life of savagery.

"Surely I am not to blame? Surely you

wouldn't leave me stripped of all I know because of the actions of another?" he pleaded. Baronna felt his guilt come thrashing forward from the hidden place where Tama had banished it. "Arghh, haaa!" he wailed like the winds sweeping up a mountain pass – like the banshees of the frozen north as the raw emotions pounded his remorse.

"What is this?" he cried. "How am I supposed to meet my fate if I cannot know it through my senses? Answer me!" He fell to his knees. "You taunt me, Killan! Without my senses I have nowhere to go." Baronna felt the creation gods had forsaken him. Killan, the greatest, he hated the most. As he held fast to the cold stone walls they began to crumble in his fingers. The ground beneath his knees rocked back and forth, throwing him on his side. Bit by bit the solid floor and walls disappeared into choking clouds of fragmented dust and floated away.

"Help me!" he cried in a hopeless, last-ditch attempt to save himself from falling into obscurity, his words echoed into the bottomless chamber. Down and down he fell, seemingly forever. Finally he realised that the fall would never be over. He would never again feel the softness of the grass beneath his feet or enjoy the sun break in the new morning, or hold a cup of freshly brewed tea. He was lost to his own weaknesses and trapped in an endless spiralling downward journey.

Desperate, he cried at first, then anger raged in his soul. "I will have my life!" He shook his fist – to which direction he knew not – but his emotions were in vain. He was alone, falling and falling. What felt like an eternity passed and he felt himself growing weaker. Falling in and out of consciousness he accepted that no matter what Maris the Pretender had done to his life, even as a wolf he could have stemmed the evil by his own death, yet he had let his greedy hunger keep himself alive. If nothing more, he knew as the wolf he had the power to choose his own death over the deaths of others. Baronna gave into forgiveness and asked Killan to save him, placing himself in the hands of fate.

"I believe in you," he whispered, breathless and ill. "I believe in you, show me the way and I will follow you, my Lord Killan. I am your servant, now and forever: just show me the way and I am yours." As Baronna spoke the falling stopped, the ground felt solid beneath him and the light of Killan's magnificence fell over his face. He took several deep breaths in relief and bowed his head, grateful that Killan had answered his pleas. Getting to his feet, still a little unsteady, he stepped out of the passage into the adjoining chamber and began to meditate.

Cathal clawed his way into the darkness, anxious about what lay ahead but not without hope that his journey would bring him some unity of life and aspiration. He walked on and his attention was drawn to a small beam of light that danced in the distance. Wanting to reach the light as soon as possible, he quickened his stride, then broke into a jog and finally a run. But the light lingered at a distance, teasingly unapproachable.

The run was tiring but, compelled to move on, he kept up the pace. Visions of his past blanketed his thoughts, but the desire to keep going was even stronger. Sweat was soon swimming across his brow, dripping into his eyes and off the end of his nose, and still he ran; faster and faster, unable to let go of the light. His muscles tightened and strangled the blood vessels within, searing hot pains clawed at every inch of his torso, yet he ran on.

Breathless and depleted, Cathal's physical self-succumbed to exhaustion and collapsed to the ground. His mind, past the pain threshold, commanded his body to fight its way to a standing position, but it would not. He had not the strength to raise himself off the ground, but he still dragged his tortured body along the dirty floor, face down and despairing. His torment grew out of the seeds that he himself had planted many years ago in his despair at being unable to save his wife. He now knew that his fate was to feel his own pain forever, to run in fruitless hope and fall without being able to save himself. He cried and begged the gods for his life.

"I couldn't save her, I couldn't save her – it's my fault! My gods, will you not forgive me? Will you not give me my dignity back and forgive me? I have always been your faithful servant. Why must you punish me now? Please, if you can hear me, let me forget my pain. I am at your mercy." Finally Cathal lay face down, clawing at the earth in his helpless longing to reach the climax of a seemingly endless journey.

"My son, you desire our forgiveness for a crime that wasn't yours, therefore it is beyond our power to forgive you for it. Only the guilty can mend the bridge with the victim. You have no bridges to mend. You will find the strength where you least expect it, but only if you open up to the possibility." The words of Kalale, warm and tender, healed Cathal's broken heart. The warmth of this pledge led him to the altar next to Baronna. There he waited as if alone, resting peacefully.

Tristane stepped into a green gilded light that shone across his face. He made his way cautiously along a great winding path of soft earth in the unknown twilight of his early memory. The familiarity of subtle fear tugged at his mind, he asked himself why the nagging thought lingered in such a beautiful dawn. Majestic pines lined the pathway. He reached around the girth of one and held its wisdom for a moment, then pressed his face and body to the span of the tree, basking in its energy. The life-force it held gently flowed into his being, yet this was not the comfort it should have been. Tristane stepped away from the tree and stood still, trying to comprehend his feelings. As he did so a young bird fell by his feet from the branch above. It was sick, he thought, and he watched as it struggled for several moments, feeling powerless to help. He reached for the bird – but quickly withdrew his hand, not daring to touch it. The bird's last breath was a deep sigh of fading hope that drifted through his mind before floating away. He sat down helplessly, feeling hope leaving his body with the breath of the dead creature. He recognised his own fear of the future manifesting itself as the death of one bird, and fell into despondency beyond all hope. Catatonic, he sat through an eternal time of numb despair, until a warm hand pressed lightly on his shoulder and roused him into a wakeful peace.

"You cannot carry a burden so great, it freezes one of all motion and activity," said the soft voice of A'shara. "I should know, for I have felt the same worries in a past time. Yet here I stand as a figure of all that is good, and still I am in your heart. You torture yourself over all you have lost and all that cannot be saved, even when in your heart you know you do not have the answers, and fate is not in your hands. Come, walk with me in the twilight of the universe as it began, and feel my hand always on your shoulder. If you accept that you are who you are, then you will heal the rift you are suffering in the dawn of your path." The goddess beckoned, and Tristane rose slowly to his feet. He felt the magical power in his heart that he had always denied. He knew his world was changing, and he would have to change with it.

A'shara drifted above the ground, her golden robes flowing behind her as she moved. As Tristane walked with her he was overcome by the glory of her persona, opaque like a ghostly vision of all beautiful things that had been or were yet to be. He bathed in the light until it slowly faded and she was gone from his eyes. All that was left to see was the doorway to the lower chamber, where he knew he would at last find his destiny.

Tama felt no fear of whatever unknown she might encounter on her path.

She entered with hope, and certainty that her gods would guide her all the way. Her belief in the gods was unquestioning, and she accepted that it was they that lit the path with a glowing light that draped over her skin with the softness of silk. She moved gracefully through a long winding pathway of golden beams, which danced willingly around her body, while she held her head high to bathe in the light. But it was a deceitful picture of reality, and Tama's confidence began to waver as the light changed and suddenly grew dim. She stumbled, and searched desperately for something to cling to as she felt herself flying apart. She realised her soul was being pulled from her body and frantically tried to drag it back. With a parting wrench her soul gyrated free from her physical self, rising upwards through her forehead. Tama screamed with anguish as her divine spirit departed, leaving a physical presence that had lost its way. A blank creature with no spirit, she ran wildly about looking for her true self, but her soul had risen far above and was powerless to return to soothe the panic of her physical body.

"What should I do? What should I do?" she pleaded repeatedly, hovering above the beauty of this created world that she could not touch. But the answer was beyond her reach. The more she strained to rejoin her body, the further away she drifted. All strength gone, she felt her life-force fading away, and saw her body slump to the ground. In terror and despair she cried out to the gods, "Help me! My body is dying, please help me!"

"As the fear of truth grows, so does the fear of telling it," said a gentle, familiar voice. "The only way to break the back of fear is to meet it in the open," Sriann continued softly as together they gazed down at Tama's body.

"But... but I don't understand. What has caused this? And what must I do?" stammered Tama.

"Your actions have split you from your

true self. Accept that you must tell Cathal about the wolf-man, so that you both may freely choose your course. Only then will your soul and body come together and make you whole," the goddess said, more sternly. Tama acknowledged the truth of Sriann's words, and felt her strength flow back. Her soul began to descend to where her body lay. The two parts of her being came together as one, and Tama came out of the darkness into the inner sanctum. There she meditated as if alone.

Though they all sat side by side, for a time they could not see or know each other's presence. When the temple was ready, it gave them knowledge of each other's presence. As they rose, the four looked around in wonder, marvelling at the peace and renewed hope they saw in the others' faces.

Looking up Tama saw a domed ceiling held together with golden support beams. The window, opening high above within the golden rafters, was the source of the soft light in the chamber. In the centre of the room stood a carved stone altar; at the back of this structure lay a book filled with wisdom and knowledge, adorned with spectacular gold leaf and lettering of lapis lazuli. Tristane stretched his neck to see over the altar, somehow aware that here the future was being written and re-written as events in the present shaped it. As the pages flicked over a mysterious hand holding a feathered pen filled them with text, flashing back and forth, to the future and the present; only the past remained unchanged.

Suddenly the book's red cedar cover slammed shut. Its silvery hinges creaked under the weight of affairs contained within. Light began to pour from the skylight illuminating the space behind the altar, where a large jewel-encrusted egg nestled inside a platinum frame. Within it Tama could see where a small white form lay curled, still and unbreathing. The foursome tiptoed forward, trying not to disturb the tranquillity, feeling that the room was alive about them.

"This is truly a place where one can lose oneself, when reality is bleak and burdensome," Tama whispered.

Now Manna appeared in the middle of the circular stone altar. His tall figure was shrouded in a grey cloak, which reached to his feet and trailed behind him. The cloak was fastened to the shoulder of his loosely fitting gown by two pearl clasps, carved with a depiction of the unborn child and joined across the neck by a platinum chain. His dark skin, long black hair and welcoming smile were just like the guardian at the gate, Tama thought, as he stepped down from the altar and began to speak.

"My friends," began the custodian of the temple, his joyful tone resonating around the adamantine walls, "it is time for you to meet the essence of life. Cailean White Stone is now in your hands. I have cared for her since time began on the Plains, and now I must go to my recreation in the dimensions beyond this time and place. My job here is done."

He raised his arms high above his head, and the child was no longer behind him in the egg but nestled in his hands, supported inside a crystal orb. He gently passed it to Tama. She took it carefully and smiled at the sight of the unborn infant inside.

Manna spoke again. "As long as you do not leave the confines of the astral boat, you shall all remain safe. It will take you to the eugenicists; they will help you now."

His last few words were almost drowned out by a harsh grating sound as huge doors opened behind them and the way up to the surface was revealed. They hurried back to their waiting transport, climbed aboard and sailed west-north-west into the night sky, taking their precious new cargo to the domain of the eugenicists.

Little was known of these mysterious beings. They lived in the heartlands, so named because of its location – equally distant from the south and north poles. It was said the eugenicists were neutral-sexed sayers, with strange powers, whose unique purpose of existence was to control birth. Tama had never seen one, as all of their kind had disappeared from Pelien society before she was born. Tristane remembered seeing one as a child when travelling here with his mother, and he was curious to see if his memories were correct: that a sayer really had no mouth, but communicated by thought alone.

"It is a strange thing that these creatures should do our birthing for us. My mother never warmed to the idea. That is why it took our city such a long time to agree to it," Tristane said as they approached their destination.

"And now we must all wear the badge of a barren future should we find ourselves unworthy parents," answered Tama. Tristane looked at her with warmth in his eyes; she seemed so wise for one so young in years.

Tama, knowing all life depended on this precious object, cradled the orb of life against her breast as she watched the ship float gracefully down into the gardens in front of the entrance to the eugenicists' domain. Nervously she climbed down from the boat, Tristane ahead of her and the others waiting their turn.

"Well, Tama, we have come this far: should we hope for the miracle of birth now we are here?" Tristane called up to her as she descended.

"Your journey has been longer than mine, so you are better placed to answer that; but any hope is good, I think. So hope away that those seas I can hear breaking far inland from the shore are not going to engulf us before we get the job done," Tama replied, feeling a spray of salty water coat her face lightly. The smell of rank seaweed filled the air. Above, storm clouds gathered – swollen with rain. Tama glanced up at them and shivered, then turned toward the cave-like entry. It seemed that Peliens of all persuasions preferred the feel of caves for their dwellings, ready-made buildings that encapsulated the Plains energy and offered protection from the elements.

Baronna stopped abruptly, midway down the ladder.

"What is it?" Cathal asked, from two rungs below him.

"I don't know. Something's not right here."

Cathal looked around to see if Baronna's instincts yielded some spectre of interest, but nothing came to view. He leapt off the ladder with a few rungs to spare; and Baronna, who could leap like a gazelle and land as gently as a feather, hit the ground two paces to his left. He stood tall and uneasy, scenting the air. What he could smell he didn't know, but it seemed... somehow wrong.

"Come on," said Cathal slapping him on the shoulder. "There's nothing in the shadows but..." His voice was drowned out as a man leapt out of nearby shrubbery screaming obscenities at them. He reached for the orb, catching Tama's arm and causing the object to spin through the darkness. Tristane dived and caught it in mid-air. He breathed a sigh of relief as he lay on the ground, then Caldor lunged again for the orb, knocking it from his grasp. The ball of crystal rolled away among the flower beds. Baronna pulled out his sword: Cathal followed, but Caldor's newfound powers had made him nimble and he slipped out of sight in the foliage, blending with the darkness.

"Get the orb!" Tama cried and Tristane, not bothering to stand up, crawled towards where it lay. Caldor thrust himself out of the greenery and laughed. "I have it, I have it! All is lost, ahahahaha." He began throwing the orb up in the air and catching it, a little higher each time, all the while taunting them: "It's mine, it's mine. Come any closer and I'll smash it." They all stood still, sizing him up.

"Listen to me," Tama said softly. "You

can't take the orb. If she dies we all die, and that includes you. If you've got the sight then you know this."

Caldor looked up at the sky. His top lip twitched then he scratched his face while seeming to study the stars. Baronna needed no nudge to seize the opportunity and lunged with his blade, but though Caldor's mind was drifting his reflexes were sharp. He quickly dove out of range, refocused – and threw the orb against the wall of the cave. Tama closed her eyes at the sound of breaking glass. She knew the unborn child was no more.

CHAPTER TWELVE:

Maelstrom

Silence enclosed the group as they wondered if their vision was but a dream and a deceit. Tama crept over to where the shards lay scattered, glistening in the moonlight. Caldor made no attempt to stay and find out if his madness was truly the cause of the end of their time, but slithered into the undergrowth and out of the area. No one tried to stop him; no one noticed him or cared.

Tama bent down to where the broken pieces lay but there was no little body lying helpless at her feet – only the glass remained. Tristane began to pick up the little pieces and put them into a handkerchief.

"What now?" asked Cathal.

"I guess we'll go inside and try to find

out where the child might be. She's clearly not here." Tama said.

"Okay." Tristane replied, and they turned toward the hillside.

The rock protrusion reached high into the night sky like a sea-carved tor, and gleamed with flickering candlelight from cut-out windows. They walked into the mouth of a great white room hollowed into the limestone rock. There were no doors, just doorways. The room was barren of furnishings, with a flat white ceiling. It was basic and stark. Baronna's nose twitched at the cleanliness, his sense of smell being particularly sensitive to such odours. In the distance the sound of a baby crying could be heard, but nothing more.

They waited only a few moments before a Sayer in a white linen gown entered the room from the eastern doorway with its eyes lowered. The Sayer didn't speak verbally.

"I know you." A voice came into Tama's and Tristane's minds and they looked up, startled. "Yes, I am Shakta. I was Aleeah's aide once, and now I am A'shara's. Give me the shards: they will complete the cycle."

"But..."

"Yes, you think you've lost Cailean: but she was never in your care. She has always been here, but to protect that secret a copy was placed in the sacred halls, and a good thing it was. The broken glass – well it's more than that – is needed to start the process, for she must be born in ways you cannot imagine.

Tristane handed over the shards and watched Shakta turn away.

"Well, now what?" Tama asked Tristane as the Sayer disappeared quickly down the long corridor.

"I don't know. Why don't you take a walk and see what our wolf friend is doing," he replied, noticing that Baronna had gone. "I guess he went back to the ship to get away from the smell here. It must be a bit much for a wolf's nose." Tama shivered over

Tristane's suggestion, feeling the guilt grow inside her; though her mind had been distracted by other things, now she had to think of him again.

She turned and left the room to breathe in some of the night air, but the smell of the eugenicists' domain lingered outside the doorway, distracting her from the garden's bounty. The night was still heavy with the promise of rain and Tama strolled around the grounds studying the clouds, deliberately neglecting to check on Baronna.

Cathal followed her into the darkness, broken faintly by beams of moonlight escaping through gaps in the heavy clouds. Watching her move, he was enchanted by her bodily form and the wisps of perfume teasing his senses. Cathal closed his eyes briefly, enjoying the sensations that pulled him effortlessly towards her. He watched her nervously pace the gardens and around their gleaming ship, then he strolled after her, choosing to remain several paces behind. Dressed in the form-fitting leather garments of a fighting man, Tama's slender and youthful body was now silhouetted against the backdrop of a giant blood-red moon that had broken free of the wind-blown clouds. She looked deeply appealing and seductive to him. Her hair floated in the wind as she turned to look at his face.

They walked towards each other in a moment of unspoken understanding and embraced. The moment seemed like an eternity that was rightfully theirs, as their lips met with the heat of passion, but it left them feeling weak and unsatisfied. They both knew there was no time for their love to blossom and they broke the embrace with a last sorrowful kiss.

"I never realised just how much I needed you until just now, Cathal. But we can't be together at this time. Can you wait for me?" said Tama breathlessly, her skin lightly glistening.

He drew her back to his heart and they kissed with a greater passion. "My only hope, sweet woman-child, is that you will wait for me. There should be no question on your lips about my love for you, and its capacity to hold on until the days are once again peaceful." Cathal touched her lips, still swollen from the kiss; gently he rubbed his thumb across her mouth, then turned around and walked back towards the building. Tama touched her own lips, savouring their tingling pleasure as she watched her chosen consort walk away with her heart. She turned to see Baronna's figure high up in the boat, silhouetted against the grey skyline. She wondered briefly what he had been able to hear, or sense, then she walked away alone in the gardens.

Tristane waited impatiently at the doorway, watching Cathal walk back towards the building. He'd seen them outlined against the light of the ship, and now he sensed an awakening in his friend that hadn't been there since their youth. Cathal's eyes sparkled with life as he looked towards his lord and friend; Tristane knew this day had been coming since the meeting at Delgare. He touched Cathal's shoulder as he entered the room and there was a brief awkward silence. Tristane broke it with a caution.

"My niece is a fragile soul with a tough exterior. I wouldn't see her heart broken for a man who is himself broken-hearted for another. Are you sure it's what you both want?"

"You know me better than anyone, Tris. I believe that I have been given a second chance for happiness. I felt this the day we rescued her. Hmm," he paused and smiled briefly, "some rescue. I should say when she rescued us." Cathal looked deep into his friend's eyes. "You can be certain that I love her."

Tristane smiled and shook the hand of his friend. "Yes, you're smitten, there's no doubt. But you still have to ask me for her hand. I am her only guardian out here, even though she has a mind of her own. It is your duty to ask and it is my duty to make sure you're a good suitor." Tristane laughed at Cathal's annoyed reaction.

"If I didn't know any better, I'd think you were having fun at my expense." Cathal's demeanour changed and the two men relaxed, then both sat down on the floor. But in his heart Tristane was unhappy about the love between Tama and Cathal. Love seemed to be at the root of all his unhappy endings, he felt.

Baronna re-entered the room, looking pale and drawn.

"Ah Baronna," said Tristane. "You don't look well. Are you still tired?"

"No, not tired, I think I am ill. I have a terrible headache and nausea. But the last few days have been very busy, it's probably nothing. I'm sure it will pass if I rest for a little longer," replied Baronna.

"I'll call Tama. She may be able to explain your condition." Before Baronna could object Tristane called out to his niece and she came running to see what was going on.

"Is there any news?" she asked breathlessly.

"No, but our friend here seems to be sickening with something. Do you know what it could be?"

She swallowed the knot in her throat and feigned a confident stance. "I was afraid of this after such a traumatic transformation. We should get him back to the boat where he can be more comfortable."

They settled Baronna as best they could away from the halls then sat for an hour in silence waiting for some movement to come from deep within the building, eating some fresh fruit and watching the cave. At last a bright light began to fill the corridor to the east, and out of it emerged a woman. Cailean stood there with an aura as brilliant as the sun's. Mesmerised, Tama stood up, dropping the fruit to the floor, with the two men quickly jumping up after her. They shielded their eyes from the brilliant glow and could see that the woman wore a green gown overlaid with a leaf pattern. Her hair was a blend of yellow and gold and flowed long like the mane of the Bacillon that roamed free on the southern grasslands. Her face was symmetrical perfection, each bone and line clean-cut and sharp. She smiled at the onlookers with thanks in her eyes. Behind her hovered the glowing forms of Sriann, Solake, Lien, and Kalale, their features hardly visible through Cailean White Stone's aura.

The gods said nothing, but drifted from the room on a whisper of air and arced into the night sky like shooting stars, until they could no longer be seen. To their amazement Kalale returned momentarily. He reached out beyond the impending storm to pluck a sparkling ember from the jewel-laden sky, and placed it on Tama's neck as an adornment for as long she wished it there.

As the vision of Kalale disappeared she heard his voice whisper through the wind. "This is my wedding gift to you. He is my son and I choose you for my daughter." At these softly spoken words of love she glanced at her betrothed and smiled, then looked across at Cailean White Stone, emerging from the doorway towards the three companions.

"I am Cailean. I am Druid. I am Shaman, I am Goddess. I am the light in the dark, I am all, yet I am nothing. I am Seer and I am Faith. Let me travel through this world and say to you all: faith. Not the rule of law, but spirituality is the conduit we take in our solid matter until we reach the thought that began us. Come, we have much to do to achieve my reason for birth. The dawn of a new time is coming."

Aboard the vessel Cailean White Stone gently healed Baronna of his sickness, then took the helm. They sailed east towards the mountains, soaring ever higher to reach the highest peak and rise over the top into the blustery night. Ahead lay the ancient forest of Fornay.

Flickering yellow lights beckoned in the distance as the boat sailed back towards the ground. The scent of death lingered and a smoky trail could be observed from above, showing bodies lying strewn across the land. Cailean looked through the smoke using the sight of those on the ground.

"If we land here we may meet Ranyel. I can sense him, and I can also arrest the evil that has spread here."

The boat landed and Cailean instinctively walked towards the dark wall of Fornay's formidable trees, disappearing inside the woodland perimeter. Its depths were darker than anything in the open world. Only the ghost gums shone in luminescence, casting lighter shadows into the darkness. Lithe willow branches shifted sleepily, and pines reached endlessly into the evening above, seeking freedom from the choking damp and ennui. Cailean White Stone chanted her mantra to the shadows.

With Baronna still weak and needing rest, Tama and her two companions stepped down from the boat, numbed by the trauma spread before them. It seemed Maris had launched his evil out into the world, and that evil had come across Ranyel's migrating tribe of Aldora Alroy, the people of the Titian Ardent region. A survivor – fair-skinned like all his tribe, and with hair the same flaming red as the long lost Jugger Short-Stop, Tristane saw – told them the Alroy had come to the north in search of their mage and had found a grisly ambush awaiting them.

"We should look for Ranyel while Cailean is busy," Tama said.

"Okay." Tristane replied.

"Who are these folks really?" she asked as they searched for the mage. "I wasn't permitted to mingle with the traders as a child, and anyway they were rarely red-heads."

"They are, I believe, the result of their first encounters with the red flames of Rhunraja, at the end of the Restoration. The flames ripped out of the volcano and poured down into the sea, hissing and spitting as they hit the waters, which boiled with magma and formed new land dividing the Barragotha region into south-west and south-east. The local tribe worshipped the spirit of the flame, Raphael, who blessed them for their devotion with the fire in their hair colour. As the flame sleeps, waiting for a reason to spark, so do the Aldora Alroy live their lives."

"Poetic," Tama said.

"I suppose it was, yes," Tristane said doubtfully, recalling the less than poetic Jugger.

"Tris!" shouted Cathal. "I've found him – look!" He pointed to where the mage was sitting and resting, chewing on a blade of grass and reading a parchment scroll.

Ranyel looked up in the direction of the voice. "Friends from afar!" he cried. "The time has come to part with my talisman and for you to collect the others. I suspect that the sky will not hold its treasure for much longer." With his words came the resounding crash of thunder, and the air heated up around them, charged with electricity. He handed Tama his necklace, with a round amulet hanging from it. She could not read the markings. "Get yourselves off to Xarjay first, then Mainheart; they are expecting you. Go, shoo, I am too busy here to ponder these problems anymore."

"We have to at least wait for our charge," Tristane said. Ranyel nodded towards the boat and they turned to look. Cailean was already there, having passed them without their knowledge. Save for seeing her leave it, Tama would have felt sure Cailean had never left the boat.

She asked a last question of Ranyel. "Where will we find Mainheart?"

"Just look for the crystal city of the Min Min, north of the Kye!"

First light was struggling to break through the clouds, but the rains had begun to pour and thunder followed lightning at regular intervals. They climbed aboard their transport and sailed up into the sky leaving the devastation behind. It was a mere hour back to the Blue Hills of Healing, but a miserable one – there was no shelter aboard this ship. Its only saving grace was that it did not hold the rainwater, which leaked through small gaps in the deck. Tristane and Cathal occupied themselves with occasional views of wild seas off the Somery Coast, and Baronna listened to waves crashing down on the shores.

To the south-east, Rhunraja had already begun to spew fire, as Ranyel the Red was the keeper of the fire element. Tama worried about the Aldora Alroy descending through the Pass of Golt and into the very heart of the mountain to gain access to their home region. Cailean smiled at her, knowing her thoughts.

"I see all futures, Tama," Cailean softly said. "What I cannot know is which future will reign here with us now. Don't try to solve the greater problem with one leap. It is akin to unravelling a ball of thread by trying to find the end that began it. Each problem must at all times be seen first as a smaller puzzle to solve, which will then add to the solving of all."

"I understand, yet I am worried for Ranyel and the Alroy. The mountain will be engulfed in fire and lava by the time they reach the pass. How will they get home? Or what if their home is destroyed before they get there?"

"Trust that someone else has this piece of the puzzle to solve. Ranyel is no fool. He will not lead them into danger. Trust this advice as you have at times trusted your own instincts. Your gut instinct will tell you what is right and wrong; your third eye will grant you inner sight. Use them, they are within you: yet you fight the powers you've been granted."

"Because I have made mistakes in my judgement," Tama sighed, thinking about Caldor's true colours. "The reforging of the Plains is within our sight because I trusted one person."

"We cannot be responsible for the fall of other people. Freedom of will to choose one's destiny is inexplicably inherent in who we are. There are immeasurable numbers of available futures at our very fingertips which may seem caused or pre-ordained, but the sisters of wyrd rarely leave you choiceless. All futures are possible, only one is chosen – it is caused by the will. Some would have it otherwise but they are not the wisest; and in the meantime, your choices err on the side of goodness and hope. Caldor never wanted anything but false glory. When he was given the choice he took the one that paid off for him, and him alone. Lastly, choosing the right destiny may not seem so ambiguous if it were known that there is only the right one, no matter what the result. Let it rest. Nothing we do is a mistake, even when the whole world is about to fall to its knees."

The ship descended to an anxiously waiting mage, who waved his torch vigorously to be seen by the ship's crew; the storm had concealed the break of dawn.

"Welcome, welcome my dear, dear friends! And you have brought your charge. Oh, it is such an honour finally to see you in person." Xarjay bowed to Cailean as she emerged into the light of his torch. "Now, I have gathered from this weather that you have two talismans." The group nodded in agreement.

"We have all spoken to each other – that is, the guild members and I. Mainheart is expecting you in less than a day. When the spirits are fully awake they will assume they are to re-form the Plains, and we will be lost once again in the maelstrom of thought."

"Is that their sole purpose, Xarjay?" asked Cathal, curious about Kalale's apparent inability to contain the weather within the sky.

"Yes, Cathal, it is their only true purpose. They know of none other, though they are conscious. They will only cease once the job is done or they are taken back to their resting place. I have no reason to go back to the darkness, and wish not that it happens to any of you. So, here – take my chain and go."

"Xarjay, defence of life is not lost to me." Cailean touched his shoulder, seeing the years that shone beyond the light of the old man's eyes. "Let me take your burden, give me the talisman, I shall carry the weight of it for you."

"Thank you." he said.

They held each other's gaze briefly as if talking without words about a time and a place they had once shared. For a moment their spirits shone like companion stars. Then Cailean withdrew, reminding the group that it was imperative for them to leave. With goodbyes said, they set off once more on their journey.

The Plains, distant though they were, could be seen to the north through a shroud of light rain. The Kingdom of Husienna shone brightly in the distant plain to their left as they headed over Lien's Divide, capped with snow. Their destination was further to the north – above the Kingdom of Valaron, where Mainheart, keeper of air, held the last piece of the puzzle.

They carried with them the cargo that forced the elements themselves to re-build their world without regard for life or love. The effects of the talismans in their possession had begun to break the world apart. The ground below began to shake and rumble as gaping cracks in the terra firma became an instant gateway for the rivers and streams to pour into. Fire spewed from the mountain range and was already forcing open new fissures.

Cailean commanded high speed from the vessel; it sped towards the Northern Plains. Below, groups of people came pouring out of the mountain's tunnels, running and screaming. The battleground of Valaron had been quenched with the blood of its citizens, but the quakes had stayed Maris's hand and his beasts were scattered in search of shelter from the elements – only to find they were to be swallowed by cascades of red, burning rock. Confusion was everywhere: without warning, a small hill appeared in the once green and flattened plain. The others watched helplessly from their vantage point while Cailean commanded more and more speed, then a glow of pale light began to surround the air ship. Time itself appeared to stand still – another trick of Cailean's, thought Tama. Soon she could no longer see the ground: it was out of sight, cloaked by the strange effects. She tried to speak but no sound came from her mouth. She felt unable to move; from the corner of her eye she could see the others standing as still as she, and Cailean chanting beneath her breath. The white light was brilliant now, as if they were viewing the image of the entire world at once and no longer able to separate colour from its parental wave.

When they finally ceased to ride through the waves of light, they found themselves landing in the outer grounds of the Crystal City. The devastation had not yet reached this far north. But the calm moments troubled Tama and her party.

"How can this be?" she asked Cailean.

"I can only tell you that with my thoughts I sped up time within the boat and slowed time down on the Plains. It requires a great deal of effort to do this. I can hold the moment for a few more hours, but you must go on without me. I'll have to use the Crystal's energy here to sustain this unnatural state for as long as I can. Go to Mainheart: he is waiting for you now beyond the city's gates. But you will find that you can't travel at speed once you step down outside the ship. You will take at least thrice the time of your normal movements. I will meditate up to the Crystal's peak where its energy is at its most concentrated. And now you're away by yourselves – this is my job and mine alone."

Without another word the earthbound spirit drifted up into the smoky quartz that towered above the ground. The four companions descended the ladder to find they had stepped into a slowed timeframe, just as Cailean had predicted. To reach the gates seemed to take a lifetime, but in reality it was only a matter of minutes. They could see tiny lights drifting in and out through the walls then disappearing without warning, to be replaced by another. Cathal slowly reached out and touched one; as it passed through him he felt the pain of a Pelien running for his life, then it was gone. He reached for another and felt the warm love, brief but distinct, of a family together hiding somewhere on the Plains.

"Min min lights," explained Tristane. "It's the thoughts of the Peliens that you're feeling. They accumulate here where the energy from the crystal draws them in, and they last for as long as the thought lasts. What did you receive?" he asked Cathal.

"Pain, then happiness. I don't think I'll try another one."

A tall man glided to meet them, his

blue robes flowing about him as he came. The air around him seemed to be whispering sweetly, and his long, smoke-coloured hair gently waved around his face. Mainheart greeted them warmly, having been forewarned by his fellow mages of the reason for their visit. He spoke little to the group and simply handed them the talisman from around his neck. He then passed a scroll to Tama; it was a spell, he said, but there was no time for her to read it now.

Mainheart guided them to a cavern below the city and sent them on their way. He told them the ship would be of no use in the currents of air that would now join in the battle for the Plains, and the city of Kye was too heavily guarded to be approached from the upper levels.

They left with nothing more to guide them than their noses, and a flaming torch. As they set off into the tunnel Mainheart's final words played on Tama's mind: "Watch out for the walkers," he'd whispered.

*****

From his hidden sanctuary the Pretender sensed their entry, and smiled grimly. "So, the seekers are coming to Kye. May it truly be the city of death for all of them. They have troubled me too long, and I must make an end of them. Rakeem! Listen carefully..."

CHAPTER THIRTEEN:

Confronting the Darkness

For a long part of the journey they saw nothing but the flickering flame of their torch. The only sound was that of their footsteps crunching on the pebbly cave floor. Tristane led the party and Baronna walked at the rear, with Cathal and Tama side by side listening intently to each other breathing in the increasingly foul air. The air became thicker and more dreadful as they went, and their pace slowed. It was a sad place; Tama felt as she had in the cave under the Blue Hills. Her sensitivity became heightened in the gloom as they descended into the spiritual centre. How inconvenient that the Adrian should choose such a place to build their city on, Tama thought, as the cave walls seemed to ooze grief.

Baronna's ears picked up the sound

of shuffling feet and he poised to listen like an animal on the hunt. The noises came from behind them, now close enough for them all to hear. The footsteps grew closer in the darkness, and Baronna's heart began to quicken, as it never had as a wolf. "Damn the heart if it makes you spell out fear with every beat," he said under his breath, not liking the feeling at all. The others moved a little behind him, hands ready to grasp their swords and eyes staring into the shadowy depths. The silhouette of an elderly man came into view. He gave no acknowledgment of their presence, but simply pushed his way through the tight space between the party and the cavern walls. As he came into the light of the torch it was clear their visitor was one of the walkers that Mainheart had warned of – a lonely body of skin and bones, without hope. He walked on and into the dark on the other side of the party, leaving the odour of death in his wake.

"So that is a walker," Tama sighed.

"The dragons called us walkers. I hope they saw more in us than what that person has become."

"Don't bet on it," Tristane said, cringing away to stay as far from the creature as possible. "My mother told me the dragons mostly showed disgust of us; they did become tolerant in the end, even respectful to some degree, though it was earned at a great price."

"Well, I suppose I don't really care what they thought; it would be nice to have such an ally right now," Tama said, and covered her nose to stifle the odour invading her nostrils. The hairs pricked up on the back of Baronna's neck for a second time; he gently pressed a hand on Cathal's shoulder to alert him. They waited for the being to pass, but as it came into the light of their torch Tama and Tristane realised that they recognised it. Tama searched for what now seemed like a distant memory of a loving light that had left her orphaned not so long ago. Tristane, too, swallowed the lump in his throat, realising just who they were both looking at. It was King Husienna, Tama's father and Tristane's brother, in gaunt skin, wearing the stained robes of his former life draped carelessly around a body whose weakened skeletal structure laboured to hold up the miserable garb. The stooping zombie ignored their presence, just like the one before; but Tama, beside herself, cried out to him in desperation. Tristane grabbed her and held her close. Several seconds passed, and then a great shuffling began, in stark contrast to the silence. Many footsteps beat around them as they inched forward through the flickering darkness of the cavern. When the walls fell away on both sides, the companions stepped into what seemed like an open chamber. As they came further into the room, they saw that it was filled with the soulless bodies of many, many more walkers. The creatures made no sound except an endless shuffling, echoing to a lost audience. Tama was grief-stricken; her stomach churned and her legs refused to move a step further. The walkers, alerted to their presence, moved in to surround them, pressing them against the chamber wall.

Baronna reached for his sword and jabbed at the pathetic creatures to force them back. Tears welled in Tama's eyes as she now came face to face with an image not only of her father but also of her mother – a pale reflection of her once beautiful and elegant self. Tama choked back her tears and jabbed with her sword, knowing that the thing before her was not her mother any more, but a sad apparition of what was once a queen of the Kingdom of Husienna. The great King Husienna, reduced to a mindless wandering receptacle, could no longer lay claim to that descent.

"Ah finally, the Marda family and company arrives. Your lovely voice, Princess, gave you away completely. Though my master knew you were here even before even you did" He smiled at them knowingly. "You didn't think you could enter my world and not get caught?" His sneering voice inquired from the shadows.

"Rakeem!" Tama cried, recognising the voice that had haunted her dreams and looking wildly around for its owner.

Rakeem stepped into the chamber from the south tunnel, waving a knowing finger and tutting reprovingly as he came into full view. Tama looked over at him, distracted from the zombie walkers. The string of eyeballs swung back and forth on chains from a crown on Rakeem's head, set above the bony face that had burned an image into her memories from their last meeting. His voice, like her own, seemed to grind through its words under Cailean's warp of time. But he had an air of self-satisfied importance, like the cat that had caught the fish without getting his feet wet. His arrogance came from having defeated Aleeah's curse, Tama thought.

"We've never had such grand company under our city," Rakeem laughed. "That's if you don't include your parents.

Don't worry, they have no idea who you are; your soul-taker god saved their souls." His voice lowered to hypnotic levels. "Remember Tama – the dark night – the storm – the feel of the howling wind as it gushed across your child brow – the way you trembled in the muddy mire. How fragile you were, your innocence charming the world – then you were shattered to find you were made to be the saviour of it. But that destiny is not yet fulfilled, my lovely girl-woman who resonates at levels that confound all in your presence." His whispered words began to enchant her. "Remember what I told you then?" he asked.

"Yes." she softly replied.

"What do you want, Rakeem?" demanded Tristane. "Do you think your mindless band is going to protect you from my blade? Well, it isn't!"

Tama was jerked out of the enchantment and shook her head, puzzled by Rakeem's power over her.

"Argh!" Rakeem was clearly annoyed

by the interruption. "I need no protection from your blade. It has no power in my world." He gestured, and their four swords slid across the chamber as if through thickened air. A small company of wights and battle mages entered from the tunnel behind Rakeem, swiftly forming ranks facing the travellers.

"You've come to the end of your journey. We'll take the amulets now – there's no sense in us all dying after we've worked so hard to live, so we'll finish the job you've started."

Baronna pushed forward; his large frame making a barrier between the dread creatures and his companions.

"Oh stop posturing, blind man. What hope is there for a blind dog with no master?" Rakeem sneered.

Baronna was infuriated by the insult and leapt over the creatures' heads, landing a foot in front of Rakeem, to his evident surprise. Tama grabbed the swords with her mind and gave them back to their owners so they could fight. But Rakeem did not stay to fight. Like the coward he was, he ran back towards his city, with Baronna in pursuit. Rakeem knew his tunnels well and slunk far into the shadows. Baronna hunted him relentlessly by sound and scent, driven by the need for personal revenge.

*****

The battle scene was made stranger by Cailean's slowing of time: each movement seemed to take forever to accomplish. Rakeem's three battle mages stood at the back of the chamber sending incendiary spells at the melee in front of them, hindering the trio's defence. Tama, sensing crystal springs below the cold stone, opened a fissure and released icy water to put out the flames.

With a swish of his narrow blade Tristane cut down several of the walkers that stood motionless between him and the wights. Cathal and Tama broke away and thrust their swords into the other walkers. Bodies came thudding to the ground like stale meat cast out from the butcher's shop. But the walkers were the easy part: the several wights behind were now cleared of obstacles and could attack directly. The battle mages had quickly sealed the fissure and began to cast their spells again.

"*Fire starters will not learn; the ways of magick must be earned*," Tama chanted, reopening the fissure directly beneath the battle mages. Out spewed a maelstrom of icy-fresh waters, ending the incendiary attack and sucking the enemy down into a stone-walled tomb. She stood back a moment, satisfied with her own quick thinking. "That'll teach them to play with fire," she said to herself.

"Less play, more work!" shouted Cathal, who was being set upon by three wights with wicked blades covered in a poisonous fluid. She turned, annoyed at his words, and plunged her sword into the back of one, then reached for Cathal with the other hand, pulling him clear of certain death. The two of them swiped their swords into the same creature and turned to pick off several more. Tristane had leapt onto a rocky outcrop and was kicking away the sword blades slashing at him. Only five of the enemy remained upright and Cathal swept the head off one, leaving four of the biggest and ugliest to kill. Tristane leapt onto the back of one, riding it like a carthorse and swinging at the others, while keeping his free hand over its eyes.

Finally, the last enemy fell and the group paused to reassess their situation. From the silence of the caverns, they heard a rumble in the distance, and began to move back into a normal time frame. Dust and fragments of rock fell into the chamber in larger and larger quantities, dislodged by the violent disturbances above. As the debris became harder and bigger in size, the three moved hurriedly to the side of the cavern.

"Where's Baronna?" asked Cathal. "We can't go into the spiritual centre without him."

"Typical, just when you need him he disappears," Tristane said, stepping over the pile of bodies he'd hewn down and trying to catch his breath. Tama was sitting silently beside the wasted bodies of her parents. She looked up at Tristane briefly.

"Where do we go from here? Cailean's power is obviously fading; we are back and forth in this conflict of time, and the cavern is not a safe place to be. Either we'll be trapped by it falling on us, or it will soon be crawling with beasts again," she said.

"I know, but we must find Baronna. The fool let his emotions drag him off after that... that animal, Rakeem." Tristane said.

Tama jumped to her feet with renewed determination. Sparing no more time for her loss she set off for the city of Kye, the two men following her into the torch-lit cavern. They went cautiously, each step they made feeling like a step closer to some doom. This sense of unease was not helped by Cailean's repeated loss and regaining of her spell over time. Feeling jerky and uncoordinated, the trio crept up into the main house of Rakeem.

It was eerily quiet. The house should have been bustling with guardians, but there was no one. Accompanied only by the sounds of a door creaking open and closed somewhere far off, and the rain pelting at the dirt-stained windows, they crept as silently they could into the upper house.

"Where on this Plain is Baronna?" Tama asked rhetorically. Her words were followed by a loud wailing that sent shivers down her spine. The sound was unmistakable. It was almost as if Baronna had gone back to his wolf-man form, the howl was so close to that of the animal. Tama froze and Tristane spoke aloud without realising he'd said anything: "They've got him."

"No!" Tama shouted, and began to search the rooms frantically with the two men in tow. They came to the last room on the second floor, where light gently spilled into the darkened hallway from cracks in the wooden-slatted door. Something about this room made Tama stop suddenly; she sensed the presence of something far greater than Rakeem or his dying hordes, and entered gingerly.

She breathed as lightly as she could and Cathal felt her passion as he watched her cautiously step forward and push the door fully open. She looked at the desperate state of the room. It was bleak, grey, and heavy with the odour of sweat and unwashed bed linen. In the corner of the room she could see an untidy bed supporting a hapless body, barely able to move. On the headboard a black raven perched as if on guard duty, looking over the man's frail and ravaged body. The raven squawked at Tama and she knew immediately who they were; but that didn't explain the power she felt about her. Tristane came around her right side to see who or what she was staring at, and realised very quickly that it was one of his half-brothers that lay abed and the other that perched over him.

"Look what the curse has done to them," Tama said softly, and reached out to touch Oraldo's brow. He opened his eyes briefly but just as quickly closed them again, obviously pained by the light.

"Two less of them to worry about, if you ask me." Tristane was not sympathetic, having grown up with his mother's hardened heart against her firstborn sons.

"They are not what you think," Tama protested. "Not all Adrian are dark by nature. I can see much more in them; they have not inherited their father's breath, but their mother's. Aleeah runs through their veins, and it is her curse that oozes from every crevice in this room. That's the power I can feel in here – can you feel it?"

"Yes, but there's nothing we can do for them now, even if you are right," Tristane replied, unhappy to be having this conversation or to even be in the same room as his evil opposites, as he felt them to be. "He's bad blood. Let him die." The bird squawked again, but this time flapped its wings frantically. Tristane stepped back and almost fell over Cathal.

"I can hear its thoughts," Tama said. "They have been waiting for forgiveness for crimes that were not theirs."

"I know how that feels," said Cathal. "It's a burden I'd wish on nobody."

Tristane stood for what seemed like the longest time looking down at the creature and its charge, and realising that he too could hear the bird's thoughts. His resolve towards Oraldo and Kerr softened.

"I can hear him too. He's been stricken with the curse also: but at least the raven spirits have kept the curse at bay for him."

"Yes, but they won't hold it off forever," said Tama.

Cathal became impatient as the rumble of the ground below resonated through the walls and floors. "We need to work out a plan to find Baronna. As important as this history of yours is, we can't save everyone."

Tama continued to stroke the head of her half-uncle and then held out her other hand for the raven to sit upon. Kerr came, sensing her remorse for their plight. Tama whispered a charm:

"Whatever sins you've carried abreast,
They are not yours and so should rest.
The rod in your back will be exposed,
The trials of your life no longer controlled;
The curse is lifted from your heads
For I shall free you from its dread.
The blight's maker is elsewhere now,
And cannot touch your tortured brows;
So I will bless them in her place,
Unbinding the curse's sharp embrace.
I release you both."

Tama blew from her palm the crushed leaves from Xylon's branches that she'd pulled from her lap pouch. The leaves sparkled like crystal shards in the sun as they drifted through the air, their long and fruitful life-force still part of their dried state. The shredded leaves landed softly across their targets, then melted into them becoming part of their essence.

A light zephyr entered the room, cleansing away the curse as it passed. Aleeah's heavy presence dissipated and the freshness of a new life began to bloom for Oraldo and Kerr. Kerr flapped back onto the headboard and Oraldo opened his eyes for the second time, but now turned to look into Tama's eyes. He was not yet aware enough to know what had happened, but the torment had left his face leaving it seeming younger and fresher. Oraldo was not a pretty man, thought Tama, but at least he had regained some of his lost years. With no time to explain the situation to him, the three left him with Kerr while they resumed the search for Baronna.

Turning left down the hallway, they found the main staircase leading out into the courtyard. There they discovered why the city had earned its name: Kye, the epitome of death itself. Cathal shivered as he looked out over at the city's expanse, stained with blood and strewn with tortured and dismembered bodies. Tristane desperately tried to convince himself it was all a horrible illusion, not reality; and Tama cringed under the weight of such slaughter. Gagging, they hurriedly tied scarves around their faces to reduce the intake of the foul air.

In the distance Baronna's cries could still be heard; and Tama, Tristane and Cathal followed the unholy sound to its source. They had to fight their way up the beaten, cobbled streets covered with a sticky coating: black dust had quickly turned to mud by the rain falling almost horizontally in the high winds. They were still unaware that Cailean's power over time had collapsed and the impending rework of the Plains had resumed fully. They hardly even noticed that the hordes of Rakeem had vanished, and no one tried to stop them coming deeper into the city. Deeper and deeper they trotted against the tumultuous weather that beat without a break against their tired bodies, following the sound of their companion wailing somewhere up in one of the towers. Up streets and down twisted alleyways they ran towards the furthest of the buildings, against the dragging weight of their heavy damp clothes and weapons, until they finally reached the bottom of the tower, and the wailing stopped.

"Now what?" said Cathal.

"In for a dobber –" Tristane replied. They both looked at Tama.

"– in for ten dobbers. Yes – we're here, so let's do it!" Tama said. "There are so many floors to this tower, and I'll bet he's at the top."

"Why make the task easy for us now?" Tristane feigned a smile, still doubting his niece's judgement in relieving his half-brothers of their curse. They began to climb and soon discovered that the staircase wound around on itself, up and up in the pitch blackness of windowless walls. The sound of the storm was deadened by the air in the tower and Tama felt herself choking on the staleness of it. Damp gave rise to a mildewed smell, and the walls were cold to the touch. They could only walk in single file, but each held to the hand of the next. A thumping could be heard above them and a chunk of stone bounced out of the darkness, barely missing Tama before rattling past them through the cramped space. The falling stone masked the sounds of shuffling feet that followed them in the dark, far enough away not to be detected by the senses. The climbers stared in awe at each in shock, but then forged on.

"At last!" Tama said, when light from the upper window spreading down the stairs marked the end of their climb.

"What now?" asked Cathal, echoing the thoughts of the other two.

"One door, one way," Tristane said, squeezing past Tama to be first into the room.

The door creaked open revealing a sea of creatures waiting for their arrival, with no way out. And now another sea of creatures blocked the stairs; they could do nothing but surrender. Tama berated herself for not having read the signs along the way and for being manipulated by her feelings towards Baronna. And now her mistakes had led her team to certain death. Baronna was nowhere about: there was just a lowly dog cowering at the feet of her enemy. Rakeem smiled, knowing that he'd tricked them into believing it was their friend.

"We don't know yet where your tame wolf is, but it won't be long before we do. This city does not let intruders go so easily," Rakeem said. "Now, the amulets – hand them over and we will let you go to whatever dimension one goes to after death. Otherwise, we will keep you alive, as slaves to torture at our pleasure. There's no way out this time."

Tama looked desperately around the room for some means of escape. The window openings let in the driving rain, but any attempt to jump would bring certain death. Her gaze was caught by two black birds battling upwards against the storm. They landed on the sill and looked on with apparent interest.

"If we must choose to die by default or live by torture, then we will go on to the dimension of light and not stay here as your slaves," Tama said, as if defeated. But she sent a quite different message to the other two. "To die in battle as a warrior is better than to be enslaved or murdered," she told them. Tama reluctantly handed over three amulets to Rakeem, glad that the fourth was yet out of reach with Baronna. Having lulled the company of wights and zombies into thinking they had won, the three went on the attack for the second time that day. Cathal turned and bolted the door against the horde outside, leaving just the twenty or so in the room with them. Rakeem seemed too shocked by this deceit to rally his forces, though Tama felt sure it was exactly what he would have done in her place.

The two ravens dived into the heat of the fray, pecking wildly at any evil soul that came within reach and seeming to enjoy the deadly battle. This fight was far worse than that in the chambers below. The trio fought desperately but were soon forced to retreat into a corner, safe from attack from behind as they defended themselves against swords and battleaxes. Rakeem stood back and watched the three tire as they jabbed, jibed and blocked the twisted army. Outside the solid timber door other battle sounds rose: weapons clanged and clashed, heavy bodies thudded against the door. Finally, Tama managed to formulate a spell that placed a block wall between her party and their attackers. Then she simply blew it down on top of the enemy, ploughing a pathway out of their corner.

"Yarr!" Cathal cried as he leapt at Rakeem. "Now we'll see how strong you are without your army."

Rakeem seemed defenceless, but he

used his powers of magick to conjure a thorny vine to bind the trio before they could bring him down. Satisfied that they were now at his mercy, he overlooked the two ravens who'd become Tama's allies. The bigger one flew up behind Rakeem while the other swooped down to peck at his eyes. The large raven transformed into Oraldo, who plunged a silver stiletto into the dark heart's back, bringing him to his knees. Unable to die like a Pelien since his pact with Maris the Pretender, Rakeem writhed in helpless pain, his senses gone, while Oraldo undid the spiky rope holding captive his new-found family.

"Thank you," Tama said as the man pulled her upright. He bowed as if the gesture of thanks was his to give, not hers.

Tristane stood up without help and looked upon this half-brother with a new light in his eyes – a realisation that forgiveness was nothing more than a reason to befriend and accept a brother. Two brothers, Tristane thought.

"You look well, Oraldo, and it seems you have your mother's ability," he said.

"Yes, I have always had it – not that it has done me any good until now. I'm told it is one of the benefits of being a mage child."

"Then that means..." Tama began, as she looked across at Tristane. Cathal put a hand on his friend's shoulder and they both looked as if they were expecting him to give some grand speech.

He felt a sudden release, as if a secret had been let loose and now an explanation was called for. "It's true, I may have that ability also. But my father dissuaded me from developing it so I haven't explored the possibility."

"You may well be the last dragon on these shores my friend, if it is your father that you take after. It's worth the try for that alone, and we could certainly use the power of the dragon right now." Cathal paused. "In case you haven't noticed we are deep in enemy territory, led into an ambush, with the king of it still writhing over there." They all turned to look at Rakeem, now blinded and fallen.

"Can you do something to stop him doing any more evil, Tama? I'd much rather he was out of the way before I have a go at using powers I've not thought to exist all these years. Oh, and don't forget to get back the amulets – we might need them sometime." Tristane tried to sound facetious, then let out a small nervous laugh at being put on the spot.

"I'll bind his powers," Tama replied, "and he will cross over to wherever his kind crosses. I believe it is his powers that saved him from the curse, and from death on the end of that blade."

She began a ritual, but was almost drowned out by the persistent clanking sounds outside the locked door. Cathal walked to the door and listened. A smile creased his face and he gingerly opened the door, letting the roar of Baronna's battle cry blast into the room. He stood awestruck at the way Baronna was able to fight using his other senses to make up for his lack of sight.

"Some help would be useful, and now would be a good time!" Baronna gasped, as he blocked another sword thrust and sent its owner tumbling down the staircase he'd fought so hard to get up. Cathal and Tristane leapt into the fray, joining Baronna's mighty arms in swinging their swords at the creatures of the dark. The three men fought on from the top of the tiny landing until no more wights or zombies clambered over the pile of bodies to get to them, then they sat breathless for several moments.

"Hey, Baronna, we thought we'd lost you for good. We need you to finish this thing – and besides, we missed your charming presence," Cathal joked, trying to hide his pleasure at seeing Baronna.

"Yeah, right," Baronna laughed. "I've been all over this place fighting, dodging, and seeking the path back down. I was quite lost until I heard the wailing, and then

I followed this lot up the stairs. I figured out what was happening when I heard you go through the door above, so I got stuck into these nasty smelling beasties."

"Aye, you guessed right," said Cathal, and proceeded to tell Baronna their story of events. Tristane looked out of the window, listening to the winds howling repeatedly as if to remind them of the job still to be done.

"...and if the Thane will find the courage to fly us down to our destination, we should not need any more luck," finished Cathal.

"So," said Baronna, slapping Tristane on the back and jolting him out of his distant thoughts, "likely you're a dragon then, and never let on." Tristane smiled an uneasy smile, as Tama shouted from beyond the door that her task was done. Rakeem was now dead, whether of his wounds or the curse – it really didn't matter which, she thought.

"We need to go from here for many reasons, Thane, not least because of how far from safety we are. You will not like how many more creatures are out in the courtyards around the city," Baronna said. "I can hear them from here."

Tristane nodded, got up, and walked back into the room where Tama and Oraldo stood by the empty husk of Rakeem. Kerr was perched once again on Oraldo's shoulder as if proud to be there again.

"Take the steps to the roof, Uncle," Tama said, pointing to a ladder at the far side of the room. She rarely called him uncle, but it seemed appropriate this time. "You will find your dragon when at the highest point, looking down."

Tristane looked at her in silence, and tried to swallow the lump that was forming in his throat. He wasn't afraid, exactly, but the call to be the last dragon of the Plains lay very heavily upon his heart; each step up the ladder seemed like a step away from grace toward possible disaster.

The others followed him up to the roof. His individual essence seemed to surround him with awesome energy as they watched his silhouette atop the grey-walled turret, thrashed with rain. The five onlookers waited silently for their friend and kinsman to find his way among the clouds of the low-lying storm. Cathal reached over and placed his hand over Tama's and she clutched it tightly with her other.

Tristane walked to the edge, and stretched out his arms ready to fall into the ether. But the wind blew cold and hard against him, making it difficult to lean over; he pushed forward and his cloak snapped back behind him. Looking down, he saw the ground as a blur of objects shrouded by the heavy weather. Deep inside himself he could feel the call of the dragon beginning, something that had not troubled him fully since he was a child. Several times he'd gone to leap from the highest point of the palace without knowing why he wanted to, and several times his father had hauled him back. "There's only one way down, and that is by the stairs," Alden would say firmly.

"Not this time, dad," he thought, as if his father was listening. His blood pounded, roused by the spirit of the dragon. He sported no tattoo like Alden's: the matching of spirits was different for the child of a dragon mage. Tristane knew there was no escaping this fate, he just had to work out the activation of it.

His breath slowed, and the air called him forward, releasing Tristane from the stone tower. He fell into the wind: it carried him as a man for a short time, but then the wings of a golden-desert dragon emerged from his arms and his fingers became the spiny bones that held their webbed shape. His tail bone grew long and ridged from his newly spiny back, making it a most deadly weapon; his scaly legs now trailed razor-sharp claws. His head and neck took on the characteristic majesty of the dragon, and he roared with a fiery breath to let the world know he'd found his spirit. Roaring a second time, just to show off a little, he shot a tongue of flame into the stormy air, turning the falling rain into steam. Carried away with the power of his new form, he circled several times using the wind to take the weight of his giant body.

The five bystanders craned over the edge, awed by Tristane's new power. Tama let out a gasp as she took in a spectacle not seen since Alden had lost his ability; yet here it was again, reborn in the dragon mage's son.

"So majestic," she whispered, and Cathal put an arm around her shoulders, enjoying the vision of his long-standing friend becoming the last dragon. Finally Tristane came in to land on the edge of the tower, shaking it to its foundations.

As Tristane came to a halt opposite their viewing point, Oraldo turned to leave. He was comforted by the connexions he'd made, feeling he'd built a bridge with his family, one that they must now choose whether to cross.

"Where are you going?" Tama asked, as Oraldo stepped onto the ladder.

"I've work to do. Kye was once Barrakye, life after death, and so it shall be again. As long as I am able to continue, the evil here will be cleansed." Kerr squawked in agreement, and the two left the rooftop with as little fanfare as when they arrived.

CHAPTER FOURTEEN:

Trapped in the Centre

Tristane ferried Tama, Cathal, and Baronna one by one to the ground, transforming back to himself the moment they were all safely landed in front of the tower. They quickly headed downhill and found their way back into the tunnels below the palace. Soon they had reached the cavern where they'd previously fought. But where they'd left a pile of slain creatures, they found a rotting, stinking, sludge.

"I'm not walking through that... that foul soup," Cathal said in disgust. The ground grumbled and the slop swished about like a lake of ooze.

"Some choices are not ours to make, and this is one of those. We have to get to that tunnel over there regardless of what's under our feet," Tristane insisted.

"How do you know it's that one?" Cathal asked, hoping Tristane was mistaken.

"Because we came up that one and back down this one, so there's only one left to try."

"Well, remind me not to come with you the next time you knock on my door," Cathal muttered.

"If I remember rightly, you couldn't wait to get stuck into our quest," Tristane retorted, stepping bravely into the putrid lake.

"I was a fool then, and now I know better!" His companions sniggered.

"Come on!" Tristane signalled for the others to leave the tunnel and they gingerly stepped from the dry cavern-ledge into the slimy remnants of their fight. Cathal could hear his feet sucking down into the slop, and Baronna covered his nose and mouth with both hands to protect his delicate senses, trusting to his heightened hearing to find the way across. The waste rose as high as their knees, slowing their progress. In Tristane's wake, an eyeball would float upwards, or a hand seemed to clutch at them. Tama was green and clenched her stomach, trying not to think about what she was wading through. Finally they reached the opposite side of the chamber, carrying with them the remnants of the stinking slop on their clothes.

"There'd better be crystal waters to bath in down here, or I'm going to heave," said Baronna, struggling for breath.

The walls in this cave were lined with flickering torches, and became smoother and lighter in colour as the quartet walked deeper. They came suddenly around a bend and found an arched doorway. It was carved from the great oak, and adorned with jewels of the world that glistened like an early morning frost in the flickering light of the torches. The door was inscribed in a language that Tama immediately recognised. She read it aloud. The others looked on, but knew nothing of the language, only that it sounded like the wind rustling through the trees.

"We come as bearers of earth, air, fire, and water. We come as servants of soil, wind, flame, and liquid. We bid you to give us right of passage into the hallowed halls of the keepers of the elements, Sera, Ranyel, Xarjay, and Mainheart. Will you not answer?" Tama read.

"I will answer in my own good time and when I feel like it," came the unexpected reply from a voice that sounded hoarse and dry and seemed to come from the door itself. "Who are you, and what do you think your business is within the hallowed chamber? Answer! Answer me!"

"Err, um..." Tama stuttered, wondering what she should do, then settled for a repeat of the inscription. "We come as..."

"Yes, yes, I heard you the first time. But what is it you want?"

"To give back to the halls that which does not sleep and which causes chaos."

"I see."

The rumbles that had followed them down the tunnel now grew louder. A powerful tremor rocked them from side to side and covered them with drifts of white dust.

"Could you please 'see' a little more quickly, before the cave falls in and crushes us all?" Tama said impatiently, exasperated by the doorkeeper's inaction.

"No need to be cross. I can see there's a problem," the unseen speaker admonished her.

"Well you're not exactly helping with your ridiculous questions," she retorted, as more white powder fell on them.

"I don't get out much you know, and my social skills are not what they used to be. But I can see your point, and if the spirits are going to bring down the walls of my home then you shall enter," the voice said, as if coming to a decision. It paused, then went on more firmly. "But heed this: if you forget me, you will forget your purpose."

It sounded like a silly warning to Tama; she was in no mood to listen to it with such a pressing task at hand, and waited impatiently for the door to open. The chains ran around their cogs and the locking mechanism was released, drawing the door back. Tama was first to see into the halls and she filled her lungs with the fresh, clean air that met her. She stepped inside the bright, opaline chamber, signalling for the others to follow. They looked about for the source of the voice, but could see no one. Tama tossed her boots off to feel the heavy carpet of grass between her toes. Baronna headed straight for the sound of the waterfall that ran down the westerly face, and was quickly followed by the other three. Forgetting their task, they bathed in the watery essence until the stench of their recent past was all but erased.

This was an enchanted place: a large spiritual garden draped with peace. Marble statues of the four mages represented north, south, east, and west. The travellers wandered through the beauty of the rose gardens, dotted with blossoms of all the colours of the rainbow. Several large oaks formed the cathedral ceilings, and the song of a skylark rose to enchant the quartet; they sat beneath the boughs and soaked up the tranquillity. It was impossible to think of anything bad here, and so easy to forget why they had come.

Tama sat looking at the view, but couldn't understand why there was a door spoiling it. "Indeed, it is a strange thing that a garden should have a door at all, don't you think?" she asked the others, who were settling in for a nap in the dry warm air.

"A door, what door?" Cathal sat bolt upright. "Oh, that door. Now you mention it, it is odd."

"A door, indeed," yawned Tristane disbelievingly, but sat up to look.

"Doors are for going, and I'm not going anywhere... although a door would be handy if we did want to leave, I suppose," Baronna said, wondering why he was even contemplating such a terrible idea.

"I've got a feeling about that door," Tama said as she watched it close tightly. "Oh, it's closed. Well I guess we can't leave now."

"Good, because I don't want to," said Baronna.

"I know, let's go and knock on the door and see who answers it," Tristane said. The others got up, except Baronna who stayed put, curled comfortably in the light of the inner sun.

"What now?" asked Cathal as they stood in front of the door.

Tama knocked on the door. She knew it was important, but had no idea why.

"Back so soon?" the door responded.

"Who are you?" she asked.

"Oh, I see: when I told you not to forget me, you went and forgot me." Tama looked at the door blankly. It sighed in response. "Then I'll remind you." The door told her the story of how they were to replace the amulets but only one could do it, and that one was now sleeping soundly under the canopy of an oak tree.

"We have to put them back on the necks of their masters," Tama remembered. Tristane and Cathal, sensing something important going on, looked at each other and began to walk back to where they'd left Baronna.

"Yes, that's it, and today would be good, because on the other side of this door a great end is upon us – so hurry, please!"

Tama ran over to Baronna, overtaking the other two in her urgency, and shook him vigorously. He woke up, but seemed to have forgotten who she was.

"Why do you wake me from my peaceful sleep, lovely lady?" he murmured.

She was bemused and the words stuck in her throat, then she blurted out, "By the Celi Mawr, because you have a bloody job to do!"

"Nay, I have no work to do. I am resting, my lady."

Tama threw up her arms in

exasperation at his odd speech and dissociation from her. "What do we do now?" she exclaimed as Tristane and Cathal approached.

"A spell, niece, a spell! Forget your ethics and just stick one on him," Tristane advised.

"Err, well, yes... Yes, of course..." She raised Baronna from the ground and put all the amulets in his hands. He protested, but she took no notice. With the help of the others she managed to make him walk over towards the statues, but he fought the spell. She pushed him harder with an invisible finger making sure its end was pointed enough to jolt him up to the first ramp. Baronna took a deep breath and appeared as if his memory was returning; he dropped the amulet down on the lap of Xarjay's statue then stood back reluctantly until her spell pushed him to the next. With each of the other three events Baronna's memory became clearer, until he no longer needed a push to fulfil his task.

The group breathed deeply in relief that the world was still intact, and that they were still in it. But their relief was short-lived. Outside the door there was a tremendous crash as the roof of the cave fell in, blocking their exit. They were trapped in this beautiful garden, forced to stay but unable to enjoy its peace because all they wanted to do was leave as soon as possible.

Cathal looked over to the door, splintered by the collapsing stone. He urged Baronna to help him move it; but even the strength of his wolf-power could not clear the way.

"Well, I guess if we have to be anywhere this is as good a place as any to stay," Cathal said, "because it doesn't look as if we were meant to leave." Then he reconsidered the problem. "Perhaps you can move it, Tama."

"I'm too tired to even contemplate such a thing at this time. I'll have a go shortly," she replied.

"That door: I remember it hissing at

you," Cathal added as an afterthought.

"Yes, its language would sound like that, I suppose. The door was made of oak, and the oak speaks – you just have to listen."

"That is true," came a voice from the background. "And only a true child of prophecy would be able to understand so much."

"Sera! It can't be!" Tristane cried out as he turned to look at the ghostly form drifting towards them.

"Yes, it is me. I have decided it's time for me to come back to my life on the Plains. There's a lot to do now, and I'm ready."

"But Ranyel said none of you mages could be here," Tama protested.

"That's true in body – haven't found mine yet. What are you still doing here? It's not good to play in the gardens of the gods for too long, you know."

"We're trapped behind the rubble and there's no way out," Baronna replied.

"You have forgotten much of the ways

of the mage, Baronna, that is clear. But there *is* something you can do. Tama, Mainheart gave you a scripture, didn't he?"

"Well, yes, but I have not had time to..."

"Time is all you have now, so look."

Tama reached into her backpack and pulled out the now crumpled parchment. She read it aloud: "*Traverse time and space, when I name the place, of our destination now – the Crystal City of Power.*"

By the time Tama had said the last word the four were travelling through a void, with no sense of time or space. When they came to a standstill, they were inside Mainheart's personal chamber, right in front of the mage.

"So, you finally decided to read my scroll, I knew you'd be tired and in need of my help. Good, good. It's good to have you back safe and sound," Mainheart greeted them, then his look changed to one of sorrow. "Alas that I should be greeting you with sad news. Cailean White Stone has left us, depleted of her entire life-force. She vanished from the pinnacle a short time ago."

"I don't understand. How?" Tama asked.

"The earthbound spirit converted all her solid matter to energy in an effort to give you the most time you could have. She was spectacular to behold, right up to the very last moment of ascendance. I will miss her in this life, because we have all known her in the past; it will be some time before we are able to ascend to the same dimension she now traverses. Her task here on the Plains is complete, and the rest is up to us. So come: you have a short time to refresh yourselves, and then you must finish your job."

"And what about Sera, did he come here too?"

"No he hasn't, but I'll call my brothers shortly to give them news of your arrival. If he's back he'll be there with them."

"Arrival only to get ready for another

departure," thought Tama wearily. "Perhaps I should have stayed in the hallowed halls. At least there life was untroubled and I didn't have to spare a thought for anything else. Will my task never end?"

*****

"So," thought Maris. "The child warrior wearies of the battle, does she? A little more suffering should weaken her so that I can bend her more easily to my will. Perhaps I will strike at the heart this time."

CHAPTER FIFTEEN:

Tama's Dilemma

Mainheart led them down the smoky-quartz hallways to their separate rooms and left them to bathe or sleep until it was time to eat. They were very hungry: Baronna in particular resented having to wait for a meal, but did his best to ignore his hunger. As they lay resting in their beds several hours later they were each called down to the dining room for breakfast, by means of a min min sent by Mainheart.

Another day begun, and they hadn't slept in their own beds for several weeks. Tama's weariness at the thought of further journeying had begun to show in her face. The last images of her parents crept back into her mind, like a slow river filling with stormwater, until her defences crumbled. She struggled to breathe, overcome by sadness. It was the first time she'd had the opportunity to really think about them since she'd left home. Tristane was worried by his niece's demeanour; he too felt the horror of her thoughts. They would never be free of that moment in the underground caverns, and no amount of kind words would ever liberate them from the useless sense of guilt over what they had had to do. Made closer than ever by their mourning, their emotional bond seemed to leave little room for the love of Cathal and Tama.

Cathal was beginning to feel that Tama had become less tolerant of his longing looks. But he dismissed the feeling as paranoia, the result of a strange courtship that had not yet had the chance to become more than an impassioned kiss in the moonlight.

They gathered for breakfast in near-silence around a table spread with bountiful food to ease their hunger. Tama found she had no interest in eating: she toyed with her scrambled eggs as Cathal watched in silence, eyeing the sparkling ember at her neck. She looked his way then turned away, hiding the lonely tear that tracked down her pale complexion. In her heart she desperately wanted to be with him, but it seemed hopeless.

The look was not one of intolerance, Cathal could see, but he was powerless to ease her sorrow.

"How are we all this morning, then?" Mainheart asked, gliding in on the wings of the air and floating to a halt at the head of the dining table. He looked around. "*Gloomy* is the word to describe you all this fine day, I can see."

"There is little to be fine about, other than the sun shining in instead of a maelstrom beating us down," Tristane said.

"Come Tris. It is a wise Pelien who understands that a day is as good as one can make it."

"Then I lack any worldly wisdom this day. I am tired and bereft, having had no time to grieve. While we sit here, I cannot even begin to imagine what has been happening in my home. How many of my people are dead? How many have been scattered to the four corners of the Plains? What will be left for my niece and me to govern, come whatever lies before us?"

"Then what about you, Baronna? How does it feel to be back to your old self again? Even if it is with a great deal more charm and a rather big set of shoulders. Mind you, I wouldn't say no to a stint as a wolf-man myself, if I knew I'd come back looking so good."

"You flatter me, Mainheart. Although I do not object to my new appearance, the downside is having this ferocious appetite to sustain such muscles."

Cathal fixed his gaze on his friend, and for a moment Baronna's face darkened in memory of his regrettable past. "There is also my conscience, Mainheart, which is more than I think I can stomach at times." Tama looked over at him, wondering why his conscience was even an issue after the spell she had used, then her mind snapped back to thoughts of her parents.

"Well, what a sorry band of soldiers we have to share breakfast with this morning. Tama, my dear, do you have the heart of a lamb this day, or can I rely on you for some sprightly conversation?"

"I, um... I... I'm sorry." She turned and fled the room, no longer able to hold back the rush of tears. Cathal leapt up to follow her and, ignoring Tristane's order to let her be alone, charged down the passageway to Tama's room. From the doorway he saw that she lay sobbing in the middle of the large bed. He cautiously entered the room and closed the door, sat down, and pulled her up into his arms. Her sobbing stopped and she lifted her head to look into his eyes.

"We shouldn't have to remain apart any longer," she said.

But in her heart a gnawing sadness reflected the memory of her encounter with Baronna. Torn between the hidden truth and the likely result of its exposure, she chose to let it haunt her instead. After all, she reasoned, there was no relationship to betray, then.

"I feel the same," Cathal responded, "yet something forebodes in me that I cannot place. It has been there ever since my father gave you that jewel. It's as if he meant for another to be your husband." Tama blushed at the mere mention of another, and dropped her gaze.

"It would be an odd thing for him to do," she agreed, "but he has the mind of a god. We cannot defeat his will by logic, in that case. You should trust in what we feel for each other, not what has been said by a mind so vast it cannot relate to us here and now," she added, allowing her subconscious to relieve her of the guilt in her own past.

He paused before answering with a smile, and then with a resounding "Yes, you are right!" as he pulled her deep into his arms. The kiss in the garden at moonlight paled in comparison to this one. It sent their souls soaring into another dimension for what seemed like the joining of two stars in Kalale's sky. Day and night passed without the breaking apart of the two, whose spirits became joined at a level few ever achieve in a lifetime of devotion. They slowly began to unravel from the fervent embrace, to the light of the new day sifting through the curtains and the sound of tapping at the door. The servant who had brought their breakfast the day before was asking if they would be attending the meeting in Mainheart's personal chamber. The two opened their eyes and smiled at each other before answering, then lay back in the comfort of the bed, momentarily breathless.

"I need to ask you something, Cathal," Tama said. "Do you trust the future?"

"There can be no doubt that the future begs me to do nothing but trust it, and I have answered with my soul."

She smiled at him. "We are sworn to each other now, so let's go and tell the Thane. Are you ready?" she asked, and

Cathal smiled back.

* * *

"What could they possibly be doing all this time?" Tristane paced about the courtyard as Baronna sat quietly on a large crystal structure desperately trying not to answer the obvious, knowing the reaction it would create in the Thane.

"My lord, it is not for me to speculate on the personal affairs of royalty." Baronna felt his own heart being torn. He knew he'd stepped out of place with Tama that night, but it was an urge that he couldn't keep at bay – a leftover from the impetuous wolf in him, perhaps. Either way he was sick with himself for his actions.

"Do not pretend you were not aware of this day eventuating. I knew it would! Everyone else knew it would too; so please don't play coy, Baronna," Tristane snapped.

"Dragon-lord, if you knew, then why the sombre disposition? Are you not happy for the two of them to finally be together? Should we not all celebrate the love that has chosen them?"

"You know, the more I know you are right, the more I hate it. She is my niece, the closest thing to family out here. What Aleeah will say when she finds out, I don't know. She is so protective." He coughed. "Tama is not wise enough for this kind of affection. She may get hurt! *He* may get hurt! I..." he paused as the truth of his heart came to the surface.

"So, it is your loss that you mourn for, and not their gain?"

"I do not remember asking you for your opinion."

"Then maybe you could ask Tama and Cathal for theirs. I hear them coming now, and I will gladly go back to sitting and thinking."

"I am sorry, Baronna. You are right and I am a fool to feel this way. I should be happy after all the sadness that has plagued my family."

"Good morning, you two. I hope we have not missed too much!" called Tama as they came into sight.

"No, niece, you haven't. We have been enjoying the comforts of the Crystal City. Before you say anything else, you need to know I am..." He paused momentarily. "I give my permission for you two to be wed at the first opportunity. I love you both and want you to be happy."

"Now that's more like it," Baronna proclaimed from his perch. "Shut up, you fool!" Tristane muttered, as Baronna jumped down onto the stony courtyard. Tama hugged him enthusiastically and Cathal shook his hand. Tristane pulled the three of them towards him.

"Come on, let's see what else we can do for Mainheart, so we can get on with planning the wedding to end all weddings."

The group re-entered the crystal passages and headed for Mainheart's rooms, where they found him busily casting min mins filled with orders for his staff. Tama thought it was an odd sight to see a man whispering to the air, then a bubble of light appearing just to carry that very thought. Mainheart's face remained intense and Tama could see a little bottle of tell-tale mead jutting out from his gown pocket. There was something about these mages and their penchant for alcohol: perhaps it was their way to escape the world they knew. But Mainheart never looked as if he needed to escape anything: in fact he revelled in being alive and in the thick of the action, or the dictating of it at least, she mused.

"Good morning, good morning." Mainheart opened his eyes as a min min collided with his forehead, letting him know he was not alone. "The min mins have been busy passing on your thoughts and I am led to believe that a wedding is planned for the not-too-distant future. Congratulations, and not before time too. It has been a long time since the Plains has had the benefit of such an affair." The word "affair" hit Tama like a dead weight and she turned away from Mainheart, who briefly lifted an eyebrow in her direction. There were no secrets in this place, she thought.

He continued. "But in the meantime, we still have one more problem to solve, that of Maris. He's still in his lair beneath the trading route. He may have been thwarted by the awakening of the spirits, but do not be fooled into thinking he has given up. The Ommers are close, but need a little guidance; their senses are being hampered by the interference of minerals in Lien's Dividing Range. The deeper under the mountain Maris's abode is, the more interference there is. We need to find him and coax the Ommers in the right direction."

"So what do you need from us?" Tama asked.

"Well, it is very simple; a magnet of sorts will pull them wherever you choose to go. They are a negative force and are attracted to a positive force. I have charged a pyrite cube with positive energy, so they are on their way now. It wasn't easy. I had to match Maris's energy signal just at the right frequency, but I am sure I have achieved this. The min mins have been picking up on the thoughts of Peliens who have witnessed their movements, so I am able to work out the trajectory they're now following, and they will be here in five celestial minutes."

"This sounds very easy, Mainheart. In which case, why hasn't Maris disguised his signature frequency? He is a powerful necromancer, after all," Tristane objected.

"That he is, but not always a very smart one. He has a tendency to overlook the obvious, the easy, hmm..." Mainheart paused briefly to find the right explanation. "When you have as high an intelligence level as the Pretender does, everything you do can become a complicated task because simple tasks just don't come to mind. I am counting on this flaw in his make-up for my plan to work. He will, at this stage of the game, be reinventing his forces. It's taken many years to build the creature base he now has. You have seen them, someone has to die for him to be able to recruit, and the process is quite inefficient."

"Can we see the crystal?" asked Cathal.

Mainheart produced a black bag and from it pulled out a gold-coloured cube that fitted snugly in his hand. In the new light it shone with a golden edge. On each of its sides runes were inscribed, creating individual circular rings on the metal. The others leaned over to peer at it, and Baronna reached out to touch it cautiously.

"Ah, fool's gold – I remember this," he said.

"What do those markings mean?" Tristane asked.

"It is the divine language, consisting of twenty-one letters in all. To feel the real power of it in one's hand, one must be a dimensional traveller, or capable of being one, such as the Ommers and Maris. I and my mage brethren, who have come to learn this art by virtue of our innate gifts, can understand its potency."

"This is the language I have in my thoughts. It was spoken at the entry to the spiritual centre," Tama said.

"Yes, that's correct. You are naturally exposed to it now."

"How can we understand it?" Cathal asked.

"To pronounce the words is not always to understand what they mean. It doesn't matter though; Tama can wield it – Tristane and Baronna too, in time. Its use is not so tricky, really. One can use a pen to write a letter without knowing how the ink flows – the result remains the same," Mainheart said, returning the cube to the bag and handing it to Tama. He glanced up. "Aha, another min min – and yellow just like the others. Step aside so I can catch it." He caught the orb light and absorbed the message. "Yes, just as I expected, the Ommers have entered the city. It is time. Keep the crystal in the bag, Tama, otherwise it will repel you, with your sensitivities."

Mainheart headed off at great speed out into the corridors and down into the stairwell, with his companions struggling to keep up. They crossed the main chamber and went back out into the courtyard towards their ship. As they approached its pearly steps the Ommers glided overhead, drawn by the positive energy of the pyrite.

"Go, quickly! Don't let them catch the crystal, or they will leave with it and we will have to wait a very long time for them to come back!" shouted Mainheart.

"Where exactly are we going?" Tama shouted to him as they scrambled onto the ship.

"Seek out the pony trail on the western side of Lien's Divide, below Sky Crag; I believe there is an entry point still open to you!"

Tama turned to look at Tristane, who had not entered the boat. She nodded to him and he morphed into his new dragon persona, preferring to be carried by his own wings.

Riding on a zephyr, led by the breathtaking form of the desert dragon and followed by the unmistakable presence of the Ommers, the ship soared over the new territories that had blended with the old country below.

"I feel like nothing has changed, yet it is not the same world we left behind when we went underground," Tama said, and leaned over the side of the ship to look down on the landscape. It was like seeing a new and unfamiliar world that somehow held a memory of another place. They were now clearing the city of Kye; they could see that some places had collapsed under the elements' wrath, yet it still had some definition. Three sides had fallen off the old lookout tower where they'd fought with Rakeem, and a solitary section of staircase held steadfast to a broken part of the structure. The rest of the buildings were in a similar state, with few remaining untouched. More interesting, thought Tama, were the many swarms of birds congregating over the unholy ground and picking at the wreckage. They were cleaning the city, she thought, and smiled. At least she now knew Oraldo was true to his word.

They sailed above the highest point of Sky Crag; from this angle it resembled a spread wing in flight. To the west the view remained as breathtaking as always; even from this distance the shimmering walls of the Rainbow City could easily be identified. Tristane looked back at his niece, smiling as if he understood how much she longed to be there.

Baronna seemed to have lost all fear of the boat falling. He stood at the helm like a centurion on guard, never faltering in his duty, one hand on the hilt of his sword and chanting some long-forgotten song. Despite the darkness of his world he had become a trusted member of the crew, dedicated to the task ahead.

Cathal, on the other hand, felt his attention to the task had been corrupted by his new found relationship. He could not take his eyes off his bride-to-be. His heart pulled so hard that he felt a physical pain in his chest, and his mind focused on the distraction of burning love, not on duty.

The tranquil blue skies gave no hint of the elemental forces unleashed on Caragh and the greater world. However, the view below the ship betrayed the reality, with new rolling hills replacing the previously flat horizon. A once straight river bed had cut a new path, twisting in and out of the tors and valleys as far as the Kastrail Straits. The open farmlands were no longer recognisable, and the grazing herds wandered mindlessly to find pastures unspoiled by the heavy rain. On the horizon, beyond the westerly seas, a new land had emerged from the depths; it was a distant and barren rock with an unknown future awaiting its virgin shores.

They set down just before the pony trail began to cut through Sky Crag's lower slopes, on the only spot flat enough for the ship to land.

"Looks like we are on Shanks's pony, then," said Baronna, climbing down the pearly steps and leaping with a thud to the rocky ground.

"Shanks's pony?" queried Cathal, following him a little less energetically.

"What I meant is, we're going to have to walk – you know, no transport."

"I think I've got it," Cathal laughed, giving Baronna a hearty slap on the back.

Tama passed the cube to Baronna before climbing down. "You can carry it for a while, it's getting heavy. Make sure the Ommers don't catch you up. It would be a disaster."

"Somehow, I don't think so, even without this lump of metal. I've seen your work. You should not be worried about anything you have yet to do."

"Thank you," she replied shyly, overcome by his admiration. Yet the whispers of the Pretender had plagued her thoughts for several days. She felt his mind watching her, manipulating the events the four had thought their own.

"Less chat and more action, please!" shouted Tristane, landing with a thud that made the ground tremble, and a skid that threw up a cloud of dust. The three others stumbled and choked.

"Oops!" said Tristane, changing back to his own body. "Sorry everyone, I haven't quite got the hang of that yet."

"So we can see, uncle." Tama brushed the dust off her once-clean garb, and dreamed of the moment when she could rid herself of the dirty leather for a queenly dress, and a stately house with a huge bath and a clean comfortable bed. Shaking herself out of the daydream, she followed the others up the stony path through the tangled scrub covering the lower slopes.

The climb was steep, though not completely unforgiving until the gravel became an impediment on the steeper slopes. Having reached the tumbled rocks below the summit of the trading route, their journey faltered. The path split into several possible trails; all seemed to lead upwards, but only one would take them to their destination – a passage leading deep down into the mountain's belly.

Tristane, growing stronger in leadership by the day, pushed onwards up a narrow ravine, without a thought to becoming lost in the wilderness of the stony mount. In his eyes, there was always the way down into the mountain. "It's just how you go about it that can get you into trouble," he thought. They followed his lead without question. Tama had noticed the change in his personality with the acceptance and empowerment of his spirit. She felt closer to her grandparents because of it, and wondered what they were doing as they waited in the Rainbow City.

The sun was high and bright in the sky, burning down on backs laden with food supplies and extra clothing to combat the cold inside the mountain. "Can we rest now, Tris? It's been a constant four-hour slog and we're all about to drop from exhaustion,"

Tama pleaded.

"I know, I know, but we can't stand still. Remember what Mainheart said about not letting the Ommers catch the cube. They will not understand that it's the proverbial carrot to lure them on."

The familiar cry of an eagle resounded above them, and the majestic creature came down to land on a nearby precipice. Mienna tilted her head and watched as they trudged up the pathway. Her keen ears picked up their conversation, and she swooped down to hover above Baronna. In answer to her soft cry he held up the sack so she could grasp it in her claws. She sailed on the winds up and around the mountain, clutching the precious cargo. Baronna waved to her as a gesture of thanks and the companions sat down to rest.

"I hope you know what you're doing, she seems a little temperamental to me," said Tristane, standing over Baronna.

Baronna lifted his head, feeling threatened by the Thane's tone and sensing how close he stood. "She will allow us rest, which we need," he said softly. Tristane looked up at the circling bird and nodded.

"What have we to eat? I'm famished," Baronna continued, rubbing his stomach.

"There's cheese, bread, and I think we have cuts of roasted meat too. They are not very cold, though, I'm afraid." Cathal passed around parcels of food.

"Here, try this," said Tama. "It is my dragon fruit from the mull at the Boulders. It is still juicy." She bit into the other half, and kept one eye on Mienna.

Tristane started a fire with what little tinder was left after the storms. The embers held their heat just long enough to boil water, as they sat in silence. Cathal passed Tama a cup and touched her hand briefly; their eyes met and he smiled warmly at her. She looked into his eyes for a fleeting moment, but Mienna's sharp cries reminded them they should get back to the task.

"She's growing tired," said Baronna.

Tristane looked up, shading his eyes

in the bright light. "There doesn't seem to be an opening into the mountain side, Cathal," he said, scratching his chin.

"I'll bet Mienna can see one, with those hawkish eyes."

"Yes," Tristane agreed. "Baronna, talk to her if you can. We need an aerial view, and there's not enough room in this ravine for me to change into dragon and have a look for myself."

Baronna raised his hands to his mouth and, making a funnel shape, squawked like an eagle, shrill and loud. Mienna swept down and dropped the cube into Tama's outstretched hands before returning to the sky. Packing up quickly they headed upwards, this time with the eagle guiding their path. At last Mienna landed, showing them the way in; as they entered a darkened cave, she cried one last distant cry and left them to their task.

CHAPTER SIXTEEN:

Into the Depths

As he had climbed through the wilderness, Baronna had spent the time recalling his training as a mage, in the days before Maris had changed him. Once in the cave he reached into his pack and felt around for several lengths of vine, which he illuminated and passed to each of his companions to drape around their necks. The vines gave off a bluish light around their bodies, casting hard shadows in the humid air. Enclosed in his own darkness, Baronna was yet comforted by the illumination he couldn't see.

Tristane examined his illuminated vine carefully before putting it on. "I remember that! You were doing it when we first met you at the guild," he said, his memory of the whole trip to the mage guild now clear in his mind.

"Yes, I was quite the happy trainee until *he* came and changed all that," said Baronna.

"Things will get better," Tristane replied as optimistically as he could.

"Well I hope so. I hate this place far more than even the last set of tunnels we were in," Cathal joined in. "And what are those things hanging from the roof? They look like old snake-skins."

Tama felt for his hand in the gloom and looked for reassurance in his face. The cave had been artificially widened to allow for the passage of several bodies abreast. It ran straight and slightly downwards. Deeper into the gloomy shadows, they came to an abrupt halt at a set of double doors. They had no hinges or handles, but there were several buttons on the grey stone wall beside the doors, with no markings to explain their use. They tried prying the doors open, but it had no effect. Tristane stood back and watched, taking a few moments to assess their situation.

"These doors have not been opened in years," Tama said. "And there is no other way that I can see, at least not without another three- or four-hour hike up the mountain. I'm sensing the direction again." She looked down, concentrating. "This is the only way, or we have to go back."

Baronna and Cathal continued trying to force open the doors, but without effect.

"It's not working," Tristane said, stretching out to press the buttons. The doors suddenly slid open, with Cathal still pressed against them. He fell through and into a yawning crevasse. Baronna grabbed at him as he disappeared into the blackness, catching his hand so Cathal swung precariously in mid-air. Tama screamed at the sight of him falling; she searched desperately for a spell to save him, but panic shattered her concentration. Cathal's weight was too much for the slippery, sweaty hand of the wolf-man: Baronna lost his grip and gravity pulled

Cathal down the hole, his rope-light disappearing quickly into the black depths. The doors began to shut with Baronna still caught between them. Tama dived through, clutching the cube and still grasping for a spell that would not come. Tristane grabbed Baronna by his leather cuirass and heaved at his body.

At that moment the Ommers caught up with them. The six red particles cut through Tristane's body like invisible fireballs and paralysed him from the waist down. He yelled in pain, his body wrenched at the severity of his agony, then he dropped to the floor weak and unable to stand. The Ommers, still chanting, arced down the crevasse after Tama and the cube, leaving Baronna wedged like an old piece of timber, with the doors opening and closing repeatedly, clamping him in place.

Tristane dragged himself towards the wall where the switch was and reached up desperately to reopen the doors. After several attempts his clawing fingers struck the button and the doors stopped beating against Baronna's ribs and drew back. Baronna dragged his battered body out of the gap before the doors closed again and hauled himself to a sitting position next to Tristane. They sat quiet in the fading light of the illuminating vines, shattered and bereft.

Tama caught her breath and her thoughts as she fell, then reached into her heart for a spell; she would hit the ground much too hard if not protected by something more than a muddled mind, she thought. She strained her eyes down through the darkness, but could see nothing of Cathal's light, and was unable to recall the spectrum of body heat. As the seconds passed she became more aware of her surroundings. They had fallen down an old mining shaft lined with gold and silver seams. Her mind reached out to search for her lover but could not find even a spark of his soul to guide her. Finally touching the bottom, she landed softly on her feet and probed the area with hands outstretched.

Hearing a faint moan to her left, she stumbled towards it.

"Cathal, is that you? I'm here, I'm coming," she called reassuringly. The light of Cathal's vine had faded to a dim wisp, and it cast a dull glow across his face, showing him grimacing in pain. He had broken his back against the hard ground on landing, and his life-force flitted in and out as she gently stroked his hair away from his face.

"No, please don't leave me like this," she pleaded. "We have barely begun to know each other. It's not your time, my love."

His voice came faintly. "It is over for me, sweet woman-child. My body will not recover, it is spent and I can't feel anything except cold. It's hard to breathe." Slowly he forced out another breath of fading life.

Tama began to sob angrily.

"No! My love, A'shara, save him, please save him!" she cried repeatedly, but no answer came to her plea.

Cathal reached for her hand then his

arm fell limp by his side, and his last breath was gone.

"No, no, not yet, please not yet!" Her heart broke a thousand times in the brief moment it took for the light in Cathal's eyes to fade and his soul to lift from his broken body. There was no sign of Salamar coming to collect the spirit of Orion's child; Cathal's destiny would be more than that. The final act that Tama could perform for him was to raise his lifeless form back up the shaft and leave him in the hands of Tristane and Baronna.

Tama rose to her feet and wiped the tears from her face as she saw the light of Cathal's spirit leave. All around her the sounds of scuffling feet broke her grieving and a storm grew inside her body. She felt her anger become pain, and the pain grow as a knot in her stomach. Then like an automaton she stepped forward, focused on the next task, and placed one foot after the other in a slow walk towards the scuffling. As the storm inside her continued to grow, she took the pyrite crystal and without a thought or a care hurled it deep into the darkness, screaming her energy into the throw. It flew straight and hard, whipping the air and releasing a howling wail that eerily touched every nook and cranny in the deep, until at last it met an obstacle and a double boom shook the subterranean chambers.

Tama's footsteps began to clash heavily with the ground beneath, leaving cracks in the surface as the torrent of anger thrust down through her feet. Faster and faster she went, until she was pounding along the tunnel. With each thundering step the storm within her blazed higher and the desire to eliminate all in her path grew stronger. Her soul became a fire and the storm the ether that carried it. No need for will to assist or intelligence to guide: her actions were stripped to their essence. If any dared to cross her path she whipped them asunder using elemental forces, scattering them like toys. While the fierce crash of the pyrite crystal still echoed through the mountain, Tama came to the place where it had shattered. Its impact on the rock wall was so powerful that it had breached the inner barriers of Maris's central sanctum.

She stepped through the hole. The fire of her spirit was now so strong that it caused all things in her path to glow as she glowed. In one corner, she heard the sobs of a man in terrible pain, and recognised the voice of Caldor. The once-great captain was no longer able to hold his head up, but lay curled in a foetal position, overcome with the worries of the universe. He seemed oblivious to her presence; his madness had destroyed his ability to communicate or comprehend. Briefly, sanity flickered across his eyes and he looked pleadingly at the glowing woman across the room, but the respite was fleeting and he went back into his terrifying world of turmoil and pain.

Tama both pitied him and hated him, but his destiny was no longer a threat to hers and she moved on through the shadows looking for Maris the Pretender, and leaving the madman to die in his own way.

The fire of Tama's soul burned with the desire to kill. She searched the comfortable corridors with their fine furnishings and their walls hung with pictures of fatality and devastation, looking for the one who had begun this cycle. She listened with heightened senses until she heard what she'd been waiting for. The door to her right opened with a grinding sound and a figure filled the doorframe. Its shadow was as unwavering as the flames her body projected. His outline was one she knew well: it was etched on her psyche just as Rakeem's had been. She breathed deeply, feeling her quest drawing to its climax.

She was filled with power; perhaps the only time she would reach this level of power and be the equal of any entity – mortal, spirit, or deity – that traversed the dimensions. Maris sensed it as he stood in the doorway. The extent of her anger and power was unexpected, though he concealed that from her.

"So you found my house, and after all I have done to dissuade you," he greeted her.

"You take credit where no credit is due, lord of destruction."

"And you show your ignorance of the powers that exist in this and all realms within the sphere of the Maker Eternal. You cannot cast out that which belongs, child of the wyrd."

"Then I shall remove you from this place and A'shara can put you back in your bottle," Tama retorted.

"There is nothing in this and all the other worlds that I cannot be part of. It matters not whether I am here or elsewhere. Surely you realise that now."

"Your physical presence is an abomination. Form is not your right: form is *our* right."

"That may or may not be so. Regardless, I like the physical life and I'll fight to keep it, so fight back, child – fight!"

Maris lifted his left hand and tugged on an invisible rope that now twined about Tama's being. Though she resisted, grabbing the rope and pulling back, Maris managed to drag her fiery image through the doorway and into an inner chamber. Realising she'd not beat him with strength alone she created her own invisible spell and cracked a whip of air that flashed over Maris; he was jolted back through the doorway and across the room, leaving her free. She stepped forward and cracked another air current over his body, and he remained on the ground. She dived on top of him, pinning him under her fiery wrath. They struggled in mind and body, her heart pounding as the fight continued. With sudden force he threw her across the room. Tama was briefly stunned, and in this unguarded moment her nemesis blasted at her fire with water that sprang forth from a wall. Tama's flame went out, and she was abruptly brought back to the gravity of her situation.

Drenched, Tama pulled herself up from the floor, battered and breathless. Her iron will would not allow her to withdraw from the fray. Inspired by the water cooling her very essence, she summoned the liquid in her veins to become one with the underground springs of the life-giver. The two fluids joined and Maris was sent crashing to the floor in a torrent of liquid energy. But Maris was quick of mind; seizing the static they had generated he directed a bolt of lightning towards Tama, who had not yet separated her organic self from the water around her. In excruciating pain, she tried to re-form her body, but the electric shock was shattering her molecules into atoms and she was unable to prevent herself turning to a vapour. She became the very air Maris breathed and was drawn deep into his lungs. Her essence recoiled in horror, but she was powerless to stop the arcane from completing his deed. Certain he'd achieved her end, Maris walked towards the mirrored wall and looked at himself smugly through Baronna's eyes.

"Let's see how the gods get out of that!" he chuckled to himself.

CHAPTER SEVENTEEN:

A Breath of Life

Tristane and Baronna had fallen silent when Cathal's body floated out of the darkness and gently came to rest on the floor in front of them. Tristane rubbed his forehead in despair. With his niece gone, his close friend dead, Baronna battered, and himself paralysed, it seemed that all was lost.

"Cathal is here. Tama has raised him to us. He's dead," he said harshly.

Baronna could hear the pain in Tristane's voice, but it still irked him that the last dragon talked with no hope in his tone.

"What does that mean?" asked the wolf-man, nursing his bruised ribs.

"It's up to Tama now. That is what this history has come to. That is what she is supposed to do."

"Are you sure? I mean, it is no easy task bringing such an entity into line, my lord," Baronna objected, wincing as he got up. There had to be at least one cracked rib in there, he thought, rubbing his chest gingerly. "Maybe you can't go and help her, but I can. I'm not so injured that I can't stand – and fight."

"Then go, if you can. My legs have not recovered, though at least now they tingle, which is more than they did after those... those things, crashed through me," Tristane spat, frustrated by his helplessness. "Don't worry about me. Go, with my blessings."

"And mine stay with you, Thane." Baronna paused as if to say more, sensing the damage to Tristane's heart but unable to find the words to heal him.

Taking a deep breath, Baronna stepped towards the open doors and felt around in the shaft for the ladder-like structure his hand had struck when trying to save Cathal. Turning, he began to climb down, untroubled by the darkness. There was no colour or light in his new world: everything he did was by instinct.

He could smell Tama's bodily signature still lingering in the air as he made his descent, overshadowing Cathal's and reminding him of her essence in the Blue Hills. He was drawn to her again, but could not fathom why his primordial emotions raged for her when Cathal's body was barely cold. Perhaps, he mused, it was because she was in danger.

Then he was down on the ground, and back in familiar territory. The last time he'd been summoned to the underground world of the Pretender, he'd undergone the agony of having his eyes removed and replaced by Maris's eyes. This time, he vowed, it would be different.

Guided by touch and smell he crept down the darkened tunnel, freezing to stillness at the slightest sound so as not to warn of his approach. His nose was revolted by the smell of charred flesh lingering from

Tama's fiery passage, and he battled to put aside the pain of rib bones grinding with every move he made. It was not real pain, he told himself, trying to convince his lucid mind of an illusion.

Baronna scented the air and knew he was close to his goal. He was filled with the savage power of the wolf and thirsted for revenge. For years he'd been the puppet of the evil that haunted this underground realm, and now an opportunity had come to take back his self-respect. He crept forward ever more cautiously, feeling the edges of exposed granite dislodged by the pyrite explosion. He slithered through the hole into the quiet room and listened, silent as a thief. Hearing nothing except a faint moan from the far corner, of no interest because it was not his quarrel, he felt his way into the next room. Tama had been here, he sensed, but her smell was all but gone and what lingered was in an unfamiliar form. "Perhaps death has taken her and I am too late," he thought. Thrown off balance by the thought, he stumbled in the water still gushing from the spring and caught his breath, waiting frozen to see if his presence had been noted. Tiptoeing forward he came to another door, and opened it soundlessly.

Maris sat with his back to the door. The wolf was stupid as well as blind to think he could come here unnoticed, thought the Pretender. He stood and walked around the chair to face Baronna, all the while maintaining his inner control to prevent Tama from escaping.

"Where is she?" Baronna demanded.

"She's gone and will not be coming back. I have her... confined."

"What have you done to her?" Baronna began to panic.

"She did it to herself by coming here. It was self-defence on my part, and nothing you can say or do can bring her back. I will hold her forever, in a place where she will never see the light – like you, in fact, you pathetic creature."

"Arghhhh!" Baronna charged forward

with sword raised. Maris stepped aside and the big man fell over the chair before somersaulting to his feet with sword still in hand.

"Impressive action, but no prize. Try again!" Maris taunted him. Enraged, Baronna slashed repeatedly at the air as Maris laughed and danced out of his way. But while Maris was distracted by Baronna, his hold on Tama weakened. The air flowing in and out of his lungs brought new consciousness to Tama, and she became aware of Baronna's presence. The purity of her condensed being fought against her host's dark matter, breaking it down one molecule at a time. With each new breath she forced herself deeper, pulsing through his veins, dissecting as she went and destroying him organ by organ. As his physical body broke down and the decay neared his brain, Maris's laughter waned and his dodging faltered. Finally he fell to the floor in front of Baronna and lay still. Baronna, recognising whose power was at work, sheathed his sword and stood back to allow Tama to fulfil her destiny.

The Pretender's body began to dissolve, until nothing was left but a pool of foul rotting matter. Tama, now free of the tissue that had bound her, was able to recompose her body. She reached out and touched Baronna's face. "Thank you for coming," she said softly.

"I thought I was too late. If only I had been able to see..."

"Oh no, your eyes!" Fearing that she had destroyed them, she looked down and discovered to her relief that they had survived. They were not of the same essence as the Pretender and so had escaped his body's fate. She bent to rescue them from the fetid soup in which they floated, and cradled them gently in one hand. "I have them," she said.

Baronna stood unmoving, anticipating the worst. "Will they still work?" he asked hoarsely.

Tama looked at the eyeballs in her

hand to his ravaged eye sockets. "I don't know, but I can try." She took his hand and led him over to the fountain in the other room, where she carefully cleansed the eyes in its life-giving flow. "Are you ready?" she asked.

Baronna took a deep breath and nodded. As gently as she could, Tama pushed the eyeballs back into their sockets. Baronna groaned once at the agony of it, which brought fresh memories of their original removal, then silently endured the pain. Admiring his strength and courage, Tama cupped her hands around his closed eyelids and breathed life back into them, and all the pain lifted. Baronna opened his eyes slowly and, for the first time in this new reality, saw the woman who had brought him out of the wolf, and out of the darkness. She smiled at him and each felt the connection, though neither understood it.

A sudden rhythmic sound brought their attention back to the room where the remains of the Pretender lay. Baronna drew his sword and took a guarded stance, one which he knew better blind than seeing. Tama boldly slipped by him, afraid of little in this new world, to find that the Ommers had come at last. Disoriented by the shattering of the cube, they had searched the underground passages one by one until they found what they had been seeking. Now they were absorbing all the foul essence, until no trace remained. Their task done, they vanished as swiftly as they had come, leaving Tama to explain to Baronna what they were.

The end of Maris brought a fresh surprise, as an old man, bent and bearded, stepped into the room and looked around in wonder.

"Who are you?" Tama asked.

Baronna, still with his sword ready, recognised the old man, though it was someone he'd not seen since the day of his transformation. "Cullen! But how... you were dead... we all thought... You're not dead!" he stammered in shock.

"Cullen?" Tama said in surprise, having read of him in Aleeah's archives, but never expecting to see him alive. "Truly, you are the wanderer, then."

"Apparently, it is me, but don't ask me how I got here," the old man answered, still looking confused. "I saw the Ommers pass, and followed them. I can tell from the pure air in this room that Maris is no more – your work, I assume, young lady?" Tama nodded.

Cullen stared at Baronna, obviously struggling to remember him. "You look like the son of Kalale, the boy that was sent to us as a child to be educated. You were never told, of course, but now you look too much like him for it to be kept a secret." Tama gazed at Baronna, who seemed shaken to the core by what Cullen had told him. The notion explained a great deal about his attraction to the princess, and about the work he had been asked to do. Tama smiled through her heartache: to marry the son of

Kalale was one of her destinies, but perhaps Cathal, the one she had thought was chosen, was not the right son after all.

Tristane came rushing into the room, having finally regained the use of his legs and determined to make a last stand for the Plains, no matter what happened to him. He stopped short, as puzzled as Tama and Baronna about the presence of Cullen in place of Maris.

"So, have you found your inner dragon yet?" Cullen demanded, as if he'd never been away.

"Well, yes. But how did you find yourself here?"

"It's hard to say, really, but I suppose it will come to me in time. I can only guess that Maris's... passing freed me from the labyrinth in which he trapped me when the mage guild was destroyed. Now, fill me in on what has happened since I've been gone."

They did so, as the group slowly made its way back out of the mountain, by a lower path than previously. Tristane told them that Cathal had been taken already, on the orders of Mienna, so there was no reason to climb back the way they had come. In return for their news, Cullen told them as much as he could remember of his trials in the bowels of the mage guild, up to the time when he was suddenly transported into Maris's domain.

Outside the tunnel stood several ponies, waiting to carry the group home. As they emerged into the light, Mienna squawked familiarly and flew off, satisfied she was no longer needed. Tama was sad to see that her boat was no longer moored at the bottom of the mountain. It seemed that on the death of Maris her control over unseen things had dissipated, and she felt rather lost without the burning flame inside. When they reached the lowlands a small bright light flickering out of the ground caught her eye. She dismounted and walked over to examine it, discovering that the boat had not disappeared: it was merely that her strength was not enough to maintain the boat's shape and it had returned to its original dimensions.

"What is it?" asked Tristane, shielding his eyes from the sun.

"It's our transport, except I don't have the power to engage it."

"Then we will continue to walk, or rather our animals will. As unceremonious as this may look, it's better than nothing," her uncle said good-humouredly.

"Never be afraid to be humble, prodigy child," interjected Cullen. "To be humble is to cleanse where our demons have given us a swollen head."

"What an odd thing to say," Tama thought, but she smiled at him anyway. If this was an effect of what he had been through, then who was she to criticise, she reasoned. But Baronna and Tristane knew that this was just Cullen's way.

They returned to the Plains and headed west for home.

CHAPTER EIGHTTEEN:

Homecoming

On their return to the Rainbow City the companions learned of all that had gone on in their absence – the deaths of many, as well as the triumphs. Change was in effect, and there was only so much Tama felt she could cope with. Worst of all, at least for herself and Tristane, was the news of Xylon's disappearance during the elemental storms. It was said that a great spiralling wind had plucked him out of the ground and carried him out to sea. As time passed and more and more searchers returned with no news of the old druid, Tama began to grow anxious. Xylon's roots and branches had been found stuck in the mire around the new virgin isles, but of Xylon himself there was no trace. She suspected that the tree and the wise old councillor were no longer joined – separating with the death of the spell-caster, Maris, perhaps – but she could not know for sure. Baronna came upon her one evening as she stared longingly through the window at the starry night, and tried to reassure her.

"You miss him, I can see that. But we don't know if he is truly gone, or just lost on an island somewhere. Your staff said they saw him being carried by the wind, so who knows where he might have been set down," he said.

"I know, but he should be here for our joining ceremony. He has been a part of our lives for longer than most of the elders can even remember. By rights, we should have been able to receive his blessing. It won't be quite the same without him. I don't want to lose my old friends as well as our old customs."

"You have scouts roaming the virgin lands to the west, and ships scouring the seas for any sign of him. What more shall we do?" Baronna asked.

"Nothing – that is all we can do." She turned away from the window, into his waiting arms.

"Then come to bed – it's late, and cold in here without you. They'll find him, you'll see."

As the next day dawned Tama and Baronna woke to the sounds of preparation for the ceremony. The joining was set for sundown in the April Hall, and the streets were already filling with citizens looking for the best vantage point. The white carpets were ready to be laid from the halls to the party tent, covering the cobblestone streets, and a multitude of cooking smells warmed the air.

Looking out from her balcony window, Tama could see Sky Crag hanging silent and snow-capped against an ice blue sky. With winter finally upon Caragh, ice sculptures were being chiselled by the local craftspeople, and she saw several ice doves being carried to the party tent. Turning back, she noticed a strange sight: three great winged shapes careering through the sky towards her. She opened the glass doors for a better view, and saw a black bear running in the shadow of the airborne creatures.

"Dragons!" she yelled, "and a bear!"

"Ah," said Baronna, seeming not at all surprised, "so the mages finally show themselves out of respect for the Dragon Lord. They've waited a long time for this – till they could show themselves, that is. As children of battle mages, like you and the Thane, they have the gifts of their parents, you know."

"And Tristane is leading them," Tama said.

Sera, the only one of the mages who didn't have the gift of transformation, was also making a grand entrance. Tama watched him arrive at high speed in a horse-drawn chariot, and called to Baronna.

"You should come and see this."

"I don't need to," Baronna said, sleepily rolling deeper under the covers to escape the brisk air coming in through the open window. Tama sighed deeply.

"Why the sigh?" he asked.

"Because I was hoping they had found Xylon and brought him home."

Craven pounded heavily on the door with the news of their guests' arrival. "Get dressed, quickly, you have to greet them – there's something they want to tell you!" Tama didn't ask how Craven had this news. He was wily, often knowing secrets that others would prefer to have forgotten.

She met her uncle and the mages in the gardens, with Cullen and Baronna following, then Aleeah entered hand-in-hand with Alden. The mages had brought with them a gift for Tama: one of the wyrd and golden threads of fate which had begun this story so many years before Tama's birth, at the beginning of Aleeah's reign. As she held the vine in her hands Tama realised that Xylon was alive. When he wanted to find his way back, she knew he would come home.